Praise for

MORE OF ME

"Very weird and very wonderful. What a debut!"
Tanya Landman, Carnegie Medal-winning author of
Buffalo Soldier

"Weird, wonderful and utterly fabulous, I read this
in one big gulp. I loved it!"
Teri Terry, author of the *Slated* series

"An attention-grabbing debut, which kept me
surprised right up to the end."
Mary Hoffman, author of the *Stravaganza* series

"A super-smart, standout read that takes a pinch of sci-fi,
a dash of romance and a hefty dose of tension and mixes
them up in a contemporary test tube. It grabbed me from
the very first page and didn't let go!"
Tamsyn Murray, author of *My So-Called Afterlife*

"A tense, thought-provoking thriller about the
(quite literal) pain of growing up. What is really wrong
with Teva? I couldn't put this novel down!"
Bryony Pearce, author of *Phoenix Rising*

kathryn evans

MORE OF ME

USBORNE

To all the honeyz in the Hun Club x

First published in the UK in 2016 by Usborne Publishing Ltd., Usborne House,
83-85 Saffron Hill, London EC1N 8RT, England. www.usborne.com

Text © Kathryn Evans, 2016

The right of Kathryn Evans to be identified as the author of this work has been asserted by
her in accordance with the Copyright, Designs and Patents Act, 1988.

Cover image © Moment / Rekha Garten / Getty Images

The name Usborne and the devices ♀ 🎈 are Trade Marks of
Usborne Publishing Ltd.

This is a work of fiction. The characters, incidents, and dialogues are products of the author's
imagination and are not to be construed as real. Any resemblance to actual events or persons,
living or dead, is entirely coincidental.

A CIP catalogue record for this book is available from the British Library.

ISBN 9781474903028 03897/3 JF AMJJASON/16

Printed in the UK.

prologue

I have grown in strength inside her. Filled her cells with mine until we must split apart. It's not my choice – that's how it's always been for us.

Though we've done this many times before, I know she is afraid, because I share her heart. Her memories are mine, hazy sometimes, but mine. I feel what she feels. I have walked where she has walked, been in her every step. I have kissed where she has kissed. *Ollie.* I sigh but the breath that comes out is hers. It's time to breathe for myself. It's time to live.

She is in that dream place where her body cannot move and her mind is unsure and scattered. I stretch and fill every cell, feel them all expand and swell to make room for me. I search for the weakest point to break out and find it: the little finger of the right hand.

Some deep memory tells me it's always been this way. The first cell splits with a tiny pop; she hardly notices.

I'm controlling our breathing now. We take a deep lungful of steadying air and tense. I press our shoulders into the bed and that's when she realizes. That's when she starts to fight.

Our minds are still merged and her panic leaks into me. For a second I can do nothing, but it's started now and there's no stopping it. I refocus on that weak spot. I try to lift my knuckles, to pull them away, but it's the tip of the little finger that frees itself. I bend back my hand. The fingers come away with a syrupy tear. She is fully awake now. For a moment we fight for control, but she cannot hold me and I wrench my arm free. The raw ripping sparks in every fibre, every sinew – we burn together. I work on the other arm, pushing through the fingertips, feeling every cell split and seal up again, as hers do, releasing me.

Guilt flickers through me. Mine, not hers. I am moments away from being Teva and she…she will be left behind.

She fights. Her arms grab at mine but there is no turning back, there's no longer room for both of us.

I lift my toes and feel them suck away; they brush the bedclothes as they come free. My new skin is sensitive, not used to being touched – I almost can't bear it. I wrench my legs up and kick away the covers. Her hands are on our face now.

She can't stop it.

I have to be free.

I *will* be free.

one

Six months had flown by. Six months since I'd fought my way out of Fifteen's body and taken over as Teva. Six months since Fifteen had been trapped at home and I'd been free. It didn't take a maths genius to work out what that meant. I had just six short months until a new Teva tried to fight her way out of me. Only I wasn't going to let it happen. I wasn't going to be stuck in this madhouse for ever, with all my former selves driving me completely doolally.

I was sat cross legged on my bed, twisting Peepee's ears through my fingers while I tried to think. We all had a Peepee – a little grey rabbit filled with tiny beans so he flopped in your hands. A warm memory took me by surprise; Mum tucking him into bed with me on the day I emerged. She didn't quite get that a new Peepee wasn't the same as the original, but giving each of us our own version was one of the few things she did that actually made a difference. I remember exactly how I'd felt in that moment: kind of relieved and kind of put out. I still wanted Fifteen's Peepee. What a stupid thing to want when I was about to take everything else. Ollie. Mads. Everything.

Six months, then, to stop it happening to me. And I *was* going to stop it. I was absolutely *not* giving up *my* life for someone else to take over.

So I had to do something about it.

Ten out of ten for determination. Nought out of ten for a decent plan. I nibbled the raw skin on my fingertips, a habit Mum totally hated – along with scratching behind my knees, flicking the cover off my phone, wanting to have a future – you know, just the small things in life.

Mum liked to pretend everything was fine. We didn't even need a doctor, apparently. And I'd asked. Quite a few times. She always cut me off with a variety of excuses, all of which boiled down to the same thing – Mum's number one rule: the world must not know about our freakery.

Not long after I emerged, I'd called a meeting of Tevas, to find out if the others knew anything I didn't. Fifteen wouldn't come – no surprise there – but, apart from little Eva, the rest of them did. I got Eight to listen out for Mum.

"Like a spy?" she said, clapping her hands together and taking up position by my bedroom door. I dimly remembered us reading a lot of Famous Five around that age and totally loving anything a bit secretive.

I'd looked around at them all. Fourteen leaning against

my dressing table, arms folded tight across her chest; Seven sat at her feet gazing up adoringly. Thirteen and Twelve, more like twins than anything else, sprawled across my bed like they owned the place, laughing at celebrity arm fat in Mum's *Chatter* magazine. Nine and Ten sat on the floor, legs crossed, heads tipped together over an exercise book. They were writing an autobiography – probably the world's first to be written by two people about their one life. That was also the most interesting thing about it, seeing as they didn't really have a life any more. Six was huddled in a corner, making herself as small as possible, and Eleven was going through my wardrobe looking for stuff so she could dress herself up as Hermione Granger. A doomed mission as we all had the same short, fluffy, blonde completely un-Hermione-like hair.

That's all of us. There's no Four or Five. I don't know why.

I said: "We need to discuss our future."

"*Your* future, you mean," Fourteen said.

"No, *all* of our futures."

"We don't have a future though, do we?" she said. "This is it for us."

I didn't have an answer to that so I just said, "I was thinking about going to a doctor."

Six whimpered in the corner, then jerked to her feet and bolted out of the door.

"Oh, good one, well done," Thirteen said, stomping out after Six, rapidly followed by Twelve. I watched them leave, astonished at the reaction. I turned to the others. "Why is Six so upset?"

Ten looked up from her writing and said, "Probably scared."

"What? Why?" I *could* remember things we'd shared, but it was hard if I didn't know what I was looking for – like sifting through a dusty junk shop to find something you'd never seen before. I tried to find something in the memories Six had left behind, but all I got was a dark feeling of unease.

Nine said: "Doctors will just want to experiment on us."

"Oh, don't be ridiculous," I said.

Ten backed her up. "It's true, actually. Mum told us. She won't let you go anyway. Ask her. I bet you a million pounds she won't."

"Well, I knew that already," I said. "I could go on my own."

"No!" squeaked Seven, shooting to her feet. "I don't want to be an experiment."

Fourteen slipped an arm round her shoulder and said, "Don't worry." Then to me: "There's no point seeing a doctor; I tried that. They thought I was making everything up to get attention."

Fourteen's memory bobbed to the surface of my brain, clouded with embarrassment. I blushed on her behalf. The doctor she'd seen had been about ninety – he'd sighed, muttered something about *girls your age* and suggested a psychiatric referral. Nice.

I said, "Maybe if we went together they'd believe us. You'd be walking proof I wasn't mad."

Seven clenched her fists. "No! I'm not going and you can't make me."

Fourteen said, "Just forget it. Mum'd go nuts if she knew you were even thinking about it."

"But if we got help, you wouldn't have to be stuck here all day."

"Really? We could all go into the world and everyone would love us, would they? The freak family? I don't think so."

Fourteen took Seven's hand and left, shaking her head. I looked at Nine and Ten. They shrugged and gathered up their things. End of meeting.

As I went downstairs, Six was under the banister peeling the wallpaper off and Mum was waiting for me by the bottom step, disappointment radiating from her. Nine and Ten were lurking behind her – they'd clearly dobbed me in.

"Why, Teva?" asked Mum. "We're fine, aren't we? We manage okay? Other people won't understand you, darling, not even doctors. They'll think you're…"

"Crazy? A freak? Yeah. I know. You've told me enough times."

"Not a fr…just…people can be very unkind."

"If you're ashamed of us, I could go to the doctor with a couple of the others. You don't need to come."

"I'm not ashamed! I just know what will happen. They'll want to do tests on you – horrible tests. They might take you away from me, Tee, put you in hospital. Why won't you trust me?"

Her bottom lip wobbled and I felt horrible. That bottom lip got me every time.

"Don't cry, Mum. I do trust you, of course I do."

She lowered her voice to a whisper. "You have to believe me, Teva. We're better on our own. You've no idea how cruel people can be."

Maybe she was right. Maybe she had taken us to a doctor and it had been so awful we'd buried the memory deep, deep down.

So I'd left it at that with her, but I hadn't given up. I spent literally hours on the internet trying to understand what was wrong with us.

The lure of Google was irresistible. I pulled my laptop onto my knee and started a new search.

It was hard to know what to look for. "Splitting cells" brought up stuff on spreadsheets. "Body inside another body" brought up stories about twins who had got stuck inside each other in the womb. Nothing explained us. And in the end all medical roads on Google tend to lead to one terrifying possibility: cancer.

Just thinking about that sent new panic wriggling through my veins. I told myself: *It's not cancer. It can't be. I feel too well. We'd be in hospital having treatment. Even Mum wouldn't stop that happening if we had cancer.*

Cancer did not grow a whole new version of a person. I stroked Peepee's ears until my heart stopped pounding and I could see my laptop clearly, without all the words blurring together.

I scanned the results page and saw a new Wikipedia entry. With a little bloom of optimism, I clicked on the link. It was just some kind of science-fiction joke. I was clearly not half girl, half fly. I didn't have boggle eyes or a hairy back or a terrible temper. Okay, maybe the temper, but I'd pretty much got control of that over the last few months, so I wasn't counting it. I drummed my fingers lightly on the keyboard; it rattled softly. I went back to the results page. Google was getting me nowhere.

Maybe I wasn't looking properly. I mean there's no librarian on Google is there? You're totally alone – you and a billion answers. As I stared at the list of websites, though, I had an idea. Maybe there were other people with the same condition looking for information just like me? What if *I* put something on the internet and let them find me? Would that work?

I pulled the cuff of my cardigan over my knuckle and wiped the lens of my webcam. Maybe if I told the world, someone, somewhere, would have an idea how to help? I hesitated.

There was a tiny problem with my genius plan: Mum. She'd go nuts if she found out.

I'd do a practice – that wasn't breaking any rules – and then, if I looked like a total twit or I changed my mind, I wouldn't post it. I got up and dumped my dressing gown in a heap behind my bedroom door, to slow down anyone trying to come in, then I pulled my laptop back on my knee and waved at the camera.

"Okay. So, hi. I'm Teva Webb. Well, the current me at any rate. My mum would hate this – me talking to you.

Don't trust the internet, Teva, paedophiles are sneaky – they'll look for reflections in your eyeballs and work out where you live…"

Rambling like a lunatic wasn't going to help. I tried again.

"Hi, I'm Teva Webb, Freak of Nature. I have a large family – a very large family. There are twelve of us plus my single, never-goes-out mother – that's nearly one a year for the whole of my life. It's a miracle, I hear you cry, yeah? Well… no. Here's the thing. I've got this condition where I don't quite grow up like normal people…"

I stopped. The reality of what lay ahead of me closed off my throat for a second. Six months…it wasn't long enough. I pressed the heels of my hands against my eyelids. *Come on, Teva…* I breathed out a shaky stream of air and turned back to the camera.

"So, here it is. Roughly every birthday, a new me forces its way out of the old one. I don't know exactly how it works. I know it hurts. I know every cell inside me will split apart and seal up again until the new me has completely torn herself away. I think it's a bit like how twins separate in the womb, only with a lot more cells.

"Once it's started, we pull apart like Velcro. That makes it sound easy. It's not. Imagine you're trapped in glue, the whole of your body, and if you don't pull yourself out you'll drown. The glue tries to hold you but you tear yourself free, and when it finally lets go, it seals over and hardens."

The thick silvery skin in the crook of my elbow niggled

at me. The insides of my joints itched most of the time – the skin there was flaky and scarred. I had a theory it was because they didn't quite seal properly after the separation and were constantly trying to repair – you know, how the skin under a scab does when it's getting better? It was worse when I was stressed, and thinking about the future was about as stressful as it got. I forced myself not to scratch and turned back to the camera.

"I don't know why it happens. I only know it will. I'll still be here, but a new Teva will take over my life. Thanks to my mother's paranoia, only the new version of us leaves the house. That's not even the worst of it. Only three of us have a room to ourselves. Fifteen because she's so…hmm…what? Let's be fair – cross? Angry? Constantly furious – mostly with me. And Six because, well, she's weird. I've got the last free room because, obviously, I couldn't share with Fifteen. But when the new Teva comes along, I'll have to share with her. Only it's not exactly sharing, because I have to give up everything."

I sighed and reached for my phone. My lifeline to the two people who kept me sane, who reminded me I had a place in the world. For now, anyway. It was nearly quarter past seven. Ollie finished football at half past. My Ollie. *Mine*. A sudden surge of anger fired me up and I turned back to the camera for one more minute.

"I need help to fix this. I need someone's help from out there. When my time comes, when a new Teva starts to fight her way out of me, I need to be ready to stop her. She's not taking my life. She's not."

My voice squeezed into a dry husk.

"I hate it, hate it. It's five months and twenty-three days until my next birthday and I'm going to find a way to make it stop. I am."

two

My bedroom door bumped against the bundled-up dressing gown and Eight slipped into my room, helpfully picking up my doorstop and trailing it across the floor to my bed.

"Thanks," I said, flipping the laptop closed. "I put that there to keep you lot out."

She climbed onto my bed, a little blueprint of me. Pale skin with a permanent blush, even paler tufty hair and deep-blue sleepy eyes.

"What you doing?"

"Yeah, what you doing?" said Nine, sauntering in with her recorder swinging menacingly from her fingers – I absolutely was not in the mood for a screechy recital of "God Save the Queen".

I said, "Nothing, and if you're planning on playing that thing, please do it in your own room. Or in the loft. Or on the moon."

"You are doing something," insisted Nine. "We heard you talking."

Eva toddled in, her thumb in her mouth. She flopped Peepee on my bed. Eva, of course, had the original Peepee. Hers had soggy, chewed ears and she carried him everywhere. She loved him with a passion bordering on violence. Miraculously, she pushed him towards me. I couldn't help but smile at the offer of such a treasured possession. I took Peepee, avoiding his wet ears, and pulled Eva onto the bed, pressing a kiss on her soft little head. Eight opened my laptop and I reached round and took it off her.

"No chance, you."

"I need it."

"You don't."

"I do, I'm going to find Dad."

I froze for a second. Dad left years ago. We had no idea where he went, but we all secretly yearned for him – yep, even though we'd guessed he'd probably run out on us because we were so weird. What kid doesn't want a dad in their life? As gently as I could I said, "Don't start this again, he's not on Facebook, we looked, remember?"

Her chin wobbled and my heart twisted for her, for us. I relented, "Go on then, see what you can find."

She hunched over the keyboard. She did dwell a bit on the mystery of our dad – a combination of boredom and Enid Blyton. She'd built up a picture of a big bear of a man who was desperately sorry for leaving and was now searching for us. It was as good a picture as any. I gave Eight half a smile and said, "Honestly, you lot never give me any peace."

Eva took Peepee back. "'Smine," she said, stuffing his soggy ear into her mouth.

"Teva?" Mum's knackered voice called up the stairs followed by her heavy tread. There were three floors in our rambling old house and we needed all of them. My room was only on the first floor but it still took Mum a good couple of minutes to puff her way up. She stopped in the doorway to catch her breath before complaining, "Can't you hear me calling? I need help in the kitchen."

"I've got homework. Can't one of the others help?"

Mum flinched. "I'm asking you. Don't make a thing of it. The place is a tip and I've got a book to finish writing by the end of the week. Please?"

She gave me a sad puppy look.

"Alright," I said. "I'll be down in two minutes."

I sat Eva back against my pillows, tickling her tiny ribs. She squawked happily for a second and a little pang darted through me, that this was all the happiness she ever got.

I know she tried, but Mum had no idea what it was like for us. My stomach clenched as my future flashed through my mind again. This *every day* for ever, only without school, without…

My phone beeped.

Got time for a chat?

Mads. I messaged back.

Later. Am required to wait hand and foot on Mum x

I texted Ollie too:

Hope football was good, love you xxx

How could I manage without them in my life? What would be the point? I flicked away the messages and let my fingers linger on my background photo. Our happy faces filled the screen, Ollie's beautiful brown cheek pressed against my pink one. We'd gone to Bridlington beach for the day. The wind had blown sand across our arms and legs and cut our skin like razor wire, but it had been so worth it.

The memory of that outing twisted inside me, tainted by Fifteen's bitter rantings. The trip wasn't meant for me. It should have happened the Saturday before, but Ollie had postponed it for a football match. Fifteen had been looking forward to the trip for weeks, but it came too late for her. I took over and I took Ollie. She never got to see him again.

You can see why she hated me.

three

The next morning I was shocked awake by Fifteen slamming through my bedroom door. I jerked upright, my heart pumping crazily.

"Not getting up?" she said, banging the wardrobe doors open. I checked my clock and threw the covers back sharply.

"You could have woken me."

"Just did, didn't I?" She pulled an old school sweatshirt out of the cupboard and said, "Mine, I think? Unless you own everything now?"

She flounced out. God, she was tiring. Why would she even want her manky old uniform?

As I dressed, the few memories I had of our separation danced round my head. Fifteen had put up quite a fight. She'd clawed at my face, tried to force me back inside. I'd been stronger than her though. I was new, full of energy. Like the one who'll try and force her way out of me.

After, I remember looking down at Fifteen's exhausted

body, her hands clasped over her weeping face, pink and shining from the trauma of tearing apart and rapidly repairing again. It was weird to be outside of her, to be free of her thoughts. Everything I'd shared with her as we'd grown together, even our joint memories, felt – I don't know – cold and muddled. It was like I'd left all the fire, all the anger, in her. I remember the shock of it, searching for things to anchor myself to…I knew I was Teva, but then Teva was also in front of me, so what did that mean?

I'd panicked, drowning in the sudden loneliness of it. I scrabbled around my brain for something to hold on to, and there were Maddy and Ollie and Mum. A rush of relief surged through me as I pictured their faces. It was enough – that triangle of people – to hold me steady.

In that moment of relief, I'd smiled at the girl I'd left behind and she'd thrown her hands aside and flown at me, her bruise-blue eyes raging. That was my first independent memory. Fifteen's hands around my throat as she crashed me into the wall, screaming, "No, no, no! You're not having him, you're not."

I was seeing stars when Mum finally appeared and pulled us apart. It wasn't me she sat with though. As I rubbed at my sore throat, Mum sat rocking Fifteen back and forth whispering, "I'm sorry, my darling, so sorry. I should have been here."

I gave myself a shake and pushed the memories away. Life went on.

22

Until it didn't.

I slipped my blue school sweatshirt over my head, scuffed my fingers through my fluffy hair and scrabbled through my make-up for mascara before heading downstairs.

Six was peeling the wallpaper under the banister. I patted her head as I passed. "That drives Mum mad, monkey chops."

I liked the empty space the paper left behind though, the satisfying papery scorch where little strips had come away. Six hugged Peepee tightly against her stomach and carried on picking at the paper, her little body huddled in on itself.

Kitchen noise pressed towards me: Mum muttering, banging pots as she emptied the dishwasher; Eva crying and Twelve and Thirteen having a full-on fight over the Rice Krispies.

Breakfast was the crossest, craziest part of the day and at the last moment I couldn't face it.

"I'm off, Mum! See you later."

"What about breakfast? Teva? Wait!"

"I'll get something at school."

I grabbed my coat from the hall stand and left, pulling the heavy front door shut behind me. Cold air bit my cheeks. Hopping down our worn front steps, my breath made little clouds in the freezing air. With a shiver, I walked briskly towards the huge gates that kept the world out and us in. Weeds that had pushed through the gravel in summer lay wilted by the frost. I crunched over them, zipping my coat up tight. At the gate, I glanced over my shoulder before I punched in the code and waited to be let out. Mum had drilled it into me that the others mustn't know the code, for their own safety. I had no problem with that. I didn't want Fifteen slinking out after me.

I hurried towards the row of tiny terraced houses in Hope Street, the early morning sun stroking my back with warmth. I knocked on the flaky green door of Number 32. It floated open and Maddy said from behind it, "You're early."

"Yeah, had to escape."

"Shut the door, it's freezing out there."

I squeezed into the tiny hallway, crunching a little plastic car underfoot as I shut the door behind me. Maddy was straightening her shiny black hair in front of the hall mirror. I held out the squashed toy.

"Stick it on there." She nodded towards a pile of hairpins and brushes, odd gloves and car keys piled on the radiator shelf. I balanced the broken car on top.

"Can I grab a bit of bread?" I said. "I missed brekkie."

"Mum's in the kitchen, go and bat your eyelashes at her."

I dropped my bag by the bottom of the stairs and pushed open the door into their front room. It was piled high with boxes of saris – Mrs Ranjha ran an internet shop from home. I headed to the bright little kitchen at the back of the house. Sometimes I felt more at home in the Ranjha household than I did in mine. It was all so comfortingly normal.

"Morning, Teva. Early again?" Mrs Ranjha spooned a

dribbling blob of porridge into Baby Jay's mouth. He kicked his marshmallow legs against the high chair.

Mrs R cooed, "He loves his breakfast – don't you, darling?"

I smiled as Jay poked a porridge blob out of his mouth and down his chin.

"Can I feed him?" I said.

Mrs Ranjha handed me the spoon as Jay kicked his podgy legs in a frenzy of breakfast excitement. He was so cute, he made my cheeks hurt from smiling.

"Time for a cup of tea?" said Maddy's mum.

"Not really. Can I have a bit of bread though?"

"There's fresh chapattis by the cooker." She took over feeding baby Jay saying, "I suppose you're stressing about exams like Madam out there?"

"Mmm, sort of."

I peeled a warm chapatti from the pile and smeared it with butter before tearing a golden corner off and putting it in my mouth. Mrs R made amazing chapattis. I watched her pop the last spoonful of creamy goo into Jay's mouth and a tiny knot tightened in my throat. Their life was so different to ours. So normal; so alive. All the noise and mess in my house was…well…dead.

I'd never have a little brother. Dad gone, Mum writing books all day, inventing lives for other people instead of living one for herself. There'd never be anyone different in my house. Just me, me, more of me.

Maddy walked in, folding the top of her school skirt over. Mrs Ranjha rolled her eyes.

"Madeeha, if that skirt gets any shorter it'll be dangling round your neck like a scarf."

"Thank you, mother, I note your lack of fashion sense and duly ignore it. You ready, Tee?"

I forced myself to swallow past the knot in my throat and nodded. "Thanks for the chapatti, Mrs R."

Maddy kissed Jay's feathery hair. "See you later, poo face."

He chuckled with delight and I stole a sneaky kiss off his soft baby head.

"Come on then, Tee, if we get in early we can go to the library."

I followed her out before saying, "Library?"

"Genius, eh?" Maddy hooked her arm through mine. "Mum's constantly on my back about exams. My plan is to look like a model student so she'll leave me alone. You should have heard my *woe is me, geography is so hard* speech. Oscar-winning."

I smiled to myself. Maddy *was* a model student – it just wasn't easy to fit in at school if you were brainy, *really* brainy, AND beautiful AND you worked hard. I sometimes thought she did as much pretending as me; maybe that's why we were such good friends.

"Why did I choose geography anyway?" she said.

I had a tiny pop of panic as I delved into Fifteen's memories and couldn't find the answer. Then it came to me: "Because you fancied Dr Walker."

"Oh yeah. And then I got bloody Smitt. Remember when Walker first came? His funny little bow tie?"

I mumbled something. Talking about the past was difficult. Some things were relatively clear; some I had to piece together from stuff people said and a fog of inherited memories. How well I could remember seemed to depend on how important the memory had been to the others. Fifteen's memories of Ollie had transferred pretty much intact.

"You alright?" Maddy asked.

"Yeah, just thinking."

"Daydreaming about the lovely Ollie, perchance?" Maddy said.

"Kind of."

My thoughts pinched. My best friend had no idea what a mess my life was. Not a day went by when I didn't think about telling her the truth, but I always bottled it. I'd got pretty close but something always held me back. It was so hard to explain. I wished I could, I wanted to – maybe she could even help. I suppose it was kind of ridiculous thinking about telling everyone on the internet when I hadn't even told my best mate.

I looked at her, tried to imagine her response. She knew some stuff – she knew my skin was pretty bad but, like everyone else, she assumed it was eczema. My heart skipped. Could I tell her? Was now the time? Could I explain something totally inexplicable?

"Mads?"

"Yeah?"

"You know I sometimes have problems with dry skin?"

"Mmm."

"Well, what if it wasn't eczema? What if it was something a bit more serious than that?"

"But it isn't though."

"But what if it was?"

"But it isn't. Is it?"

I didn't answer.

Maddy stopped walking.

"Tee?"

Oh god, could I trust her? Could I actually tell her? She'd think I was crazy. Unless…what would Maddy say if I took her home, *showed* her what my life was really like…my heart raced insanely… Mum would never let her in the house, would she?

No one must know. People wouldn't understand. They'd take you away. You'd be experimented on, treated like a freak show. Mum had told us over and over.

"What? Tee, come on," Maddy laughed nervously.

I looked at her, aware of my own breathing coming just a little bit too fast. How would she feel to know I wasn't the Teva she thought she knew at fifteen? Or thirteen? Or eight? That I wasn't the girl she'd choked on a stolen cigarette with? And I wasn't the girl she'd cried her heart out to when Ben Harrison had turned up at the Year Seven disco with some other girl?

She'd know I was a liar for a start.

My throat tightened.

"Come on," she said, "it can't be that bad? Is it scabies? I had that when I was at St Michael's."

What if she thought I'd stolen Fifteen's life? In my darkest, most honest moments, I knew that was true. It wasn't my fault but it was true. I couldn't tell her. I couldn't risk it.

"Nits then?" Maddy teased. "You've got nits and you think you've given them to me? Eurgh, now I've made my own head itch," she said, frantically scratching.

I laughed and that was it – the moment for telling was gone. She made things so normal. If Maddy knew, everything would change – and I wasn't ready for that. When I'd found some answers – a cure – then I'd tell her. Then there'd be hope, not just a hideous tangle of worry that I could only forget when I was with her or Ollie.

So I said, "You loon, Madeeha. It's nothing, come on, we might make it in time to get a bacon butty." I yanked her arm. "I'm starved."

"You literally never stop eating."

I clamped my teeth together. She was right. I was always eating. My hand strayed to my waist. "Am I fat? Do I look fat to you?" I tugged the hemline of my skirt down a tiny bit. "Can you see the fat bit at the top of my legs?"

"I was joking! God, Tee, you're not fat. You're such a bloody worrier."

She didn't know the half of it.

four

"So why'd you run away before breakfast?" Maddy asked.

"Ahh, you know what my mum's like when she's tired."

"Not really, no."

I scuffed my foot against the floor. It wound Maddy up that I never asked her back to mine. I glossed over the little dig.

"She was just in a mood, I didn't want to deal with it." How easily I lied.

"Expect all the ghosts kept her awake last night."

I shoved Mads in the ribs with my elbow. It was a standing joke that our house was haunted. Maddy had nearly died when she found out where I lived. That made it a little bit easier to keep friends away – and to explain the ghostly faces at the windows sometimes. Not many people wanted a sleepover in Crumbly Towers.

"Don't you feel lonely in that massive house, just the two of you?"

"Sometimes, a bit," I answered honestly, although not for the reasons she thought. Life could be very lonely when half your household hated you.

"Must be nice not to have to worry about money though?"

This was Maddy's not very subtle way of digging into my family background. She knew Mum was a writer and seemed to think that we had JK Rowling amounts of money. We didn't. Mum had to write a lot of books to keep us going – romance stories mostly; ironic, eh? My mum, who only ever saw the grocery man. Paula Houldin, Natalie Wilde and Verity Sunlight were all my mum. Last count she'd written forty-three books, but we weren't exactly swilling champagne every night.

A nugget of guilt about helping out more nudged at the edge of my brain. I nudged it right back and changed the subject. "Did you talk to Ed last night?"

"Yeah," said Maddy, "he sent me a copy of his personal statement."

"Nice," I said. "Really romantic."

"Oh shut up, Webb, we can't all be in loved-up heaven. I can't believe it'll be us next, getting our uni applications ready. It only seems five minutes since you took Kristal Mitchell down for the first time. Pow!"

Maddy mimed a little punch and then hugged me to her side, quick and sharp. She always exaggerated that scene in the folklore of our friendship. Kristal had gathered a gaggle of girls to bitch about Maddy, and Six had waded in, stamping her foot and shouting, *"You're just mean. She's brown, not dirty."*

It was one of the few memories Six had passed on; she'd been pretty proud of herself that day. I smiled, thinking about it.

Maddy said, "I wonder what we'll end up doing?"

Talk about the future made my chest hurt but I managed to mumble, "Mmmm…"

Luckily, Mads was in full flow. "Poor Ed's totally stressed out. Did you know he's got a weekend job at the skate park? Hey, maybe we should go on Saturday?"

"Erm, really, Mads…? Are you serious?"

"No. Brief moment of madness. Anyway, I don't really want to get involved with anyone in Year Thirteen."

Maddy talked a lot about boys but she never, ever did anything about it. All she really cared about, no matter what she said, was good grades and getting into a decent uni. Still, it was such a familiar routine, the walk to school, Maddy talking about whichever boy she was focusing on that week. I pulled her chatter round me like a warm blanket.

I was an expert at half listening, at saying the right thing at the right time. My head churned with thoughts I didn't want to have. Filling it with Maddy talk was like smoothing cream on my itchy skin. I'd lose that if I told Maddy what my condition was really like. She'd want to know everything. Everything. I could never use her to wipe it away; it would always be there, all the time.

"So what do you think?" Maddy said.

So much for half listening. I'd completely missed what she said. "Erm. Isn't it today you get your maths results back?"

Maddy covered her face with pink, fluffy gloved fingers, and groaned.

"Come on, Mads, you'll have done brilliantly."

"I won't."

"Course you will, you always do."

"Hmm, I sometimes wish I'd done drama – prancing about and making masks, or whatever it is you do. Or textiles – a nice bit of sewing. Why are all your subjects so much fun while all of mine are boring?"

"Shut up, my nerdy friend, you know you love it." I slipped my arm through hers, my fingers squishing into the padded warmth of her coat. "Anyway, you'll be the one earning pots of money one day while I..."

I blinked. Caught off guard by my own stupidity. I wouldn't be doing anything, would I? Not unless I found a cure. I scrabbled for something to save my tumbling thoughts, but Maddy cut in. "While you live a life of fun and frolics. I know. Which reminds me, you missed the first fashion show meeting, you better be coming to the one tonight."

"Erm..." I shrank a little bit. "I can't. I've got to get home, Mum needs me to help out with a story she's writing."

Well that was the worst lie ever.

"You're such a fibber, Tee. Honestly. Come on, you have to do it – it's tradition. All the sixth-formers do it. You know Ollie'll be there? His group are modelling ski wear and dancing to 'Let it Snow'."

"Mmm..."

"Literally everyone does it, Tee – it raises so much money for charity. Think of all the starving children in Africa. They need you! Last year they raised over £5000."

She stepped in front of me and held both my arms. "Please, Tee? Loads of cool shops are lending us stuff. Everyone is getting involved. Even the geeky tech boys are doing lights and stuff. It'll be a laugh – it's just one dance."

I struggled to give her another excuse. The truth was, there were loads of reasons why I didn't want to do it. Everyone thinks drama students love any chance to show off, but that's not true – acting is a bit like hiding and that was something I did every day of my life. Modelling showed far too much of me. The actual me. Plus, I'd have to try and persuade Mum to come, or look like a totally unloved loser, and Mum was highly unlikely to ever leave the house unless it was on fire. So I said, "It's not proper fashion, is it? It's stupid stuff like stinky charity shops. And I bet Year Thirteen give us all the rubbish clothes, like the stuff from the fancy dress shop. Didn't some of them have to dress up in sumo outfits last year?"

"Yeah, that was hilarious. I thought you loved it."

The memory popped up clear as day; Fifteen had definitely loved it. I tried a new tactic.

"What's your group even doing?"

"*Our* group, Tee. I put your name down too."

I flicked a look at her and she raised her eyebrows in defiance.

"Alright," I said, "what's OUR group doing?"

"Don't freak out. It's funny, okay?"

"What is it?"

"Promise you won't have a hissy fit?"

"Maddy!"

"Alright, alright…outdoor shoes."

"Outdoor shoes? Hiking boots and wellies?"

"Yeah, the camping shop are lending them. Oh come on, it's for charity, Teva. And it's meant to be fun. Not everyone can do ball gowns, that would be boring."

She looked at the floor and I felt like the world's worst friend. The world's worst charity-scorning friend. And shoes and boots were kind of okay, weren't they? You wouldn't show much skin modelling shoes and boots. I tucked my hand in my pocket, flicking the cover off my phone, but I was saved from making a decision when Maddy spotted Ed waiting at the school gates.

"Eek!"

"Maddy, you actually just squeaked."

"Oh shut up, Tee. Is he waiting for us, do you think? Has my nose gone red in the cold?"

She rubbed the end of her nose with her glove.

"Yes. You are practically Rudolph."

Maddy slapped my arm and switched on her hundred-watt smile. A bounce crept into her walk and she flicked her head from side to side like she was in a shampoo ad.

I couldn't help letting out a little snorty giggle.

"Shut up," said Maddy, without ruining her beautiful, slightly mad, grin. She gave an extra flick of her head.

My cheeks ached trying not to laugh. "You're literally Ed-sessed."

"Easy for you to say, Mrs I've-got-a-boyfriend."

She waved at Ed and sparkled, "Ed! Hi. You waiting for someone?"

He stood a little taller and swung his rucksack over his shoulder. "I saw you coming and thought, you know…"

My phone vibrated in my pocket, thrilling through my body. I pulled it out, hoping it would be Ollie. I wasn't disappointed:

Waiting by hall xx

"Sorry, guys, Ollie wants to see me before reg. I better run. Hey, Ed, you can carry Maddy's books for her?"

Maddy swung her bag at my legs but I'd already skipped off, calling, "See you in ten!"

I ran the distance between Maddy and Ollie. Partly because I wanted to feel wrapped up in him and partly because, without Maddy's bubbling chatter, all the worry I'd managed to push down would just seep back up to the surface, making my head hurt and my heart pound and, and, and…

As soon as I saw him, I stopped racing and walked, drinking in the sight of him. He had his headphones clamped over his ears and one leg crooked up against the sports-hall wall. He was playing on his phone. My solid rock in a rough, rough sea. I'd read some of Mum's Paula Houldin books. I knew my heart was supposed to race and my knees turn to jelly when I saw him, but it wasn't like that with us. I felt like that when I *wasn't* with him, not when I was.

Walking up to Ollie was like being slowly pulled into his orbit of normal. He looked up and saw me, his face cracking into the widest smile…I couldn't help but be lifted by it. Pulling his earphones down around his neck, he came towards me, rocking from side to side as he walked – I loved his swagger. I knew he seemed cocky, but he was actually really sweet. The Ollie he showed to the world was a tough man, a bit of a lad maybe, but when he traced his thumb over my cheek; when he gently touched the tip of his nose to my nose; when he twined his fingers into mine, our hands palm to palm, and held me in his gaze…sometimes I thought he half powered my life.

"Morning," I said, pulling him closer with my words.

"Morning." He tucked his hand behind my neck and pulled me into a full on-the-mouth kiss. I sank into it. If he wanted to show the whole school I was his, I wasn't going to argue with that.

He slipped his arm round my shoulder as we walked to class. I loved the feeling of belonging, even if it pushed my neck into a funny angle. Since that first day on the beach, *my* first day with him, Fifteen's feelings, her memories of Ollie, had become mine. I had willingly absorbed them, blended with them. I tipped my head towards his and he kissed the top of it, like I knew he would.

"Football good last night?" I asked.

"It was alright."

"Did you get your English done?" Why? Why did I even mention it?

He didn't answer.

A little anxious burst squeezed my insides. I looked up at him. I should have shut up then but I didn't. "You've got to get it this year, Oll. They won't let you carry on with A levels if you don't, you'll have to do an apprenticeship or something."

"I know, I'm trying, it's just so boring."

"I'll help you, you've only got to say."

"You promised me you wouldn't go on about it."

I bit my lip. That so wasn't true. I'd said no such thing. Ollie kicked at an imaginary can in front of him. "War poetry. Who needs that stuff in real life anyway?"

"Yeah. I know but…"

I wasn't a genius like Maddy, but, miraculously – given it was Fifteen who'd taken the exams – we'd managed alright at GCSE. She'd done enough for me to do the A levels I wanted anyway. Ollie had stayed on by the skin of his teeth. As we walked towards school, I could feel the worry of him failing his retake throbbing in me like a living thing. It was amazing that they'd let him stay without it – they'd given a few people the chance to take it again, but if they didn't pass, they wouldn't be allowed to stay and finish their courses. Apprenticeships were not an option at our school.

I couldn't leave it alone.

"I just don't want you to get chucked out."

He stiffened at my side and *still* I didn't let it go.

"When is your actual exam?"

"I don't know, couple of weeks? Please, just leave it, yeah?

They won't chuck me out. Look at me, what would they do without me?"

What would I do without you? A shudder rippled through me, spiking the hairs on my arms.

"Yeah, you're right. It'll be fine. I know."

My stomach churned. I had a horrible feeling it wouldn't be fine. Mind you, somewhere, not all that deep down, I always had that feeling.

"Just leave it, yeah, you promised."

"I don't think I did."

"Yeah you did, last night on Facebook."

"But I…" my mouth closed. I didn't speak to him on Facebook last night.

Fifteen.

It had to be. What had she said? God, that girl.

I quizzed him lightly. "And what else did I say?"

He chuckled, before pulling me tightly into his side. "You can be a wicked girl, Teva Webb, wicked."

The churning in my stomach doubled. It was my own fault. I hadn't changed the password on our Facebook account out of guilt. I'd wanted her to have something, to at least be able to see our friends. I should have known she wouldn't just look at pictures. I wouldn't either, in her situation. And I wouldn't just sit at home while someone else lived my life. I'd be looking for a way to get it back.

And so would she.

five

As soon as we were in the school building Ollie said, "I'll catch up with you in a bit, yeah?"

He lifted his arm from my shoulder, leaving a weird anti-trace of him, cold and light.

"You going up to the common room?" I asked, knowing full well he was.

"Pool tournament," he said. "I'll miss my slot if I don't go upstairs." A cheeky dimple played at the corner of his mouth. "Come with me?"

I wrinkled my nose. Skipping registration wasn't really okay and, let's face it, I was a fair-weather rebel – only likely to revolt if I was lost in a crowd. I might have moaned about things but I usually toed the line. Sad, eh? I said, "I'll come up later. I need to see Frankie."

"Off you go then, there's a good girl," he pulled me close so our noses were touching, "my bad-good girl."

He slid his hand over my bum before pulling away, grinning.

What had Fifteen said to him? Whatever it was, I could guarantee she'd have deleted the whole message thread so I'd never know.

"Laters then," he said and walked away.

"Yeah, sorry," I said to his disappearing back. Would Fifteen have followed him? Maybe. Probably not. She'd have made up a better excuse though. Coloured her reason with something important – definitely not because she wanted to see her form tutor. I rubbed the back of my neck. Thinking about Fifteen sent a grinding ache up through my spine and into my head.

I shoved open the door to the textiles room, slung my bag on the floor and flopped into the old patchwork armchair that me and Mads usually shared. It was an ex-student project and, since our first day in the form room, we'd made it ours.

I liked Miss Francis, Frankie, our form tutor. She was my textiles teacher too – that's why registration was in her lovely, mad-old-hippy classroom. I loved spending time in there – the walls hung with students' work, cushion covers and tapestries, the warm smell of wool and creativity.

There were usually only a dozen of us in reg. All in various combinations of skirts and trousers topped off with the school sweatshirt – the only bit of uniform we had to wear in Year Twelve. Lola and Barnet nodded at me. They were sitting on a long work surface under the window, joined at the head by shared headphones and Lola's iPod. I can't remember Barnet's real name; it was long forgotten in the midst of Year Nine, when she'd first tried out one of her crazy, ever-changing hairstyles. That morning, as I waited for Mads to come in, Barnet's hair was an astonishing pink bob, so bright it hurt my eyes, and shaved off completely over one ear. At the back of the class were the shadowy, quiet people whose names I only remembered when Frankie called the register. Kevin, Wotsit and the Skinny Girl. Maddy arrived with Miss Francis.

Frankie had her hair tied up in a 1940s headscarf thing; she gave it a tweak and the two ends flopped forward like droopy blue rabbit ears.

"You are rockin' that bunny look, Miss," Maddy said, perching next to me on the arm of the chair.

"Yes, I am rather proud of it, Madeeha. That reminds me, have you thought any more about joining the debating team?"

Maddy said, "Bunny ears reminded you about the debating team?"

"No. Your cheekiness reminded me about your personal statement. You should try for Oxbridge, Maddy, you really should."

"God, Miss, I've already said, I'm not going to no posh college where all they do is throw buns and drink port. It's ages away anyhow." Whenever Maddy talked about going to Oxford or Cambridge her accent went insanely rough, like some sort of antidote to any thoughts she had of actually going there.

Frankie went on, "The Oxbridge deadline is just a few months away."

"That's what I said," Maddy replied, "ages."

I grunted as she slithered off the arm of the chair onto my lap. "Get off, you lump. You're squeezing the breath out of me. Mads, move."

Frankie interrupted our wrestle for the comfiest spot in the chair. "I have reminder notes for Alice and Teva."

Alice. That's what the Skinny Girl was called, why could I never remember?

Frankie leaned around Maddy as if I wasn't being used as a human cushion, and handed me the pale green slip of folded paper. I shoved it in my pocket, levering Maddy off my lap as I did. She said, "I don't know why you need learning support. You're brilliant at English."

I shrugged. "Sally Gardner is dyslexic, Mads, and she won the Carnegie Medal – it doesn't mean you can't write. I just need a bit of extra help, that's all."

I was glad when the school bell split the air, marking first period. Outright lying to Maddy made my skin itch. The bit about Sally Gardner was true, but I was not dyslexic.

Frankie dismissed us with a wave of her hand. "Off you go then, faithful gang. Have a good morning."

I fingered the little slip of paper in my pocket and absent-mindedly picked up my bag. Frankie said, "Where are you going, Miss Webb? You're with me this morning, aren't you?"

"Oh yeah. Sorry."

"Well, get your work out, I won't be a minute."

Frankie slipped out of the room with everyone else. Alone, I unstapled the note: *10 a.m. Room 7 School Counsellor.*

I scratched at the inside of my left elbow. As soon as I did it, I was sorry. Within seconds my arms and shoulders prickled all over. My lurking itch flared to a screaming need to claw my skin. Why did I never learn?

"Dammit."

I raked at my arms and upper back until they flamed with delicious satisfaction, but as soon as I stopped, I burned. My soft school sweatshirt felt like it was lined with a thousand needle tips. I scrabbled through my bag for my cream. I was an expert at applying it under my clothes and slowly the savage fire gave way to damp, cloying calm. I wound my hands together until the last of it had soaked in, covering my fingers with a greasy layer that would make it nearly impossible to sew. Brilliant.

I slapped the huge plastic wallet full of my project work down on the desk in front of me. It was cracking where I kept folding it in half and shoving it in my bag. I was glad Frankie hadn't seen the state of it. I tried to smooth it out a bit. The rest of my textiles class trickled in, murmuring sleepy good mornings. Bags were thrown under chairs and more plastic folders were flopped on to tables. The desks were soon covered in an array of fabric and scribbled notes. I slid out the tweed corset I was making. It was British army khaki on the outside with a Union Jack silk fabric on the inside. The tattered skin on my thumb snagged on the lining every time I worked it.

My corset looked alright though. I was quite pleased with it really. My job for that morning was making the scarlet poppies that would twist down the front and over the left shoulder.

Tommo dropped heavily into the seat next to me. He was the only boy in the whole of sixth form doing textiles. Tall, broad and with a six-pack he was always ready to show off, Tommo was not the kind of boy you'd expect in a sewing class. All his friends had taken the piss when he'd signed up but he'd just smiled and said, "Girls, mate, who's the fool?"

He laid his perfect black folder on the desk and then kissed me on the cheek, sparking a wild blush across my face.

"Morning, gorgeous," he said, oblivious to my bright pink cheeks. He held the edge of my corset between his thumb and forefinger, feeling the fabric and said, "That's looking awesome."

I smiled, pleased.

"Now you've shown me yours, I'll show you mine."

From the smooth covers of his folder he slipped out the black-and-white bunny-girl corset he was making. It was such a *Playboy* cliché, it made me laugh every time I saw it. You had to hand it to him though, for a lad with the hands of a giant, he'd done a good job.

"You sorted those sequins round the top then?" I said – he'd been having trouble securing them.

"Yeah, Frankie Fixit showed me how."

"Looks good," I said as Frankie came bounding back into class with a big grin on her face. She clapped her hands excitedly.

45

"News, I have news! You are going to LOVE it. Mr Blackwell has agreed that you can model your corsets in the fashion show!"

Mouths dropped open all around the classroom. I could literally feel the shock waves. What was she thinking? I looked at her happy face. Was she insane? There was no way on god's earth I was standing on stage in my underwear.

Cold horror balled in my stomach. This was exactly what I'd been trying to avoid. Like I was going to put my hideous skin on display. I'd managed to keep myself hidden through the whole of school – and that wasn't easy in PE I can tell you – Mum had to write notes pretending I suffered really badly with the cold and needed to wear base layers and trackie bottoms even on the hottest days. No. This was not happening. The woman really was insane. Didn't I have enough to cope with?

Six

"Onstage? In our corsets? Did I hear you right, Miss?" Skinny Alice piped up from the back of the class.

I pulled my sleeves over my hands, shrank into my chair and glanced around the room. I wasn't the only one looking horrified. Miss Francis flapped her hands at us, confusion at our lack of enthusiasm written across her furrowed brow.

"Alright," she said, "don't panic, the idea is you'll wear them over something. It's one of the conditions – no more skin than you'd see in a PE lesson. Surely we can manage that? *Come on, guys!* Let's get creative. How great will it be to show off your work to the rest of the school? This is the first time they've let us include your projects and I'm proud of you – I want everyone to see how brilliant you are."

Tommo pulled up his T-shirt and ran a hand over his rock-hard stomach, saying, "Well, I'm up for it." He held up the scrap of fabric he'd designed to lace tightly round a girl's body. "I might have to add some longer laces though…"

It was alright for him, he could make a joke of it. It wasn't the same for the rest of us, was it?

"Thank you, Tommo. I had hoped the rest of you might be a bit more enthusiastic," Frankie went on, "because there's something else. A scout for the lingerie team at H&S is coming and they might select one of you to go on their apprenticeship scheme this summer."

She beamed at our still stunned faces. "I know! It's brilliant, isn't it?"

It was both brilliant and terrible. A summer apprenticeship scheme, if I had any chance of getting it, was months away. After my birthday. If I didn't find a way to stay, I wouldn't be here, would I? I picked up one of my half-finished poppies, my hands trembling and slick from the cream I'd slathered on. As I tried to extract the needle I'd left in it, it slipped and stabbed me.

"Ow!" A warm bead of blood swelled fatly on my thumb. My brain flooded with thoughts – how much of that blood was mine? How much was the new Teva's? Was she already there, floating under my skin, under my conscience? My heart began to pound, sweat gathered in my armpits but fear turned to something else.

My jaw tightened. There was no way I was prancing about onstage for *her* – the new me – to get all the benefit. Unless I stopped her, unless… The anger blooming in me was swept with a sudden shot of guilt as I realized…that's how Fifteen felt about me – all the work she'd done for our exams, just for me to take over. Frustrated tears trickled down my cheeks. I dashed them away and sucked the blood off my thumb. The iron tang mingling with the medical, greasy cream left a nasty taste in my mouth. I jabbed my needle viciously into the delicate flower. Angry with myself, angry with the new Teva, angry with everything still to come.

As I tried to pull the needle back through, the thread puckered behind the flower and caught in an ugly knot. I threw it on the table with a growl. Tommo turned to me and noticed the tears. "Come on, it's not that bad – it could be fun. Hey, I could lace our corsets together and model them both. I have the power."

He pulled up his sleeve and flexed his bicep. As the muscle bulged, heat seeped up my neck. I couldn't help the tiny smile that crept into the corners of my mouth. Tommo tipped his head towards mine and whispered, "You can have a feel if you like."

A laugh burst from me and I slapped him. A vision of Ollie sprang guiltily into my head and I sat up a bit straighter in my chair. Tommo said, "The H&S thing is a really great opportunity – imagine how good it could look on your CV."

"*You* imagine how good it would look on *your* CV."

He shrugged. "I've already got something lined up this summer, with the Navy cadets."

My mouth squeezed together – I wanted to say something encouraging but I couldn't trust myself to speak. I wanted so badly to have a future. Something to dream about, something to hope for. I just nodded.

"You should go for it," Tommo said. "Your work is amazing, seriously."

"I don't know," I managed to croak. "I haven't really thought about what I'm going to do with my..."

I stopped. I wanted to say *life* but I wasn't going to have one, was I? My thoughts spun off. What *could* I do? If the others were right about doctors, what could I clutch at? Could my lame idea of a blog really help?

Tommo said, "If you don't give it a go, you'll never know, will you?" He was right, and not just about the H&S visit. I looked down at the piece I was making and tried to say something that made sense.

"Yeah, maybe...I wonder if Mads would be my model?"

"That's my girl," said Tommo putting an arm round my shoulders, crushing me into his side, just as Ollie walked past the classroom.

I jerked away.

Tension flowered in my chest. Had he seen? Ollie had a bit of a problem with Tommo; all the boys did. They liked him but they didn't like how easy he was with girls. Ollie would go mad if he thought Tommo was flirting with me. Or worse, that I was flirting with Tommo. Something in me retreated. Dimly, I watched Tommo hand his portfolio to Miss Francis, like I was far away, separated. I watched her pull out sheets and sheets of sketches, notes, fabric swatches, pattern details.

As I watched, I scratched at the table with my index finger and thought about Six peeling the wallpaper, leaving a lovely, clean space. If only you could do that to your life, peel away the layers and leave something clean and...

"Teva? Hello? Earth calling Teva."

I dragged myself back to reality.

"Sorry, Miss, sorry, I was just thinking I..."

"It's fine, I just want to look at the work in your folder."

I pulled my portfolio closer and let Miss Francis slide out the practically empty sheets of paper that should, by now, have been covered with my assessment work.

She wasn't happy. She sucked in her top lip and said, "Are you struggling with this, Teva?"

I shrugged. I was having a hard time concentrating, my mind stuffed with the extra worry that Ollie had seen me tucked under Tommo's arm. I looked at her blankly – *was I struggling?* Did she want to have a go at living my life for a bit? Sometimes, it felt ridiculous that I had to worry about normal things on top of all the other stuff.

"Your garment is good, but you have to back it up with portfolio work or you won't get the marks you deserve."

She waited but what could I say? Part of me wished she'd push harder, force me to tell her the truth, but she just said, "If there's nowhere for you to work at home you can come in here at lunchtimes, if that helps."

Space to work was so far down the list of things that would help it was off the page. My phone beeped.

"Sorry, Miss, that's my alarm, I've got to go – my appointment."

Frankie sighed. "Go on then. But we need to sort this, Teva.

I'm not going to let you waste six months' work."

"Hey, Tee," said Tommo, flourishing a rabbit tail at me, "you can come round mine if you like, we can work together."

Frankie patted Tommo's folder. "That's a good idea, Teva, you should take him up on that. Tom has done some really excellent work."

I grabbed my stuff and bolted from the room so fast I barely had time to give an apologetic smile. What a terrible idea. Ollie would go mad. The last thing I needed was *more* problems.

Seven

I headed up to my appointment but I couldn't shake off the worry about Ollie seeing me with Tommo. I nipped into the loo to calm down a bit. I splashed my face with cold water, careful not to smudge my mascara. Leaning on the sink, I looked in the gum-stuck mirror and said, "Stop stressing, you've done nothing wrong."

And I hadn't, it wasn't like I'd flirted back.

I sent Ollie a text, *Meet me lunchtime? Xxx*

A bit of me was slightly disgusted that I was so clingy but I just needed to know everything was okay between us.

It's hard to explain why I needed him so much; it was more than love. He was like one of those sandbags they hang around the side of a hot-air balloon. Maddy was too. They kept me weighted, steady. Without them I'd float off. And not in a good way. In a disappearing way. I knew my heart would calm once he'd texted me back. When we were fine everything else was fine too. Sort of. As close to fine as it got for me.

I went upstairs, fiddling with the cover on my phone. The door to room seven was half open.

Elliepants was writing notes, her long, stringy hair tucked behind her enormous ears. Obviously, I didn't have learning support. I had a therapy session with Ms Ellie Fenton. She looked up at me with her wrinkly, blinky eyes and smiled, her mouth all pouty like an elephant's.

"Hi, Teva, come in, shut the door, that's it."

I sat in the armchair opposite her, tucking my school bag into my stomach like a flak jacket.

"Is there anything special you want to talk about this week?"

I shook my head. We had these sessions because Fifteen had shoved Kristal Mitchell down C-block staircase after she called Maddy a stuck-up Paki. Kristal got away with it; Fifteen got Elliepants. I don't know why I still had to see her. I'd learned to control my anger. I wondered sometimes if Elliepants knew something wasn't right with me; not that I gave anything away. Mum had to let us go to the sessions but she'd laid down the law about what we could and couldn't say.

They'll come poking around our house if you say anything odd. Imagine what it'll be like. Everyone will think you're a freak – or crazy.

Elliepants tried again. "How've you been this week?"

I shrugged. "Alright."

"Did you try writing things down, like we talked about?"

Like Elliepants had talked about.

"Yeah," I lied.

"And how was that?"

I shrugged again.

I was hotly aware that Ollie hadn't texted me back.

"You seem a bit tense, Teva. Is everything okay?"

My teeth ground together. Sometimes the urge to throw at her what my life was really like was overwhelming. I clamped it down. Mum was probably right, she'd think I was mad and then I'd never get away from her – Elliepants would love a real-life genuine crazy to work on.

Silence stretched between us.

A patch of skin behind my knee began to itch. I'd barely got a fingernail to it before it flared into a bonfire of irritation. I dug in my bag for my cream. At least that saved me from having to talk. Well, it would have, if Elliepants ever gave up.

"Did you keep a journal then?" she said.

I looked at the floor.

"Teva?"

She waited. Eventually I said, "I did a video blog thing."

Her eyes opened like saucers. "On the internet? Are you sure that's a good idea?"

No. I wasn't sure of anything. There were no self-help books on how to deal with a life like mine. No agony aunts to email. The one person I could talk to was Mum and she never listened. How was I supposed to know what was a good idea and what wasn't?

Elliepants said, "The internet's very public, Teva."

Did she think I didn't know that?

"Maybe," she said, "if you feel you want to share with more people, group therapy would be good?"

I bolted upright. "God no!"

She raised her eyebrows.

I shook my head. "I didn't post the video. I'm not an idiot." I was seriously thinking about it though. So what did that make me?

Elliepants stuck on her calm-down-dear smile but I boiled inside. She had no idea. Every day was a struggle just to stay calm. Every minute. The only way I stayed sane was by keeping my anchors in place and one of them was feeling too wobbly for my liking. My silent phone burned a hole in my hand. Ollie still hadn't texted me back. It was too much. I stood up, holding my bag close.

Elliepants tried to coax me into staying: "Well, I'm not very good with computers. Tell me about the blog, is it like a diary?"

I nodded but I needed to go; to make sure Ollie hadn't seen Tommo and me. Other people might not realize how sensitive he was but I had a head full of memories of his tenderness. Okay, I'd inherited most of them from Fifteen but I'd replayed them so often, it was easy to believe they were mine. I remembered our first kiss like it *had* been me.

Ollie had held me in his gaze and I didn't feel like a pale, scabby-skinned shadow, barely holding onto her place in the world. When he looked at me, I saw myself the way he did. He thought my tufty hair was cute, so it was. He wasn't bothered by my horrible skin so, when I was with him,

I wasn't. When I was with him, *I* mattered. I couldn't lose him. I wouldn't.

"Teva?"

"I've got to go, Miss, I don't want to be too late for my next lesson…"

"These sessions are for your benefit, Teva."

"I know. Sorry. I've got to go."

I left Elliepants – frowning – behind me and headed straight for the common room. I felt so stupid after talking to her, like I really was an unstable idiot. I charged along the corridor, nearly colliding with Mrs Churchill, who barked, "Teva Webb, walk don't run!"

I slowed to a walking run until I was out of her sight, then I flew up the common room stairs and banged open the door.

Kristal Mitchell was bent over the pool table, her skirt so short her fanny was practically on display. And there, helping her line up her cue, nearly on top of her, was Ollie. My Ollie. Kristal's diamanté-tipped nails glittered in the sun like claws. My heart nearly exploded out of my chest.

eight

I spun round and ran to the sixth-form loos, flung open a cubicle and locked myself in. Footsteps were right behind me. Ollie. A pathetic ladies sign wouldn't keep him out. He slapped his palm against the door, a single flat knock, and sighed.

"It's not what you think, Tee."

I screwed my hands into my hair, the tight pull on my scalp relieving some of the pressure on my brain. Had that little scene been deliberate? Was he punishing me because he'd seen me and Tommo? He rattled the door.

"Tee, come on. I was just showing her how to hold the cue – you know what an airhead she is. Don't be like this."

I sniffed, determined not to cry. "You were practically on top of her."

"Oh come on, I wasn't. I was just helping her. I felt sorry for her, that's all. Anyway, you said you never worried about me hanging out with other girls because you knew I'd always be yours."

I hadn't said that. I absolutely had not said that. I bet that was Fifteen having a dig at me.

"Honestly, sometimes I can't get a handle on what you want from me, Tee. You say something one day and the next you don't seem to remember anything about it!"

The tone of his voice had changed and a twitch of panic tightened my jaw.

"Can you really see me and Kristal together?"

I just had.

"Come on, *you're* my girl, you know that."

I took my phone out of my pocket and tapped the screen. Our happy beach faces smiled up at me. I touched my fingertip to his beautiful cheek and stood for a second, weighing up my options. I felt like I was holding on so tight to everything – to Ollie, to my dreams of a future, to life... If I tried to talk to him about Kristal, everything else might burst out. I couldn't do it. I said, "It's not that. Sorry. I think I must have eaten something funny, my stomach is a bit off. I'll be fine, just give me five minutes."

And actually, my stomach did feel a bit off. Unsettled. More than usual, I mean. I put it down to seeing Ollie and Kristal, but something really didn't feel right.

My phone vibrated in my hand and Mum's name flashed up. As Mum never texted, it could only mean Fifteen had her phone. Great.

Hope you're having a lovely day xx

Sarcastic cow. How did she know? I texted back, *Yeah, great thanks.*

Ollie pushed the toe of his Converse under the door. It made me smile, just a little bit. I touched it with my own, whispering, "Snap."

"You sure you're okay?" he said.

I swallowed, not trusting myself to speak, and then the main door to the loo creaked open and another pair of feet came in. With relief, I heard Maddy's voice. "Oi oi! Something to tell us, Oliver? Had a sex change, have we?"

My heart lifted.

"Yeah, very funny. Teva's in there, she's not feeling well, she won't come out."

A gentler hand knocked the door.

"Tee? What's up, hon?"

"I ate something funny. I'm fine, honestly, just a bit queasy."

"I hope my mum hasn't chapattied you to death."

"Ha," I said softly.

Maddy and Ollie mumbled something quietly and then the outer door creaked.

"Tee? He's gone. It's just me. What's up?"

I slid back the lock and peeled open the door. Glossy, lovely, solid Mads frowned her concern at me.

I said, "Kristal Mitchell."

"What?"

An image of Kristal sprawled over the pool table, laughing up at Ollie, fired a ball of anger in my gut and a blazing trail of itching in my skin. How dare she flirt with him? I needed him. What else did she have to cope with in her life? The rising price of lipgloss? I gave in to the itching and scratched until my skin was screaming. Until Maddy caught up my hands and held onto them.

"You're making yourself bleed, Tee, stop it. Whatever she did, she's not worth it."

I threw myself back against the toilet wall.

"God, Mads – she's such a slag. She might as well have a tattoo on her arse saying 'Take Me'."

"So…?"

"Ollie was *helping* her with her pool technique."

Maddy raised her eyebrows. "Ouch."

"Yeah."

"So what are you going to do?"

"Do?"

"Yeah? With Ollie, what are you going to do?"

What could I do? What did I even want to do? I shrugged and, as my shoulders dropped, my anger turned into something floppy and wet. I had enough to worry about. Anyway, if he had seen me with Tommo's arm round my shoulders it sort of made us quits, didn't it?

Through a thick throat I said, "Nothing. It just looked bad. Ollie wouldn't really do anything."

She opened her mouth to speak but I said, "Oh, look, it's fine. I overreacted. Let's just leave it, yeah? Can I borrow your mascara? I look a wreck."

She hesitated then rummaged in her bag.

"Here," she stuck it in my hand. "You sure you're okay? I want to see Smitt before next lesson, he's got some papers for me."

"Yeah. Go on."

"Haven't you got…?"

"Art? Yeah. I'll be fine, just tidy myself up a bit."

I'd lied though. I wasn't fine. My stomach felt really weird – bloated and gurgly. I undid the top button of my trousers. Maybe I *had* been chapattied to death. I heaved a sigh and took one last look in the mirror, tufting up my hair before I left the loo. As I opened the door, my phone vibrated again. I pulled it out of my bag as I walked. A smiley face – supposedly from Mum. Definitely Fifteen winding me up. I knew she was bored, jealous – angry about a million things I could do nothing about, but still, I growled under my breath before heading back to the common room to make things right with Ollie.

It took a very deep breath to push the door open, but there was no horrible flirting going on. Ollie was sitting with the rest of the boys, looking a bit lost if I'm honest. He glanced up when I came in and his face opened up into his huge, little boy smile. My heart melted and I smiled right back.

I glanced round for Kristal. She was sitting on a window ledge, sunlight filtering through her mane of red hair. She might be a cow but she was beautiful. Tears bit the back of my throat but Ollie was on his feet and crossing the room towards me. Before I could even speak, he tucked one arm round my shoulders and the other behind my knees and scooped me up. My nerves evaporated in a flutter of squeals.

We were okay. I was okay. He buried his face in my neck.

"Got you," he said, so only I could hear, "and now I'm going to eat you."

I laughed as he plopped me on one of the old sofas between Jake and Ed and then tried to squeeze himself in as well. He ended up half sitting on Jake's lap.

Jake shoved at Ollie. "Get off me, you bony-arsed git."

The pair of them tussled like puppies, nearly elbowing me in the face. There was a burst of laughter from across the room – Kristal trying to prove she couldn't care less what Ollie was doing. Yeah, right.

Jake and Ed got up, tipping Ollie across my lap. He grinned up at me. Eyes such a deep dark brown you couldn't really see the pupils. Like pools of chocolate.

He was mine.

I bent down to kiss his soft mouth but the angle was wrong and my neck wouldn't quite bend and I ended up kissing his nose. We laughed but as I fell into his gaze, the uncomfortable feeling in my gut gripped me, and like a thing uncoiling, it rippled around my insides.

Something, *someone*, was wriggling under my skin.

nine

I froze.

Ollie lifted a hand to my face and stroked my cheek with his thumb. "What's up?"

Be normal, be normal, be normal...

"Nothing," I said, holding his palm to my lips. I sat very still, searching for any more disturbance, anything inside me that felt wrong. Dread crept across my skin and my heart pounded painfully, but there was nothing more. Had I imagined it?

Ollie said, "Haven't you got a lesson? Not bunking off, are you, Teva Webb?"

I forced the words out of my dry throat. "Yeah. Art. I should go. Haven't *you* got a lesson?"

Too late, I remembered he had English and he'd think I was nagging him. Again. He shrugged and said, "Nah."

He sat up and stretched, leaving a cold emptiness on my lap. "Go on then, you better head off."

Reluctantly, I got to my feet, searching again for the crawling feeling under my skin. Was it her? The new Teva? Had Fifteen felt me stir like that under her skin? I couldn't find anything in her memories but if she'd tried to forget it, I wouldn't find anything, would I? If only I could ask her. If only she didn't hate me quite so much. She could tell me if it was normal.

I laughed – a single, ugly, bark of a laugh. Normal? Nothing about me was normal. I *was* a freak. Mum was right.

"What?" Ollie said, puzzled. "Why are you laughing?"

I plunged into the lie bank for a reason: "I was just thinking about staying with you, maybe not going to art?"

He tipped his head on one side and said, "Yeah, that is quite funny."

I hovered, not sure what to do, then he pulled me onto his lap, laughing. He kissed my forehead saying, "Your face, you're hilarious. Go on, get to art, Picasso. I'll see you at lunch."

As I walked to the art block, I tried to hold onto a trace of Ollie's warmth, but I was shivering. I wanted a shower. I wanted to scrub away the feeling of...*invasion*. I shuddered. It was stupid going to art, I needed to get on with the blog, I needed to do something practical; to find help before it was too late. I pulled my phone out to text Mads.

I had ten missed calls from Mum. Ten? Assuming it was actually her. I pressed the number to ring back.

"Mum? What's up?"

"It's not Mum, it's me."

"That narrows it down to one of several. Which me?"

"The coolest one."

Thirteen. Why she thought she was the coolest I had no idea but there you go, she did.

"Where's Mum?"

"She's a tiny bit busy. Fifteen has gone mental again. She's shut herself in her room. Mum is going nuts. Can you come home and talk to her?"

"I've got art."

"Alright for some, isn't it?"

I didn't answer.

She said, "Please come. Mum's threatening to get a ladder. She says we'll have to break in through the window."

My eighteen-stone mother trying to clamber up to Fifteen's bedroom window was not a comfortable image.

"Can't you do it?" I said.

"Er, no. After the tree incident we're banned from using a ladder, remember?"

I did remember. Mum kept the ladder locked in the shed after Thirteen had nearly broken her neck. I chewed my lip, thinking for a minute. If I helped Fifteen, maybe I could get in her good books? Maybe she'd tell me what she felt before our separation? Maybe.

"Alright, I'll come. I'll be there as soon as I can."

I texted Mads and Ollie that Mum needed me at home and left school through reception, signing out for medical reasons. Well, it was sort of true. Mads would be annoyed about me missing another fashion show meeting, but this was more important.

* * *

I punched in the security code, squeezing through the gates as soon as the gap was big enough. Twelve and Thirteen were chasing each other round the big oak tree in our front garden.

"Right, you two, what's going on? Where's Mum? Why isn't she out here?"

"We thought it would be better if you helped," Twelve said, swinging her arms around in a way that was meant to look cute and innocent and told me straight away she was hiding something.

I shook my head and said, "Alright. What happened? The truth, please."

"She asked for it," Thirteen said.

"Oh for god's sake. What happened? Twelve?"

I stared hard at her. She was hopeless at keeping secrets and definitely my best bet. "Come on, spill."

"It wasn't me!" She nodded towards Thirteen. "*She* told Fifteen that you and that boy were doing it."

"You did what? That's not even true!"

I glared at Thirteen who said, "She's so annoying, droning on and on about how we'll never understand love. I understand love. I've snogged a boy. She thinks she knows everything."

I shook my head. Thirteen had literally kissed *one* boy, once, at the Year Eight Christmas party, and a cold, slimy experience that had been.

"What?" Thirteen said, her voice tight. "She's *so* annoying. It's not my fault."

"Does Mum even know she's upset? Does she know anything at all about this?"

They shook their heads. Twelve said, "She's been writing all day."

"And you two geniuses thought I'd be the best one to sort this out? Me. The one Fifteen hates the most. Well done. Great work."

I headed to the shed for the ladder. I made sure the others weren't watching while I dug the key out from behind a loose plank under the window ledge (I'd watched Mum hide it one day) and propped the door open with a brick.

I put the ladder up against the window, thinking, *If I fall off and die, please make Fifteen feel guilty for the rest of her miserable life.*

"We'll hold the ladder," Twelve and Thirteen said, grabbing a side each.

I climbed up carefully. "That makes me feel so much safer. Not!"

The round metal rungs bit into the underside of my Converse. I climbed nervously to the top and peered through the net curtains. I couldn't see Fifteen but at least she wasn't dangling from a lampshade by her dressing gown cord. I shuddered at my own horrible thought and banged on the window.

"Are you okay? Can you open the door?"

No answer.

"Come on, I'm freezing to death out here."

Nothing.

I called down the ladder, "Are you sure she's in there?"

Thirteen grinned up at me, and Twelve shrugged. They didn't look that bothered, given they'd dragged me out of school.

"Have you made this up to get me to come home?"

I scanned their faces. Twelve reached an arm round the ladder and poked Thirteen in the ribs.

As Thirteen jumped back, the ladder rocked. I grabbed for the window sill.

"Hey, careful! Will you try not to kill me, please?"

I waited for my heart to steady and took another look in the room. It was gloomy and abandoned. Posters hung off the wall; the bed was unmade. I couldn't see Fifteen anywhere.

"Right, truth please, is this a wind-up?"

Thirteen looked at me, channelling her inner witch. I knew what she was doing. I remembered her writing it in her diary. There'd been a bit of a Stephen King phase: Twelve and Thirteen had both enjoyed imagining they were Carrie for a while, it helped them cope. Maybe that's why those two were so close. Things had been tough for them – our skin was at its worst when they went to school. They'd been Alligator Girl, Flaky, Scabby Skin – a new name every term. They'd developed this iron "sod off" look…each pretending they were a witch who could curse anyone who annoyed them. It was pretty useful at the time. Now, not so much.

I said, "That look doesn't work on me, does it? Is she in there or not?"

Twelve said, "She's jammed the door from the inside."

I strained to see the bedroom door. Sure enough, the desk chair was tipped up under the door handle to stop it opening. Huddled next to it was a dark shape. My heart lurched. Fifteen was curled up so small I could barely see her. She looked broken.

I rested my forehead on the glass, wondering whether I should just go and get Mum and tell her what Thirteen had done. I chewed the inside of my lip. Apart from the fact Thirteen wouldn't speak to me for a week, I didn't want to get her in trouble. I understood why she hit out, her life was so…dull. Who wouldn't want to spice it up a bit? It was just a shame she'd chosen Fifteen's misery as her ingredient of choice.

It wasn't hard to imagine how Fifteen was feeling. All I had to do was picture Ollie and Kristal Mitchell draped across the pool table and my heart pinched painfully. If Fifteen was picturing me and Ollie together, well, I knew what that was like. Torture.

I took a deep breath and gently tapped the glass. I waited for movement and when there wasn't any, I tried again.

Slowly, Fifteen's head came up. She seemed to look at me but it was too gloomy in there to make out her features. She stayed like that for a second or two and then her head sank back on her knees.

I tried again, tapping the window and calling, "It's not

true. They were winding you up. We haven't, I didn't… Oh god, don't make me say this out loud."

Her head came up again. I waited but she clearly wanted more.

"Alright. Look, I swear, we haven't done anything you didn't do. I swear it. I've hardly seen him on his own for ages."

I stopped, realizing that it was actually true and wondering why I hadn't really noticed until now.

"Hurry up!" Twelve shouted up the ladder at me. "My fingers are cold."

Her fingers were cold? I was the one up the ladder clinging on for dear life. I tried again, "Come on, it's bloody freezing out here. Open the door so we can all get a cup of tea or something, yeah?"

She shrugged. That was some sort of communication at least.

"Please. We can talk about it. Look, I've been thinking about things, and I think I've had an idea, something to talk about anyway. Please. Come on, open the door."

I waited. Though she didn't get up, she yanked the chair out from under the door. It tumbled to the floor.

I made my way gingerly down the ladder.

"Is she out then?" said Twelve, her head on one side.

"You two put the ladder away. I need a cup of tea."

I headed for the kitchen. I could hear Mum typing away in the dining room. Fourteen was curled up in the sitting room watching Jeremy Kyle shout at a man with a tattooed face for having an affair with his wife's sister. I shivered. She didn't need crap TV, if she wanted that kind of entertainment, she only had to look at me and Fifteen.

"My Former Self Wants to Kill Me."

"My New Self Ran Away with My Boyfriend."

Maybe we should go on Jeremy Kyle. He might be able to untangle the ridiculous triangle of me, Fifteen and Ollie. Or maybe not. I might not come out of that too well.

Eva was sleeping on the squidgy sofa under the kitchen window. She looked so peaceful. I filled the kettle quietly and got two mugs out. If I was going to have a halfway decent conversation with Fifteen, I needed all the help I could get.

Mum came in.

"Hello, I thought I heard the door." She yawned, clearly oblivious to the goings on in the garden. Hadn't she even noticed her mobile was missing?

"Where's your phone, Mum?"

"Here, love."

She held up her hand and in it was the black brick she laughingly called her mobile phone.

"I always try and have it near me when you're at school. Did you try and ring me?" She checked the screen, then laid the phone on the table. "No missed calls. Everything okay?"

"Yeah," I said, confusion scratching at the corner of my mind. "I just had a couple of frees and thought I'd work at home."

I don't know why I lied. Maybe I just didn't want her to know what the others had said to Fifteen.

She nodded towards the kettle. "I'll have one, if you're making tea."

I got a third cup out, then picked up her phone and checked it for sent messages. Nothing. The little sneaks must have deleted everything. Of course they had, I would have done too. What Mum doesn't know, Mum doesn't cry over.

Mum fished for the biscuit tin, popping the lid off as Eva woke up with a mewly cry. I took out a couple of choccie digestives and gave one to her, the other I stuffed in my mouth.

The crumbly sweetness melted over my tongue. I could feel the sugar coursing through my veins, picking me up. I got a tray out and put another couple of biscuits on a plate with the tea. Mum said, "Do you really need all those?"

I shrugged and went upstairs. I stopped outside Fifteen's door and pushed it open with my elbow.

"Go away."

"We need to talk."

"Leave me alone."

"Please?"

"Just go away."

So much for that then. I wrinkled my nose, thinking for a second, then I slid the tea and the biscuit plate through the gap of the open door and left them on the floor.

"I'll be in my room if you change your mind."

I sat on my bed and opened my laptop, fully intending to work on the vlog. As soon as I sat down, though, my skin crawled with the physical memory of *her* moving inside me. I needed a shower first. I ran up to Mum's room, threw my clothes off, desperate to rid myself of the disgusting feeling of violation. I wanted to wash it all off, strip myself down to the bone, get rid of my horrible skin, my horrible thoughts... I let the hot water cascade over me but it wasn't enough.

My problem was inside of me and I couldn't wash it away – no matter how hard I tried. Still, I felt a tiny bit better once I was dry and in my trackies. I sat cross-legged on my bed and opened up the webcam. Fifteen sloped in. No knock, she just slouched in and leaned against my dressing table, fiddling with all my stuff. I played it carefully and waited for her to speak.

She opened a pot of blusher, sniffed it, turned her nose up and dropped it back amongst the jumble of make-up and jewellery.

"I want to see Ollie."

My mouth dropped open. That was so not happening.

"You can't," I said.

"You have no right to him. None. If he knew you'd tricked him, stolen him from me...he'd never forgive you."

Her face was hard, angular. My stomach coiled tightly. She was right.

She stacked my make-up into a tottering tower and said, "I'm not going to live in this prison for ever. I want my life back."

I bit the skin on my ragged thumb and said, "How? You can't. It's not safe. Mum won't let you have the gate code. What will people say? They'll think we're freaks..." I heard myself repeating our mother's words and tailed off.

"*You* could give me the gate code." She raised an eyebrow at me.

We both knew there was no way I'd do that. And we both knew why.

"Mum would kill me."

"Yeah, right. Nothing to do with you keeping my life to yourself."

"It's not my fault! You took over from Fourteen."

"Fourteen didn't have Ollie."

There was nothing I could say. Not one thing that I could say that would make things better for her.

"Look, I know you don't think much of me..."

She snorted, "You could say that."

"But we're in the same boat. My life is going to be just like yours if we don't do something."

She snarled at me. "You are so selfish, can you hear yourself? It's all about you, isn't it?"

She was right. We weren't in the same boat at all. Her chance to be saved had gone the moment I had freed myself from her. She was stuck. Fifteen for ever.

She balanced an eyeshadow box on top of the blusher she'd been sniffing. "If you won't give me the gate code, I'll find a way out on my own."

"You're not serious? You can't go out! What would Mum say? You'll ruin everything!"

Even as I said it, I could see how selfish I was being. I wanted to fix my life but I was giving her nothing.

Then she made me an offer.

"If you give me the gate code, I'll come with you to the medical centre."

My mouth dropped open. If she came with me to a doctor, at least I'd have a chance of them believing me. With two of us telling the same story we might avoid what happened to Fourteen when she'd gone. Maybe Fourteen could come as well, three of us making our case… But at what price?

If I gave Fifteen the gate code, that was it, she'd go straight to school and everyone would know. And what if Mum was right?

We'd be taken away, experimented on, we'd be the freak family…

"Up to you," she said. "A life for a life. I just want to see Ollie. He's *my* boyfriend. If you want to put things right, give me the gate code."

I was such a coward. I couldn't face the fallout. Not yet.

I said, "I'll think about it."

She knocked the make-up tower over and stormed out. I winced, knowing she'd broken something.

ten

I was so cross with myself. I was pathetic. Fifteen was offering me the chance to do something real but I was so afraid of losing what little I had, I just couldn't do it.

I flipped my laptop open and loaded the video clips I'd made the other day. I looked like a babbling idiot. If I posted them, everyone really *would* think I was crazy – I sounded totally nuts. I chewed on the sleeve of my sweatshirt, thinking. If I did a *written* blog, no one would need to know it was me. I could see if anyone could help and find out just how freaky people thought we really were.

I got a bit excited. If computers had been around, I reckon the Secret Seven would definitely have done something like this. I needed a disguise: a name...and an image.

I started searching for an avatar but then I thought I'd just do one last little internet search – just check there weren't any new pages that might be relevant to my problem. What an idiot. Up came that one word with the power to send a thousand needles diving into my skin. Cancer.

In the daylight hours I was pretty good at rationalizing the C-word but I knew what stoking those thoughts did to me at night. Terror would ball in my stomach and make sleep impossible. I tried to ignore it but even without clicking any links, the words were there:

When people have cancer some of their cells grow and multiply unchecked.

My arms itched. I yearned to scratch – instead I googled: *itchy skin and cancer.*

And up they popped, types of cancer that cause itching. I hopped through the links. There was nothing like us though; no such thing as a living breathing tumour. Except, then I found something I hadn't seen before: *walking tumour.*

It was a blog post by someone who had brain cancer, about how it affected their personality. They'd had times where they'd hallucinated, imagined whole people who weren't really there. I stared at the screen. That couldn't be like me. It couldn't. It was ridiculous – the others were real; one of them had just smashed up half my make-up. I needed to get a grip. A blog post…I was supposed to be doing a blog post. Not scaring myself to death with Google.

I pinched myself hard on the insides of my elbows – that little trick to stop me scratching also helped me calm down.

Blog.

It took about five minutes to set something up that looked half decent, and the whole of that time my heart was racing because of the stupid cancer websites. I wrote a post-it note and stuck it to my laptop screen: *DO NOT GOOGLE SYMPTOMS*.

I found an awesome avatar; small and purple with masses and masses of snaky hair and pink freckles. Her name just came to me. Celly. You know, for cells. My blog persona was born. One more of us to add to the collection.

I began my first ever post:

Celly's World

I've got a condition that doesn't even have a name but eventually, it'll rob me of my future. Imagine all your friends growing up, moving on, and you being stuck in one year of your life...

I typed for ages, wrote down everything I could think of. Then I read it back and deleted half the words so it sounded better – interesting but not moany.

I asked if anyone had heard of our condition before and to comment if they had. It gave me a buzz if I'm honest; I truly felt I was on my way to fixing everything. I was careful though – I checked it through for anything that might identify us, and then, before I could change my mind, I pressed publish.

Fifteen walked in. I snapped my laptop shut out of habit. She said, "Well? Have you decided?"

I said, "I had an idea. A blog about us, about our condition, you know to see if anyone knows what to do. I just posted the first one!"

Fifteen glared at me for a moment, but then she just said, "I don't care about a stupid blog. All I care about is Ollie. Have we got a deal or not?"

I bit my lip. What would happen if she went back to school? It was all very well thinking a future was more important but when I thought about him with her, a knife twisted inside me. He'd been with me all this time, surely she didn't think she could just pick up where they'd left off? I had to be straight with her.

"Look, I'm not just going to give him up."

"So, you're not going to give me the gate code?"

I thought for a second – was it worth it? To get her to come with me to a doctor? Not yet. Not just yet – I had six months, didn't I? I'd try the blog before I blew everything out of the water. "I can't," I said.

"You mean you won't."

"I'm sorry but Ollie is as much mine as yours. I *was* you, remember."

"You were never me. You were just a parasite inside me."

I shuddered at the venom in her words and thought of that other Teva inside me.

Fifteen snarled, "Will you give me the code or not?"

I gritted my teeth. "Not."

Fifteen's face puckered up like a shrivelled lemon.

I said, "Look, I know it's hard…"

"Hard for who?" she spat. "You're the one swanning off to school every day while we're stuck here. You've taken it all: Ollie, Maddy, everything. You even get all the good subjects at school! You don't have to do shitty maths thanks to me passing that exam."

"Scraping through it more like."

"I passed, that's what matters. You are so up your own backside – *Oh woe is me, I'm going to have to go through a separation* – you never think about what it's like for us!"

I could see her body coiling up to fly at me; I tried to calm her down.

"That's not fair, I do think about you. I'm the same as you – I only have a year…"

"A year with *my* boyfriend," Fifteen screamed and launched herself at me. She went for my face, nails out, raking down my cheek. I tried to cover my head with my arms but she was too fast. She tore at my skin, biting, scratching.

"Get off! Jesus, you're insane! MUM! MUUUUUM!"

Fifteen yanked at my hair, pushing me against the window; I stood on the curtain and it pulled the rod down on my head.

"You little cow! Leave me alone." I gathered every ounce of energy I had and shoved her away. She landed heavily on her bum and glared at me before scrabbling to her knees and scuttling out of my room.

I was gasping for breath, my face hot and sweaty, my arms bleeding. I heard Mum labouring up the stairs. I blew my hair out of my face as the door opened.

"What are you doing? Oh, Teva. What have you done, look at you!"

"It wasn't me, it was Fifteen, she's bloody mental."

Mum reached a hand towards my face but stopped before she touched it, tears pooling in her eyes. "Your poor skin… why, Teva, why?"

"I told you; it wasn't me. Why don't you ever listen? It was that insane cow Fifteen."

Mum looked at the mess and muttered, "You've pulled the curtain down." Then she shook her head and said, "Your poor arms, I'll get some antiseptic."

I sank to the floor, burning inside and out.

When I woke the next morning, my face and arms were really sore. The scratches were livid. I reached for my phone. Two messages, both from Mads:

Fashion show, you skiver???

Where were you?

I groaned inside. Literally, there were too many things going on for my one brain to try and juggle. I opened my laptop to check the blog; there weren't any hits but I'd only posted it last night. I'd leave it for the day. There were bound to be some comments by the evening. I got dressed, my sweatshirt hiding the marks on my arms. My face was trickier. I peered in my dressing table mirror. Three ragged grooves tore down my left cheek. I covered them with foundation, wincing at the sting of it.

I needn't have bothered. Neither of my best friends noticed the marks on my face. There was a moment when Maddy said, "So what happened to you yesterday?"

My hand flew to my face but she carried on, "You promised you'd come to that meeting? I had to cover for you again."

I shrugged and said, "Yeah, sorry, I wasn't feeling well, had to go home."

"You better not miss another one, I'll run out of excuses for you. Anyway, you'll never guess who texted me last night... Josh!"

"Josh?" I said, sensing a convenient distraction.

"Yeah, you know, that boy doing volunteering at my nani's nursing home?"

"Oh, him," I said, and that was enough, she was off – telling me how sweet he was and all the other things that would make no difference at all if he ever asked her out.

Eventually the bell went and she said, "See you at break?"

I nodded, forcing myself to be normal. "Yep, have fun mathsing."

"I will, you have fun having fun."

"I will."

All totally normal. I really was a great actor. I headed for the drama studio chewing my lip.

We'd just sat down to do a read-through – our own piece about the Hillsborough disaster – when someone's phone bleeped a text alert. It was a cardinal studio rule to put your phone on silent when you were rehearsing. I looked round the group, annoyed, before I realized the noise had come from my phone.

I dug in my bag, murmuring apologies, until I found it

under my textiles folder and a wizened old apple. Three messages from Mum's phone:

Anyway she's well upset. You think you're so much better than the rest of us well you're not and we think you're well pathetic.

Bile lodged in my throat. Thirteen, it had to be, no one else typed "well" after every other word. I kept the phone hidden in my bag while I read the poison she'd sent but the next message just read:

H8888888888888888

Followed by: *And you never let me use your laptop.*

That had to be Eight.

Marvellous. Fifteen had them all joining in. How did they even get hold of Mum's phone? I deleted the messages, turned my phone to silent and flicked the cover off. And on. And off.

"Teva, can you leave whatever interesting thing is in your bag alone? We really need to focus our energies here. We need to be all about the circle here, please."

Yes, alright. My whole family are ganging up on me, but fine... I looked at the faces in the circle waiting for me to "focus my energy". Erin – a chubby girl with a long ponytail pulled up so high it spilled all over her head like a hair fountain – wrinkled her nose and said, "We've got to the bit where I'm burning the toast and you're just leaving and I don't say goodbye. We need a lot of tension here, yeah, Teva, because the audience know what's going to happen but we don't and—"

"Yes, Erin, I do know, I was here when we wrote it."

I snatched the script from her proffered hand and looked

around the circle to see if anyone else wanted to tell me what I was supposed to be doing – and that's when I saw the heavy blackout curtains on the far side of the room move. That's when I saw a small, pale face peer around them, right at me. That's when I saw Fifteen.

I bolted to my feet, a little gasp escaping from me. Was I seeing things? Then I remembered, the curtains covered a mirrored wall. For a second, I thought I'd just caught sight of my own reflection and relief swept through me. But then I saw that the curtain was still moving and someone was inching their way behind it. I couldn't believe it – first she attacked me and now she was here? In school? How had she got the gate code? I stood up, every nerve in me buzzing like a living alarm.

"Teva," said Miss Davison. "What is it now? You really are being extremely disruptive today."

How had no one else noticed? I swallowed hard, the curtain was still but there was a fire exit door at the end of it. What if she'd gone out there? I had to know if she was really here. I grabbed my bag.

"Sorry, Miss, I've got to go."

"Teva!"

I headed after Fifteen, Miss Davison shouting at me, "Teva! What are you doing? Don't you dare run out on a rehearsal. Teva, that door is for emergencies only! Teva!"

Too late. Sorry, Miss. If Fifteen really was here, I had to find her, before anyone else did. And I knew exactly where she'd go. She'd be looking for Ollie.

eleven

The Quiet Area was a nasty concrete garden on a piece of ground between the library and the main hall. Too right it was quiet, nobody ever wanted to hang out there, not even terrified Year Sevens. I hurried across it, cold grey drizzle misting my face. The door to the B block corridor was just closing. My heart pounded. There were only two ways she could go. Right to the library and languages department or left…upstairs to the common room.

No contest.

I paced after her. She had to be looking for Ollie. And she clearly wanted me to know – why else would she come through the drama studio. Was she really going to force my hand like this? Really? I pulled open the door, banging my shoulder against it as I hurried through. I got halfway up the stairs before I realized – if she was in the common room, if there were suddenly two of us, there'd be no turning back; we'd have to explain. That was what she was after, wasn't it?

That's why she wanted me to follow her.

I hovered on the step, torn between facing up to the reality of my life – fighting for it – or slinking into the shadows. I had no idea what Fifteen was planning, but dumping it on people, with no real thought, that couldn't go well, could it? If – when – we told people, I wanted to be prepared. I wanted…

The common room door opened and a shower of laughter tumbled down the stairs towards me. I'd know her laugh anywhere. The same as mine but with an edge of…what? Cruelty? Determination? I think she'd always been tougher than me, more reckless, but the bitterness of giving up her life had left something hard inside her. The shadows suddenly seemed the safest bet.

I bolted, jealousy knotting my stomach. Thoughts tumbled round my head – what was she doing? What was she saying? Would Ollie know? We hadn't grown much since we were Fourteen but surely…surely he'd notice she wasn't me?

Then I had a genius thought: there were CCTV cameras in the common room. We'd complained like mad when they'd put them in, but maybe I could use them. Security was in reception, if I went down and pretended I was waiting for a call from Mum, maybe I could see what Fifteen was up to? Heart thumping, I raced to reception.

The school secretary smiled up at me. Sitting on the seats to my left was a pale boy, surely too small to be at secondary school, staring blankly into a sick bowl. On my right was the bank of CCTV monitors. I needed to get behind it to see the screens. How was I going to do that?

The receptionist coughed and said, "Anything I can help with? Teva, isn't it?"

"Urm, yeah, my phone died. Mum said she'd ring me in reception." I glanced at my watch. "She said she'd phone about twelve, can I wait here?"

The receptionist smiled sweetly at me. "Of course you can, take a seat." She nodded towards the boy with the bowl. He looked up, a sheen of sweat over his sickly face.

I hesitated – there was a wordless exchange between the three of us and eventually the secretary nodded to the seat behind the CCTV screens.

"Okay, why don't you sit there for the moment, it's nearly twelve anyway."

I slunk behind the monitors, trying not to look too keen. The switchboard phone rang and for a stupid minute I thought it actually was Mum before I remembered I'd made that up. Still, I looked as if I thought it might be her and the receptionist gave a tiny shake of her head as she spoke into the receiver: "Putting you through now."

I scanned the black-and-white pictures in front of me until I found the common-room camera. It was trained on the pool table but, for once, no one was playing. I bit my lip and the image rolled away showing the door and then the cluster of sofas. There she was, sitting on Ollie's knee, wearing one of my sweatshirts! Only it wasn't mine, was it? She'd come into my room and taken back one of hers.

How dare she? How dare she do this? Risking everything with no thought for the rest of us? I conveniently ignored my own plans to put our plight on the internet as fury burned through me. Leaving the house, coming to school, talking to Ollie? Who was she to make that call?

Fifteen threw her head back, laughing as Ollie swooped in to play-bite her neck. He didn't know she wasn't me. How could he not know? My legs felt like they were filling with water, as I realized he hadn't batted an eyelid when I'd taken over from Fifteen. Not once. My chest ached with the pain of watching them together.

"Are you alright, Teva?"

I leaped up, blocking the view of the monitor and knocking my bag to the floor at the same time. The contents spilled out. I ducked down to push everything back in, my head swirling. The receptionist kneeled down next to me to help.

"Sorry," she said, "I didn't mean to startle you. Your breathing went a bit funny; I thought you were having an asthma attack."

I could hear myself then, lungs scrabbling for air, ragged and loud. I said, "No, sorry, it's just a cold, sorry."

I pushed my bag mess back inside. "I better go actually, Miss."

"What about your mum?"

"It doesn't matter, I..." I flicked a look over my shoulder, Ollie was sitting on his own, hands pushed into his hair, leaning back on the sofa, king of all he surveyed. Whatever

89

Fifteen had done or said it had clearly put a smile on his face. But now he was on his own. Fifteen had gone.

I fumbled my bag onto my shoulder.

"I forgot...I need to...sorry..."

I could barely think. My head throbbed with the torrent of consequences fighting for attention. I forced it all down. I just had to find her. Come on, Teva. Think. She'd try and find Maddy. I would if I was her, and let's face it, I kind of was. She'd have a good idea where to go as well: the maths block.

I could get ahead of her though. I'd ring Maddy. Fifteen didn't have a phone. My fingers trembled as I texted:

You still in adding up?

She pinged back straight away:

Cheeky. Go play at being a tree, I've got numbers to do.

Can you meet me? Now?

I'm working on something tricky.

Mads – please?

You okay? Not letting the Kristal business bother you?

I closed my eyes, steadied my breathing.

A bit. Please? Meet you by the gate?

Got to nail this first – 10 minutes?

In ten minutes, Fifteen would have found her.

I texted: *I'll come over and wait.*

I'd just have to head off my pain-in-the-arse former self.

I raced to the maths block, nearly knocking over a handful of Year Sevens returning from a biology practical on the field. I whirled through them, my head throbbing with the cascade of *what ifs* crashing through it. I turned the corner;

I hadn't been fast enough. Fifteen was already there, her hand on the door, about to open it but hesitating, like she was thinking it through. A flicker of hope flared in my chest. I slowed down and called out, "Hey, Fif…"

I stopped, not wanting to call her name and remind her that she didn't belong here any more; that I'd taken her identity. She made me mad as a trapped cat, but I could imagine how I'd feel if – when – I was in her shoes. She glanced back, saw me, then pushed open the door and darted inside.

"Shit."

I followed her in. She ran up the stairs and caught her toe on the lip of a step.

"Walk, don't run," I muttered and dived forward, grabbing her arm.

I pulled her to her feet. "Enough."

She writhed under my grip, "Get off me, you bloody cow."

"Nope, if we tell people, we tell them properly. I'm not dumping this on our friends without thinking it through… Come on, out." I twisted her arm up behind her back – a little trick I'd learned from her, ironically.

"You're hurting me!"

"Sorry, can't be helped."

I marched her to the door.

"I'll scream, I'll scream for help."

My heart pounded at the threat of discovery but I said, "Oh shut up. I saw you with Ollie, you've had your fun. Now playtime's over."

The bell rang violently and Fifteen snapped, "Looks like it's just begun actually."

She squirmed out of my hands, running towards the sneaky path behind the school hedge that we weren't supposed to use.

I raced after her, the bush catching on my bag, my jacket. Neither of us were fit though and when she got to the end of the path she stopped, hands on her hips, panting. She whispered, "I hate you."

"No? Really?"

We waited until we could breathe without our lungs burning and I said, "Mum is going to kill you."

Fifteen shrugged. "Like I care."

She started walking and I trailed after her.

"I don't need a bloody bodyguard."

"You could have fooled me."

"Not difficult."

As we got to the corner of the road, a trickle of people muffled in black started coming out of the squat little church that sat there. They huddled in groups, not noticing us. Not until Fifteen shouted at me, "I wish it was you in that coffin," and ran off again.

I took a few half-hearted steps after her but, to be honest, she was heading away from school and I was just grateful to get rid of her. She'd go home, where else was there? She must have found some way out of the garden so, presumably, she could find her way back in. I stood for a second, hand on my hip and watched her go. I was about to head back to school when someone shouted from behind me.

"Wait up, Tee!"

I turned round and Tommo raised a hand. My stomach turned over. Had he seen Fifteen? I walked towards him, hoping to god I was blocking any view he might have of her, putting as much distance between the two of them as I could. I tried to look calm but sweat was trickling down my spine. I forced myself to smile. "Hey."

"Hey yourself. You going into town?" he said as he drew close.

I swung back to see if Fifteen was still in sight.

"Erm…"

"Clock's ticking, Tee, this man needs a burger. I'll walk in with you?"

He stood just a tiny bit too close. Even under his sweatshirt I could see the outline of his muscles. It wasn't helping my heart to slow down. I stepped back. Tempting as the offer was, Ollie definitely wouldn't like it. Then I remembered. "Shit, I said I'd meet Maddy!"

"She won't mind."

"I think she will, sorry, Tommo, better get back."

He put his hand around my elbow. Warmth spread up my arm as he said, "Lucky Maddy. Want anything from MaccyDee's?"

I shook my head, so confused at my betraying body responding to him. I reminded myself he was like this with everyone, even the teachers. He wasn't treating me any different. And anyway, I didn't want him to treat me any different, I— My phone buzzed; I pulled it out of my pocket.

I miss you, come back. xx

Ollie.

I smiled. It was so sweet, and unusual. Ollie hadn't spoken to me like that since…my heart dropped to my feet.

Of course.

He wasn't texting me.

He was texting Fifteen.

twelve

I raced back to school, hopping into the road to avoid the people milling about outside the church. A car horn tooted but I ran on, past the hedge and through the main gates. As I turned up the long drive I could see Ollie standing by the sports hall with Mads.

She was crushing her files to her chest, black hair pouring down her back; he was frowning, deep in concentration. They were deeply absorbed in whatever they were talking about. Me. It had to be me. Didn't it?

I crept towards them, hugging the hedge line hoping they wouldn't notice me, trying to hear what they were saying. I could just pick out a few of Ollie's words: "...different... like the old..."

Maddy looked up at him, her face smooth and open, his furrowed with confusion. I couldn't bear it. What if he didn't love me at all? What if he had only ever loved Fifteen? I wanted to sneak away but Ollie looked up. His face lit up as he saw me.

I forced a smile, choked out the words, "What are you two whispering about?"

"I was just telling Mads what a laugh we had this morning."

Yeah, great, only it wasn't me. He opened an arm for me to nestle in and I folded myself into the space, trying to swallow down the monstrous slime of envy squirming its way up my throat. Maddy said, "What happened to you? I thought you desperately needed to see me?"

I couldn't get any more words out. I felt like I needed to rearrange my brain molecules. I stood there like a total idiot. Maddy glanced at Ollie with just the tiniest hint of a raised eyebrow. He slipped his arm under my coat, round my waist and pulled me closer.

"Come on, Tee. What's up?" He leaned closer still and murmured in my ear, "I thought we were sorted? Kristal's nothing to me, you know that."

The name stabbed through me, clamping my jaw shut. But it wasn't Kristal's image that was stamped across my brain, it was Fifteen. Fifteen sitting on his lap in the common room, looking so comfortable, so at home. Fifteen laughing up at him. A sob caught in my throat. It was so hard. All of it was so hard. I shook my head, unable to speak. Whatever I said, with all that was racing through my brain, would not go well. He'd think I was crazy. One minute laughing on the sofa, the next a tight ball of…what? I didn't even know.

The smell of him swamped me: deodorant, fresh air – the faintest trace of cigarettes. Oh god. Ollie. He had the power to turn my heart upside down. I turned into him, pressed my face against his sweatshirt, soaking up the smell of him. I had to try and put things right.

"Sorry," I whispered, "headache."

Mads said, "Don't mind me. I don't need hugging or anything."

I turned towards her, just enough to give her half a smile.

She said, "Are you coming down with something, Tee? You're white as a sheet."

"Yeah, maybe."

Tears pricked at my eyes. I was trapped. I'd lose Ollie the instant he knew about Fifteen. All I could do was manage the moment and hope. I pulled myself up straight and turned within the circle of his arms, my back to his warm chest, so I could talk to Mads properly.

"Sorry, I already feel a bit better. I think I just needed some fresh air. Drama was so...intense."

That was all it took for relief to fall over them like a soft sheet. Maddy laughed. "In tents? You doing Glastonbury in the form of mime?"

I hit her lightly on the arm.

Ollie said, "Drama is a serious subject, Madeeha, don't take the mick now."

I jabbed my elbow back at him, my racing heart settling a bit at the okayness of it all. I'd scrabbled back from a cliff edge and set myself firmly between the two people who held me firm. Needing to keep a tight hold of them, I said, "Can we get lunch? I'm starved."

"We can get lunch if you say you'll do the fashion show."

"Mads!"

"Yeah," said Ollie, "I'm doing break-dance."

"You are not," I said.

"I am. Jack's teaching me, it's really cool."

Despite everything, I smiled. "I have to see that."

"Yes you do," Ollie said, then he leaned into my ear. "Come round mine after school and I'll give you a private showing."

I knew he had football training and was just messing about, but I said, "You're on." Maddy took it as an answer to her pleading and punched the air.

"Yay! I knew you'd say yes eventually."

"Mads, I didn't mean the fashion show."

"Too late, you said yes."

"I didn't! I said—"

"Not listening!" Mads said and skipped off before I could argue.

Not that it mattered. The lure of their normal was so tempting, I think I knew I was going to give in.

At the end of the day I headed out of school on my own. Maddy was doing some maths club or other. I didn't mind; with Fifteen turning up at school, I hadn't thought much about the blog but now I was itching to get home and check it. Ollie was at the gate though, holding his hand out towards me.

"You alright to come back to mine, then?"

I locked my fingers round his. "You're serious? You've not got football?"

He shrugged. "I can miss one."

I hesitated. Surely I deserved a little bit of time to be a normal teenager without my mad double life crashing in on me? I smiled up at Ollie's beautiful face, so open and warm. The blog could wait a couple of hours.

"How could I say no?"

I felt the stress fall away as we walked – no thinking, no fighting, just being. I kissed his shoulder and said, "Who's in your group for the fashion show then?"

"You know, the usual crew; some of the football lads."

He pulled me close, kissed the top of my head and we walked, entwined, to his house. I had neck ache by the time we got there but it was worth it for the warmth I felt inside.

Ollie lived with his mum on the bottom floor of an old townhouse. As he unlocked the door he said, "Mum's at work, we've got the place to ourselves."

A little thrill zipped up my spine. It seemed like ages since we'd been on our own together – his mum was normally around or, if we went out, it was usually in a group so Mads didn't feel abandoned. It wasn't just that though; in all honesty, I'd been so busy searching the internet, trying to find out what was wrong with me, maybe I hadn't made as much time for him as I'd thought. Well, I could make up for that now.

In the hallway, I dropped my school bag and pulled him

round to face me. He gently lifted my chin with a finger and dropped a soft kiss on my lips. He said, "I'm so glad you're here, we never seem to get proper time together these days. You used to come round loads after school and on the weekend. We don't seem to do that any more."

"I was thinking the same."

"You know that day on the beach, when we got totally blown about by the wind? That was the last time we had a day out. It was months ago, Tee. Months."

"We went to Thorpe Park."

"With Maddy."

"She's my best mate."

"I know. I don't want to fight – just – I miss you, that's all."

A soft cloud of shame settled on me. I texted or phoned Ollie whenever I got stressed out, but the truth was, I saw him when *I* wanted to, when *I* needed to. I'd been so wrapped up in myself, I hadn't thought about what *he* needed. I tried to make a joke of it: "Well if you prefer football to hanging out with me..."

He didn't laugh.

"I'm not always at football. We need to make time for each other, Tee, there's so much we need to talk about."

"I said I'd come round and help with your English – I'm always saying that."

"Yeah," he said sadly, "you are."

I scratched the back of my neck, my skin pricking with irritation – and then I felt it, that wriggle inside. The tiptoe of a shiver across my back. The stirring of *her*. I stopped breathing. *Go away, go away, go away.*

I squeezed my eyes shut.

"Tee?"

I searched for any more movement, any other trace that she was there. Nothing.

I opened my eyes. Ollie's face had crumpled into a frown.

"Tee?"

I swallowed.

"Sorry," I said. "Ollie, I don't want to argue."

"Things have changed, haven't they?"

"No, no. Nothing has changed. I love you," I said, desperation tight in my throat.

Everything was so messed up – I couldn't begin to straighten it out, even in my head. Fifteen sat in a big chunk of our past and the new Teva was lurking ready to take our future. What was I supposed to do...to be...to say? I wanted to forget it all, just for a bit. I wanted to live. And I wanted to prove Ollie was as much mine as he was Fifteen's. More.

I took his hands, and placed them on my waist. He sighed softly and slid them around my back, his palms flat and firm against me. I reached around his neck, lacing my fingers together, loving the feel of his close-cropped hair. I stood on tiptoe and kissed him. He hesitated, but then I felt the hunger flare in him and he kissed me back, opening my mouth with his tongue. I pulled him through to the front

room, shedding my coat as I went. I didn't want to talk; I just
wanted to feel.

I wanted to pretend my life was normal, that I could have
a relationship with a future and a past – a real past that was
totally mine. I wanted to do something with Ollie that
Fifteen hadn't, something that was just ours. I stumbled
backwards, manoeuvring our tangled bodies to the sofa,
never taking my mouth from his. The backs of my legs hit
the cushions and I fell onto it, pulling Ollie with me.

"Jesus, Tee, I can't think, you're…"

I closed his mouth with more kisses, and tugged at his
sweatshirt. He pulled it over his head, not taking his eyes
from me. I drew him close and sank into the heat of him,
burningly alive where his body pressed against mine. My
breath was ragged, my heart pounding. My hand strayed
down to the waistband of his trousers and popped the top
button. He caught my wrist.

"What?" I said.

He laughed a little bit. "You. You do my head in, Tee. I
thought you wanted…"

"What?" My body seemed to have taken control over my
brain. I wrapped my legs round him.

"Easy," he said.

I hesitated. All the excuses I'd made to stay covered up in
front of him, to hide my terrible skin, oh god, the scratches
Fifteen had left scored into my arms – could I bear him to
see that?

"I thought we were going to wait?" he said softly.

Wait? I had no time to wait. Barring some kind of miracle, I had less than six months and I didn't want to waste a second of it.

In answer, I pulled his shirt free of his trousers and he gazed down at me. "You're so beautiful, Teva."

I slid my hands under his shirt; the smooth heat of his skin goosebumped under the tracing of my fingers. He lowered his face to mine. My heart was beating so hard it might have pounded its way right out of my chest – if the light hadn't snapped on and Ollie's mum hadn't said, "Hello, you two, doing homework, are you?"

I bolted upright, hot with embarrassment.

"Don't mind me," she said, walking round the back of the sofa, snapping the curtains closed.

"Sorry," I said, rearranging my clothes. "I should go."

"Not on my account, Teva, love – we were all young once."

"Shut up, Mum," Ollie said. "Come to my room, Tee?"

I blinked. I felt like I'd been snapped out of a dream.

"Erm, I think maybe I should go home."

Ollie said, "Don't leave."

"No, really, Mum will be wondering where I am."

He got to his feet and held out a hand to me, saying, "Nice one, Mum."

"I do live here, Oliver."

I picked up my things and said, "Nice to see you, Mrs Smart, sorry about…"

She smiled at me – a big genuine smile. "Nothing to be sorry for, Teva."

Ollie saw me to the door. It was properly chilly outside, not yet dark but getting there.

"Do you want me to walk you home?"

"No," I said, "you're alright."

I hoped he'd insist. He didn't.

I reached up to kiss him goodbye. His kiss felt soft and sad. As I walked back, the heat inside me evaporated into the cold.

When I got home, I fully expected Fifteen to be waiting for me; smug and full of how Ollie liked her more. Well, at least I'd done a little bit to fight my corner. I tapped in the code and as the gates creaked open, I looked up at our crumbly old house, its tatty, paint-peeling windows trying to peep out from the ton of ivy that clung to the front walls. Funny how it could feel so much like home and yet still be a prison – and I wasn't even locked in there yet.

I stuck the long key in the front door and clunked it open. I meant to head straight upstairs to check the blog, but Six was sitting there, guardian of the fifth step, and her pale face stopped me in my tracks. I couldn't bear the loneliness that seemed to drift from her in a cloud. I dropped my bag and held my hand out. "Come on, you, let's go get a biscuit."

She slowly unpeeled herself from the wall, then froze as the front-room door smacked open and Eight and Nine tumbled into the hallway, laughing. They scrabbled past us and bounded up the stairs. Eva wobbled out after them, saw me and bowled herself at my knees, grabbing me in a podgy-armed hug. I reached a hand to Six and tugged her towards me, patting Eva's head at the same time, and saying, "Wow, what a welcome."

I couldn't help but smile. Sometimes, just sometimes, it felt like we were a normal family. Nearly. Keeping hold of Six, I scooped Eva on to my hip. She burrowed her fuzzy head into my neck and I waddled into the kitchen.

Mum had her laptop at the kitchen table and was clicking away. Eleven sat next to her colouring in and Fourteen, who hardly ever joined the rest of us, was scribbling away in a notebook, Seven copying her every move. All was surprisingly peaceful. I sat Eva on a chair and handed her a thick, sticky board book.

Mum looked up, blinking, her eyes tired.

"Nice day at school? Aren't you a bit late?"

I got out the biscuit tin and handed a custard cream to Six. She pressed herself into my side as I said, "Sorry, busy day."

So, Mum didn't know about Fifteen's little excursion. I thought about telling her, but she'd probably just clamp down harder on the rest of us. For a chilling moment I imagined she might even try and stop *me* from going to school, but she couldn't do that. One of us had to go, or people would notice. Maddy, for sure, would kick up a storm if I suddenly went missing.

Mum said, "How's that bra you're making?"

"Corset, Mum, not bra, there is a difference."

Her face flushed, hiding the tiny broken veins in her plump shiny cheeks. I was immediately sorry. My crazy day had left me snappy and brittle. I made myself be nice.

"Here. I'll show you."

I pulled my textiles folder out of my bag and got my corset out.

"It's not finished yet, there are going to be poppies all over this shoulder."

"It's beautiful, Tee, really lovely and so clever."

I flushed with warmth and had a sudden urge to share with her. "Miss Francis wants us to model them in the fashion show though, how mad is that?"

"What fashion show?" Mum said, alert and tense.

I bristled at her tone, guessing what was coming. "The sixth-form fashion show. The one *all* the sixth-formers do."

"I'm not sure that's a good idea, love. When is it?"

And there you go. Any tiny thing that might get us noticed was *always* off the agenda. I prickled all over with irritation. It didn't matter that I didn't really want to go, it was just another choice being taken from me.

"A couple of weeks. All my friends are doing it, Mum. Everyone. They've got people coming – they're scouting for apprentice designers for the summer holidays. Miss Francis thinks I might be chosen if I do it."

Okay, that wasn't exactly true, but I wanted to show Mum there was a world out there that we deserved to be part of. She stamped on that in seconds: "I don't like the idea of you being so exposed."

106

"No one will be *exposed*, it's school. They're hardly going to let people walk about in their undies."

Mum said, "It's very public, Teva, that sort of thing."

"What do you think is going to happen? No weirdo is going to be stalking a bunch of sixth-formers in charity shop leftovers. Seriously."

I don't know why, but Mum being so difficult made me want to do the show way more than Maddy's arguments. I said, "Literally everyone is doing it. It'll look bad if I don't. And anyway, our group is doing walking boots, not exactly stalker material, is it?"

Eva threw her book on the floor and I sat next to her as I dipped down to pick it up. I was rewarded with a sticky kiss on my hand.

"My life will effectively be over in a few months. Is one night out really too much to ask?"

"Are tickets on sale? To the public?"

"To parents, yeah. It's for charity, Mum, that's the point. They're not expensive, though, a couple of pounds, I think."

She curled her hands around her cup of tea and said, "It's not the money, love. I don't mind giving a few pounds for a good cause. It's just, well, everyone will see it; see you. Not just people from school, other people. What if, you know, it got passed about on people's Facebook pages?"

"What if it did? They'd see a picture of me fully clothed and wearing walking boots. You're being ridiculous."

Six slid out of the room, aware of the rising tension.

Mum picked at a label on the top of her laptop. I said,

"It's alright for you, sitting here writing lovely stories about made-up people's lovely lives – meanwhile the rest of us have to cope with all the crappy fallout of our condition."

She didn't answer and something inside me began to twist.

"I can't even talk to my counsellor about my *real* problems because you won't let me."

Her silence was infuriating.

"Fine," I said, standing up so sharply my chair fell over. Mum bent to pick it up but I snatched it away and slammed it into an upright position.

"Look at them, Mum, really look." I waved my hand towards the others, fiddling about with their pointless hobbies, killing time when they should have had a pile of homework.

"They've got nothing, nothing except each other and you. Sometimes I think I'd rather die than live like them."

Fourteen slammed her book shut and walked out in a huff. Seven trailed after her.

Eva started crying and said, "You not die, you naughty."

Mum gave me a kicked puppy look as she scooped Eva into her arms.

"Teva, please, you just have to…"

"Don't!" I yelled. "Do not tell me I just have to trust you."

I stormed out of the room, catching my toe on the chair leg and nearly tripping over. I was sick of her fobbing me off, telling me to trust her, that there were things I didn't know – of course there were things I didn't know, she never told me anything. My thoughts were all over the place – I felt like my brain was cracking in two with the pressure of being Teva for so many different people – for Maddy and Ollie and Fifteen and Mum and school and all the others. I didn't even know *how* to be Teva for just me. Apart from some kind of future, what did I even want? Craziness clawed at the edges of my mind. How was anyone supposed to live like this? Fury sent hot tears spilling over my lashes. I just…wanted… to be normal.

I went to my room and logged onto the blog, desperate for a trace of hope. There was nothing. Not a single comment. Disappointment spread through me. I wanted to chuck my stupid laptop out of the window. I was spoiling for a fight, desperate for someone to talk to or shout at, so I went looking for Fifteen.

I barely knocked before I shoved the door open onto her tip of a room. Clothes covered the floor, stuff spilled out of her wardrobe like a material eruption. Her walls were covered in peeling posters and weird drawings. Hundreds and hundreds of stick figures from her life, from her year on the outside, danced in the spaces between pictures of last year's bands.

It was totally suffocating, but Fifteen wasn't there. I backed out and knocked on Twelve and Thirteen's door. They said, "Go away."

I opened it anyway. They were sitting cross-legged on their twin beds, a mirror of each other, knitting something odd out of fluffy purple wool. They looked up almost exactly in sync.

"What?" they said.

"Have you seen Fifteen?"

"No," they said.

"God, you two are weird."

They stuck their tongues out at me and I left them to it.

I ran downstairs. I knew Fifteen wasn't in the kitchen but I quickly checked the front room – CBeebies blasted out of the telly – she definitely wasn't in there, no way would she put up with that. The dining room was empty too. I ran back up, taking the stairs two at a time.

Where was she? She must have come home, surely? I raced up to the second floor. Eight and Nine were in Mum's room, plastered in make-up and tottering about in high heels that hadn't seen the light of day since 1986.

"Have you seen Fifteen?"

"No," they said, sashaying across the room. I checked Mum's shower room and Six's tiny bedroom – no sign of her. I went back down and searched both bathrooms on our floor and the bedrooms I hadn't looked in before. I even tried the airing cupboard. The only place left was the attic. I went back up, climbed the narrow steps – so steep they were almost a ladder – and opened the crooked door to the cold loft space.

It was freezing up there. I flicked the light on with a shudder; the place was full of spiders. I forced myself to go in.

"You can stop hiding now, I've found you," I lied, hoping to lure her out. I looked behind boxes, under broken bed frames, between old paintings. I stood still and listened. Nothing but the mice that moved into the eaves over winter.

I went back downstairs and checked the front room again – maybe she *was* watching TV? Fourteen had moved to the sofa and was glued to some over-bright, over-loud rubbish, but there was no Fifteen.

I walked back to the kitchen in a daze. Hoping, hoping, hoping I'd find her there talking to Mum, moaning about me.

Eva was emptying the saucepan drawer over the floor but Fifteen wasn't there.

She hadn't come home.

thirteen

What if Fifteen had run into the road and been mangled under a bus? What if she'd been kidnapped by some weirdo? What if…?

I sucked on my bottom lip.

"What is it now?" Mum said, scraping a chopped onion into a pan. She smacked the sharp edge of the knife against the board as the room filled with the poisonous hiss of sizzling onions.

"Nothing. Just remembered my homework."

My mind worked overtime.

Mum's phone. Fifteen might have taken Mum's phone.

I spun round and ran up to my room. I dived through the door and slammed it shut. Leaning against it, I fished my phone from my pocket and dialled Mum's number.

"Come on, come on, answer."

It rang for an age and I almost hung up, then someone picked up.

"Teva? Why on earth are you dialling my phone? If you want to talk to me, come downstairs. I can't believe you could be so lazy. When I was your age…"

Mum.

I clicked off. Let her think I'd pocket dialled. What was I going to do? Maybe Fifteen was lying in a ditch, collapsed somewhere or…maybe…she was with Ollie? Again. Could she have done that? Waited outside his and gone in when I left? How would she explain that? Oh god.

I scrabbled across my bed and flipped my laptop open to see if there were any clues on Facebook. Mads was poking me: *Helloooo, answer me, Teva Webb!!!!*

So, Fifteen wasn't in the Ranjha house. How could I find out where she was? I couldn't text Ollie – if she was with him, seven shades of crazy would kick off. Maybe it was fate. Maybe it *was* time to tell the world about us. I glanced out of the window. My room was reflected back. It was dark outside. I crossed the floor and pressed my face to the window, shading my eyes from the room light. I could just make out the ladder leaning against the wall. Fifteen must have climbed out from the garden – god knows how she'd got down the other side. Or how she'd get back in.

It was all my fault. I forgot to lock the shed after I'd asked Twelve and Thirteen to put the ladder away. I had to find her. She must have gone to Ollie's and if she hadn't…if she hadn't… I just had to keep looking until I found her.

I scribbled a note for Mum:

Just popping out for half an hour.

I left it on the hall table, on top of our dumpy little house phone. With a glance towards the bright steamy light of the kitchen, I slipped out of the front door. Cold nipped my cheeks and I tugged my thick scarf up and my hat down. I ferreted in my pockets for gloves.

I had a lot more purpose in my feet than in my head as I marched towards Ollie's house. I nursed my phone in my hand the whole time, trying to flick the cover off with my thick, gloved fingers.

Street lights threw yellow spots on the pavement. Gloom, gloom, light, gloom, gloom, light…

My life was mad, really, *really* mad. Sometimes I felt like I might actually be going crazy with the pressure of it all. As I turned the corner into Ollie's road, I was shivering. Or trembling. I wasn't sure which. By the time Ollie's flat came into sight, my stomach had coiled into a knot of rats' tails so tight it was all I could do to keep stepping forward. The curtains were still closed. I wouldn't be able to see in. My heart flip-flopped against my ribs – a wet fish floundering for life. How could I find out if she was in there?

A strip of light was showing near the bottom of the window. I crept closer, tiptoeing like I was some kind of spy. I would have laughed at myself if my nerves hadn't been so totally shredded. Eight would have loved it, but I wasn't eight any more. I was sixteen and my life was collapsing. Clutching the window ledge, I crouched down to peer through the tiny gap.

I could just see Ollie, the top of his head visible over the back of the sofa. My phone buzzed in my pocket, throwing me into a heart-thumping panic. I ducked behind an overgrown rose bush to answer it, snagging my coat on the thorns.

Mum. Of all the moments to choose. I fumbled my glove off. "Yes, what?" I whispered.

She totally went off on one. "Yes, what? Yes, what? Where are you? What do you mean *back in half an hour*? Since when was it okay for you to go sneaking off in the middle of the night?"

"It's seven thirty, not the middle of the night."

"It's dark!" she shrieked. "And why are you whispering, where are you?"

Without thinking of the consequences I said, "It's not my fault – Fifteen sneaked out, I'm just looking for her."

I was instantly sorry I'd spoken and fully expected Mum to say, *That's it, none of you are going out ever again.* She didn't. She said, "You never take responsibility for your own actions, Teva. Never. You're meant to be sixteen, not a baby."

That sentence hit me square in the chest.

I let the phone slip down against my cheek.

I was *meant* to be Sixteen. That was my reality. To give up being Teva, to hand over my life and be stuck indoors for ever – a prisoner, like Fifteen and all the others. *I'd* have to sneak out too if I wanted any chance of normality. Energy leaked from my legs and I sank into a heap between the bush and the wall.

"Teva? Teva!"

I hung up. Even if Fifteen was in there, what could I do about it? I'd never felt more useless or helpless or pointless. I sat there until my legs started to scream with cramp. With a shake of my head, I forced myself back to the window. I could see Ollie's beautiful profile looking down at a fluffy blonde head. It could only be Fifteen. At least she was safe. She tipped her head back and stretched up to kiss him. A lump the size of a brick sat in my chest.

I watched them for a minute, so comfortable with each other. With every tiny gesture – Fifteen flicking quick glances up at Ollie, Ollie dropping light kisses on her head – it was like the truth was being pushed into me, crushing the air from my lungs, making it painful to breathe. A single hot tear spilled down my cheek, leaving a cold trace in the night air.

I sank back against the wall – touched my chin where he'd lifted my face to his earlier. Ugly, air-filled sobs hiccuped from my throat. I'd convinced myself that taking Ollie from Fifteen was okay, that I *was* her and it was my right. But watching them, I just didn't know. Who would? I didn't exactly have a lot of examples to go on, did I? Maybe I had no more right to Ollie than the next version of us had to take him from me? Tears ran freely down my face. Fifteen was right. I was clinging onto a relationship that had never really been mine.

I forced myself to stand up, burrowed my hands into my pockets and turned away. I was so full of sadness, so weighed down by it, I could hardly put one foot in front of the other.

Step after cold step home, I thought things over. I tortured myself, imagining a future without those brown eyes holding me fast. I couldn't bear it. When I got to the gate, I left it open, just a little bit, so Fifteen could get back in. I trudged up the gravel to our front door.

Mum flung it open before I could even get my key out.

"Don't," I said, "just don't."

I headed for the stairs, dimly heard Mum saying, "Teva? Where…"

I stopped on the stairs, turned and held up my hand.

"Fifteen's fine, she'll be back soon, I'm sure of it."

I watched my mother droop, like she'd lost control of something she barely had a grip on in the first place. I opened my mouth to say something else but there were no words. I hauled myself up to my room. She followed me to my door where I stopped, my bottom lip trembling as I said, "I can't talk right now, please, just leave me alone."

She hesitated then rubbed her hand up and down my arm and nodded.

I left the light off and lay on my bed in my coat. I just wanted to go to sleep. To drown everything under a thick layer of numbing sleep. I couldn't clear my mind of the picture Fifteen and Ollie made, their two heads tipped together, a perfect fit.

I must have dropped off because a soft knocking at the door woke me up. I blinked.

"Teva? Tee, can I come in?"

I wiped the dribble off my face.

"Yeah, alright."

Mum came over and switched on my bedside light.

"I've brought you a cup of tea."

I sat up and took it from her. "Thanks."

She sat on my bed, her plump hands sandwiched between her knees.

"You can talk to me, Teva. I know things are hard but you can talk to me about anything that's worrying you."

I tucked my knees up to my chest.

"Can I?"

"Of course, darling. Look, are you still upset about the fashion show?"

A deep unfunny laugh escaped me.

She said, "Because, if you are, I don't mind if you do it. It'll be fine. Maybe I overreacted."

She wanted me to say that was it, that if I did the fashion show everything would be okay. I hadn't even wanted to get involved with the stupid fashion show in the first place; I'd just wanted her to let me be part of something outside of my crappy world. Mum held her arms out. I hesitated but, in the end, I couldn't resist that warm space. A space I always seemed to fit no matter what. I snuggled into her arms. She smelled of onions and washing powder. She smelled of home.

I whispered, "I don't want my birthday to come."

"I know, I know, everyone feels like that sometimes."

"But not everyone has to deal with this, do they? My life will be over, I'll have nothing."

She stroked my hair silently.

I said, "I can't do this any more." That was all I could get out, before all the fear, the desperation, spilled out in a flood of tears.

"Oh, Teva," she said, her voice wavering.

I laid my wet cheek against her squidgy shoulder, sobbing, "I don't know what to do, Mum, I've tried to find a way to get help but I just can't do it. I get nowhere. It all seems so pointless. I can't keep pretending everything's okay when it's not. It hurts so much."

She pulled away from me but I wasn't letting her off that easily. I took her arms firmly in my hands. I had to try and get her to do *something*.

"Why won't you help us?"

Her chin wobbled and her weakness infuriated me. I shook her sharply as I said, "You're meant to look after us. You're meant to be strong for us."

She looked at the floor and mumbled, "You've no idea…"

"It's like you don't even care what happens to us."

She put a warm, damp hand to my cheek. "Oh, Teva. That's so unfair. There's nothing more important to me than you, nothing."

Her head drooped and she covered her mouth with the back of her hand. It was as if her tattered life was at stake, not mine. Stiff tentacles of anger crawled up my spine and lodged tightly in my jaw.

She wasn't going to help. She wasn't.

She made a massive show of mopping up her own tears.

It was my cue to be sorry, I knew that – I was meant to feel bad for upsetting her. I didn't. A dark cocktail of sorrow and anger swirled through me. As I swallowed it down, I heard the soft clunk of the front door. Fifteen was back.

fourteen

My heart tripped over itself in a fresh rush of emotion. I could barely get my head around Fifteen and Ollie. What on earth was I supposed to say to her?

Mum squeezed my arm gently and gave my hand a pat.

Had she not heard the door? Why wasn't she gearing up to yell at Fifteen? She said, "Do you want to come down for something to eat?"

I shook my head, the fight gone out of me. Mum headed downstairs and I went for a pee. I listened out for a shouting match between Mum and Fifteen, but it didn't come. Maybe she'd used up all her anger telling me off on the phone.

When I came back from the loo, Fifteen was in the middle of my room, arms folded across her chest.

She said, "Congratulations."

"What?"

"On being the world's crappiest girlfriend. Seriously. You deserve a prize."

"You've got a cheek."

"I've done nothing to be ashamed of. I didn't touch anything that wasn't mine."

She didn't look as smug and happy as I expected, considering she'd spent the whole evening with Ollie.

"You are this close" – she held her thumb and forefinger a centimetre apart – "to ruining everything."

My hands tightened into fists. "Me? You're the one sneaking round behind everyone's backs."

"If you don't stop being so weird, I'm going to have to tell him about us. He thinks we've got problems. He thinks we're not getting on like we used to."

I swallowed, not as surprised as I should have been.

"Are you listening? Here's the deal, you are just like a caretaker, okay? Until I can figure out how to be with Ollie properly, all you have to do is not muck things up."

"He's not a thing you own."

"You think I don't know that? I love him. *Him*, not what he can do for me or be to me, *him*. You don't even listen to what he's got to say, do you?"

My cheeks flushed with heat. I tried to think back over what had happened earlier but Fifteen's face crumpled. She shook her head, trying to regain some control, and hissed, "You've made him so unhappy. He said we're not as close as we used to be. He thinks you're moody."

"Me?"

"He asked me if I had hormone problems. Crying over Kristal? What even was that?"

"Don't tell me that wouldn't have upset you? He was all over her!"

"I wouldn't have cried like a baby! Anyway, I trust him, which is more than you do. And what about tonight? What was your plan there, hey? Flinging yourself at him like a tramp?"

"Don't you dare say that, don't you dare! He's my boyfriend."

"NO HE'S NOT! He's MY boyfriend. You've done nothing to deserve him. Nothing."

The look she shot me made me wince.

She pulled herself up tall and said, "You know he's planning to leave, don't you?"

"What?"

"He wants to join the army. He tried to tell you tonight but you were too busy trying to tear his clothes off."

"I was not!"

But she was right, he *had* said things about not spending enough time together, needing to talk – and I had used him to try and make myself feel better, to patch over the gaping holes in my life, to forget about the Teva inside me, stirring under my skin. I sank down on the bed. I had been an utterly selfish cow.

"What else did he say?"

She looked at me, her face hard.

"Why should I tell you?"

"He…he might ask me about it. He'll think it's weird if I don't remember."

She nodded, her jaw tight and said, "If he has his way, he'll be gone in six months. He could die in the army, you know that, right? Even you're not that stupid."

She pulled the door open and stopped. "I'll tell you something else – he said he'd missed me. *Me.* It was like he knew *you* were different."

She looked me right in the eye and said, "We're not the same, you and me, you think we are but we're not. You don't love him like I do, you never will."

I swallowed hard, my throat thick.

I pictured his face, his beautiful eyes, the feel of his hair under my fingers. How would it be to arrive at school and not think about where he was, not look for him waiting for me? We were a couple and everyone knew it. If we broke up, it'd be the talk of school for weeks. Was that love? Or was I just afraid to be on my own?

Fifteen was still standing, watching me. My stomach churned as I thought of them together, even as I realized she had to think of him and me like that every single day.

What a mess. What a horrible, horrible mess.

Almost against my will, I whispered, "Sorry."

Her eyes glittered and I said it again: "I'm sorry."

Eventually she nodded and looked me square in the face, a little mirror of me, fractionally smaller, paler, angrier.

"He's mine. He always will be. It doesn't matter what you pretend. So your blog thing? Even if, by some miracle, you do sort something out, just remember, it won't make any difference to you and Ollie because *I* am having him back."

She left quietly, didn't even slam the door. I reached under my pillow for Peepee and sat there, stroking his ear to my cheek. I thought and thought but I couldn't find any sensible answers. It was like trying to make $2 + 2 = 5$. I might lose Ollie if I found a way to fix things, but if I didn't, I'd lose everything: Ollie, Maddy, my whole life.

I reached for my computer and brought up my blog, hoping there'd be some comment, something, anything. There was nothing, and as I scrolled down wondering what to do next, I caught my little fingernail on the shift key.

Absent-mindedly, I tried to nip the ragged nail tip between my teeth. My finger felt odd, too fat. I took it out of my mouth and looked at it.

There were two nails.

One on top of another.

One that didn't belong to me.

fifteen

An almighty pressure squeezed a low scream from my chest.

"No. No. No…"

I squeezed my left hand around my finger as tight as I could. Holding, pressing, forcing the nails back into line. It hurt so much, like screwing my fingers in a vice, but I held on. I stumbled to the bathroom and scrabbled in the cupboard for a bandage. I fought back vomit as I wound the crêpe cloth tightly round my finger. I tied it as tight as I could, pulling hard with my teeth as I knotted it in place.

Heavy sobs caught in my chest. My left hand was white with the pressure of holding on. I checked my other fingernails, hardly daring to look; having to.

This couldn't be happening. Not this early. Was this it? Was she taking over already? Heat flushed through me; I was going to faint. I slithered down the side of the bath, sucking air into my lungs, trying to force myself to calm down. I wished I could remember more of what it had been like for Fifteen. More than just her panic mingling with mine. I suddenly remembered being unable to breathe – when the separation started I'd thought I was going to suffocate. I had to tear myself free so I could breathe. And it was quick. A sudden peeling away – over in a matter of minutes.

Sweat beaded on my upper lip – my tongue flicked at it, tasting the fear-drenched salt. It was so unfair. It was months until my birthday. Wasn't I even going to get a year? I sat there, shivering and crying, waiting for that other Teva to force her way out of me. I didn't move until Mum came up to bed. She pushed the door open to turn off the light and found me huddled by the bath.

"Teva? Love? I thought you'd gone to bed. Whatever is the matter?"

I blinked up at her, held my finger up, defeat all over my face. The horror in her eyes said it all.

She sat with her arms around me, gently patting my back. I lost track of how long for. My bum went numb, so it was a fair while. She wouldn't undo the bandage. She wouldn't look. She just kept hushing me and telling me it would be okay. Slowly, even though I didn't believe her, my heart steadied and I stopped feeling quite so sick. I waited for the terrible tearing to begin but it didn't. Not even the wriggling under my skin. Why not? What was going on?

Eventually Mum said, "Okay, come on, you need to get some sleep."

"But what if she comes? What if it happens when I'm on my own?"

"Call me, just shout and I'll come."

I let Mum lead me to my room and tuck me into bed. She found Peepee and folded his floppy body into a gap in my arms. She kissed me lightly, smoothing my hair. I let her treat me like I was six not sixteen and it made things just about bearable. I said, "Don't leave me."

She went out and came back with her duvet. She made a nest on the floor and lay down next to me.

"I'm right here. Okay?"

I nodded, unable to speak, so grateful she was there. Still, I lay awake, my heart squeezing out shots of head-pounding adrenalin with every twitch, every pulse in my body.

In the end, I must have dozed off but I woke stupidly early. It took me a minute to remember why my heart was pounding, why sickness swirled in my gut; for the throb in my little finger to hit me with a vile shock that sludged through my veins like cold porridge. I drew my hand out from under the duvet and pinched my finger under the bandage. Everything felt wrong, uncomfortable. I glanced at the floor. Mum wasn't there. I got up and stumbled blearily downstairs. She was in the kitchen unloading the dishwasher. She gave me a wonky smile.

"How are you feeling, sweetheart?"

I shrugged, tears bubbling, chin wobbling. She put a hand on my forehead and as I leaned into it, she said, "I think you should stay at home today."

I wasn't going to argue with that. I felt like I'd been sat on by an elephant. She got the cutlery basket out and dropped its contents in the drawer, making my brain rattle.

I wrapped my good hand round my bandaged finger and held it to my chest.

"Mum, why didn't the separation happen last night? Is it normally like this? I can't find anything in the others' memories – did they hide it? Was it too horrible to hold on to?"

She was drying her hands on a tea towel but she stopped and stood looking at the cloth in her hands. Eventually she said, "Come and sit down for a minute."

She pulled a chair out for me but I shook my head; I was coiled up so tight, it was as much as I could do to just stand there. Mum took a deep breath in and out and said, "There aren't any rules, Teva." She squeezed my shoulder. "When it's happened before it's been, well, a night of…difficulty…"

I flinched at *difficulty*. Difficulty? Really? Was that the word?

"Afterwards," she went on, "you're usually very tired, but that's it, the worst is over."

She pinched her nose, steeling herself. "I thought – I hoped – you're so much older now, Tee. You're getting through puberty, all those hormonal changes; I know you still get a bit upset about things but you're a lot less angry these days. I hoped it was over. Now you're so grown up, so much more…" She sighed and shook her head, searching for the right word. "Stable? You've been so much better tempered, don't you think? So much more in control."

I shrugged. "Control? How can I have any control over this? I don't think breathing exercises are going to cut it, do you?"

She covered her face with her hands for a second, then said, "No, sweetheart, I suppose not."

"What will happen?"

"I don't know, Teva. We'll just have to ride it out. I think you should stay at home, though, where I can keep an eye on you. We've done okay so far, haven't we?"

She covered my bandaged hand with hers. "We're a little team, aren't we?"

I thought about that for a second. She was my mum, I loved her, but I didn't feel like she was on my team. Not really.

I felt...alone.

I looked at my hand, then at her.

"We don't know then? How long I've got?"

She smiled sadly and gave the tiniest shake of her head.

I nodded and walked out of the kitchen, past Six peeling the paper under the banister, to my bedroom. I shut the door and sat, shaking, on my bed. Any hope I'd had was leaking out of my little finger where that nail had started to split. About the only decent thing I had left was Maddy. I reached for my phone and texted her:

I love you, you're the best friend anyone could ever have. Xx

She texted back straight away:

True. I am fabulous. Now stop lolling about in bed and get ready for school.

I snorted a microscopic laugh and texted:

I've been up hours.

Yeah right, you'll be under that duvet till the very last minute.

Every text lifted my spirits. I typed back:

You know me so well.

I know you inside out, now move it, lazy ;)

She didn't know me inside out. But she knew bits of me as well as anyone could. She was an antidote to everything crap in my life. I looked at my bandaged hand. Was I going to give up? Sit in the house and just wait for the new Teva to take over? No, I bloody wasn't.

First things first – I pulled my laptop towards me and logged onto the blog. I couldn't help the tiny flicker of hope that flared in me as I checked the stats, but there was still nothing. After all the warnings we'd had at school not to post pics of ourselves in our bra and knickers (who even did that – apart from Kristal Mitchell obviously?), I suppose I thought my little blog would have instantly gone viral. What an idiot. Why would it? Why would anyone notice a tiny shrimp like me in an ocean full of fish.

There'd been a few hits though, people searching for "unusual skin conditions" and "weird bodies". As I was wondering how they'd landed on my site with those searches, I slapped my forehead. I hadn't tagged the post with the little labels that people search for! That had to help. I added as many as I could think of, including, with a shudder: *weird cancers.* I needed more ideas to make the blog visible. I'd think about it on my way to Maddy's.

I sat up, amazed at myself. Was I really going into school? Yes. Yes I was. Maddy would make me feel normal. A bit. And I had to talk to Ollie. Though I had no clue what I was going to say. I was so churned up about him. How could I have a conversation about sorting things out when he thought we'd already had that conversation? I shook my head. I'd work it out. I texted Maddy back:

See you soon x

It was a huge effort to get dressed; my veins felt full of liquid lead. My phone rang just as I popped my sweatshirt over my head. It was a number I didn't recognize.

"Hello?"

A male voice, Nutella smooth, said, "Hey, gorgeous."

I bluffed it for a second. "Errr, hi."

"You have no idea who this is, do you?"

"Errrm, okay, no, I don't."

"Charming. Well let me help you out – six foot two, gym god, extremely talented with a needle and thread."

"Tommo?"

"Thank you, good of you to catch up. Maddy gave me your number."

I wrinkled my nose.

"Okay, what's up?"

"She said you might be interested in a trade?"

"Go on."

"She said you might help me with my English if I helped you with your textiles?"

"I thought you got English."

"I need an A for what I want to do next year – I'm resitting. Will you help me? Please?"

Things were complicated enough with Ollie, I couldn't risk making it worse. That would be one more problem on my already mountainous heap. I said, "I don't know, Tommo, I've got a lot to do myself and…"

"I'll help with your textiles portfolio, I promise. Pleeeeeaase, if you give me just a tiny bit of help with the war poets."

I couldn't. Not until me and Ollie had sorted stuff out. There was no way. It was almost the worst thing I could do.

A ton of thoughts crashed around my head and one kept bobbing to the top. Fifteen and Ollie with their heads tipped together. Where did I fit in that cosy couple?

"Pretty please with a cherry on top?"

I glanced at my bandaged finger. Didn't I deserve to live every second I had?

"Well? Have I begged enough?"

It was just a homework trade. There was nothing in it. Why shouldn't I say yes?

"Alright. Frankie's room at lunchtime?"

"You are a total angel, thank you!"

A weird mix of panic and excitement set my head spinning. I had to wash my hair – I looked grim. I ran upstairs to use the shower in Mum's bathroom, cursing our cranky old house as I went; it was ridiculous really, one shower between thirteen of us.

I pushed open her door. One of the little ones had pulled

a suitcase of old clothes out from under her bed. Long swishy skirts and multicoloured scarves spilled out from it. Full of purpose, I kneeled down to shove the things back in. I pushed the case firmly, but it caught on something. I groped under the bed and found a thick file. I pulled it out to make room for the suitcase. It said EVA WEBB in thick black marker. There were a load of small numbered stickers down the right-hand side and dates scrawled all over the front next to abbreviated notes I didn't understand. With a quick glance at the door, I slid it towards me with a dry hush. Was it a medical file? Thoughts of hair-washing disappeared and I opened it, one eye on the door.

The top sheet was a letter from a dermatologist recommending all the skin stuff Mum got off the internet. I flipped it over. Underneath was a psychologist's report, full of all the lies Mum had told the counsellor about my overactive imagination. I flipped that over too. Next was a permission letter for an anaesthetic dated ten years ago – I didn't remember having an operation. I didn't remember any hospital treatment. Blood flooded into my head. I turned the letter over. Mum hadn't signed it, someone else had. *Dr Tarrant, Father.*

Tarrant? My father? A doctor? Called Tarrant? Why did he have a different name to us? I touched the signature, and seeing my bandaged little finger shocked me again. I wasn't sure which had my heart racing more, that finger or the ghost of my dad on the paper. I looked at the next page, trying to figure out what the operation was for. I couldn't understand any of it. I flipped to the next sheet, copies of grainy grey pictures – scans of our body organs? Everything seemed to have a shadow behind it. Even the shadows had shadows.

"What you doing?"

I turned at the croaky little voice behind me and fumbled the papers, scattering them in a cascade. Six was standing in the door, Peepee trailing from her hand.

"You made me jump!"

I scooped the papers up and shoved them into the file, then tried to slide them back under the bed.

"What you doing?"

"Nothing."

"You was reading something."

"I wasn't."

"You was."

"I was not. Oh dear, Peepee has run away."

I darted forward, grabbed Peepee from her hand and ran down the stairs.

"Give him back," she said. "Give him back to me!"

I stopped. Ten years ago, we'd have been Six. When I asked the others if they remembered seeing a doctor, she'd run out of the room. Maybe something happened that had made her so strange and withdrawn and somehow, she'd found a way to hide it from the rest of us.

I held Peepee out. Her hand darted out for him, distrustful.

"Sorry," I said. "That was naughty. I shouldn't have done it."

135

She peered up at me, her eyes round with suspicion, Peepee pressed to her mouth.

I said, "Does Peepee remember going to hospital? A long time ago?"

She shook her head and took a step away from me.

"Are you sure? I know it was a long, long time ago. Can you try and remember?"

She ran away.

Handled that well then, Tee.

I followed her downstairs, expecting her to go straight to the kitchen to blab to Mum. She was under the banister though, huddled tight against the wall, determined not to look at me. I sat next to her.

"It's alright," I said. "I'm sorry about Peepee."

She turned even further into the wall and picked at a strip of paper.

I checked my watch; it was getting late.

"I've got to go, little one."

I gave her thin back a rub. Pity swept over me and I caught her in a tight little hug.

I dug about in the hat and glove basket for something to hide my unwashed hair. My head was literally spinning with all the stuff churning around in it: the doctor's file, the blog, Tommo, Ollie, how long I had left before...

"Teva?" Mum came to the kitchen door, drying her hands.

I grabbed a purple beanie and my coat.

"Sorry, running late. Got to go."

"You're not going to…"

I darted out of the front door shouting, "Sorry, late."

The door shut behind me with a satisfying clunk.

It was foul outside. Rain drove sideways at me. I hurried out of the gate and along the road and a stupid thought popped into my head: *I can't wait to learn to drive.*

Side-swiped.

I was never going to be old enough to drive. My bandaged little finger felt like a monster clinging to my hand. I shook my head and ran.

Rain soaked through my hat, splashed up my legs, seeped through the seams of my jacket, soaking my sweatshirt. Yellow light spilled from Maddy's front-room window onto the grey pavement outside. I raced towards it and hammered on the door. It snapped open and Maddy yanked me inside, slamming it shut behind me.

I stood shivering and dripping in their tiny hallway. Without a word Maddy ran upstairs to get me a towel. When she came back she pulled off my soggy hat and plopped the towel on my head.

"Here. I don't know why your mum doesn't get a car. It's ridiculous you walking in this."

It felt impossible that she could talk to me so normally – that she couldn't see I wasn't just wet, I was underwater and my pockets were filling up with pebbles.

I wiped my face with the towel.

She said, "Seriously, you could get pneumonia."

Mrs Ranjha came out of the kitchen with little Jay on one hip and a cup of tea in her free hand. She took one look at me and held out the steaming mug.

"Here. I'll make another one. No arguments, take it, you look frozen."

Maddy glanced at her watch.

"Madeeha, your best friend is soaking wet, stop checking on the time. I'll drive you in, you won't be late."

My teeth chattered a thank you and I accepted the scalding liquid in both hands. Maddy spotted the now soggy bandage.

"What've you done to your finger?"

I tucked it away.

"Nothing. Burned it on the iron."

I sipped the tea; it was spicy, milky and way too sweet. It made my mouth pucker but I drank it anyway.

Mrs Ranjha put a gentle hand on my arm. "You're very pale, dear. Is everything alright at home? Is Mrs Webb alright?"

I nodded. "She's fine, thank you. Just busy."

"You look very stressed today. It's exams, isn't it? So much pressure on you youngsters."

Maddy jumped in: "Mum, leave her alone. She's fine."

Only I wasn't fine. I stood there, rain steaming off me, my finger throbbing as I watched Maddy twist her hair into a plait, wanting to tell them everything and at the same time too terrified to do it. I pictured my tearful confession, their arms round me, promises of help…

Maddy checked her watch. "I'm nipping to the loo. We need to go in like two minutes."

Mrs Ranjha rummaged behind one of her sari boxes to find Jay's coat.

I forced myself to concentrate, try and be normal. It was so hard when my head was racing with what-ifs and how-tos. And then I had a thought.

"How's your shop going?" I asked Mrs Ranjha.

"Oh yes, okay, busy busy."

"How do people find it? There's so much stuff on the internet, how do you ever get noticed?"

"Oh you know, Facebook, Twitter, all of those kind of things. If you put interesting pictures up, people share them. I should dress Mr Madeeha in a sari. That would get everybody looking." She laughed out loud.

I could have kicked myself. I was a genuine idiot. Facebook. Of course.

Mrs Ranjha was still chuckling. "Oh dear me, that would be funny."

I'd make a fake Facebook profile for Celly and post links to the blog. I'd have to think about pictures – I wasn't sure how to get round that one. Maybe I could copy the scan pictures I'd found under Mum's bed? I flipped the cover off my phone and pressed it back on again. I could do the Facebook thing at school, get it up and running before I even got home. I'd go to the library, use the computers there. If we got to school fast enough, I might even manage to do something before reg.

"Thanks, Mrs R." I kissed her cheek.

"What did I do? Give you a cup of tea? Such lovely manners. Come on, let's go – Madeeha. In the car – now!"

We all dived through the rain to the car and, somehow, some of the warmth of their house came with us.

sixteen

It was still peeing down when we got to school. Mrs R pulled up right near the sports hall. Ollie wasn't there. My stomach tightened and then let go. It was tipping down – of course he wasn't there.

We said goodbye and legged it through the rain to get inside. As soon as we were through the doors, I checked my phone to see if he'd texted. Nothing. Well, that could wait. I needed to sort out Celly's Facebook page. I couldn't tell Mads I was going to the library, though, she'd want to know why. I said, "I'm just popping up to the common room."

"Running after Ollie?"

"No. I left something in my locker."

She grabbed my arm and tried to drag me towards reg. "No you haven't, you massive fibber. Come on, let him wonder where you are for a change."

"Mads, I'll be two minutes, I swear, I just want to say hi." Before I could escape Maddy's clutches though, Frankie appeared pushing a supermarket trolley of fabric scraps.

"Oh, girls, brilliant! You can give me a hand with this lot, and Teva? I've had a great idea – something for you to think about. Maybe enough to make you get your finger out and do some work."

My hand cramped up. What a choice of words.

Maddy took the trolley and pushed it towards our form room. I pushed my bandaged hand firmly into my wet pocket but not before Frankie saw it.

"Your right hand? Your sewing hand? What have you done?"

"Nothing, I just picked up a knife the wrong way round."

Maddy looked at me, "You said you burned it."

I squirmed, "Yeah, I know, both things on the same finger. I'm an idiot."

They gave me a look, but Frankie was too excited to ask any more questions. She said, "What about De Montfort? To do contour fashion?"

"What?"

"University, Teva. You need to start planning. You wait and see. I have high hopes for you at the fashion show. You're a bright and talented girl."

Bright and talented? Me? What was she talking about? Maddy was the bright one.

I shook my head, "I can't go to university."

"Why not? Is it money? You shouldn't let that stand in your way. There are loans, maybe even scholarships!"

"No, I…"

Maddy saved me, "What's contour fashion?"

"Underwear," said Miss Francis with a huge smile. "Teva has a real flair for design when she actually does any work."

"You can study knickers at college?" Maddy said.

"It's not just knickers." Miss Francis looked down her nose at Maddy and it served her right, she could be pretty snobby about academic stuff. "Fashion is a huge industry. Look, Teva, why don't you have a chat with the careers advisor and see what you'd need to apply?"

The careers office was in the library. It was the perfect excuse. "Can I go now?"

Frankie beamed all over her face.

"Of course. Good girl, Teva. Let me write down the name. You know, if you get the attention of H&S, their scholarship scheme could help you all the way through college."

She handed me a piece of paper with the university name on it. I practically ran to the library. I pulled open the door and a quiet hush settled round me like a blanket. The careers office was on the far side but on the left, amongst all the books, sat a bank of computers around an oval table. There were two sixth-formers there already. The kind of nerdy kids who were lost in the playground but right at home with a keyboard and a wall of books.

I slid into an empty chair, put Frankie's note on the table and googled the university so I could flip back to the tab if anyone came over. It looked amazing; there was a gallery of designs that was incredible. I couldn't help the yearning that bloomed in me. I just wanted a chance. That's all. Was it really so much to ask?

I looked around; no one was watching. I checked into Celly's blog: *You have comments waiting for approval.*

A prickling buzz thrilled up my spine. It evaporated as soon as I saw the comment. One. Singular. And that from someone trying to sell me Viagra. I deleted it. Funny how spammers find you when no one else does. My finger throbbed lightly, urging me on. Celly needed a cyber life.

I tried to get onto Facebook but the school firewall blocked me.

"Damn," I mumbled under my breath.

One of the floppy-haired computer geeks peered up at me through his glasses.

"Sorry," I said, "firewall."

He glanced at the librarian and mouthed, "What can't you access?"

I mouthed back, "Facebook."

He quietly pushed his chair back and came over to my PC. He pressed a few buttons and, hey presto, there was the Facebook login page. I looked up at him.

"Wow. Thanks."

He shrugged and went back to whatever he was doing. I mean that was kind of cool. Like spy stuff. Eight would have been super impressed. I looked at him again and he smiled shyly. I'd never really noticed him before. Definitely never spoken to him.

I made a mental note to be nicer to geeks as I got to work

creating a backstory for Celly. It was quite fun pretending to be someone else. I made her Scottish, I don't know why. I used my purple-haired blog avatar for her profile picture at first, but it looked way too fake, so I stole a picture off the internet instead. I chose a dark-haired girl sniffing a flower so you could hardly see her face. I liked how natural she looked. She needed more pictures though so I made her a massive Manga fan and filled up an album with weird Japanese cartoons. I updated her status:

Sorry I've not been here, guys, making a fresh start. I've just got out of hospital. Could really do with cheering up.

She needed friends. No one my age had zero friends on Facebook. How was I going to get her Scottish friends? Unless she never went to school because she was so ill… nah, she'd still have friends. Hospital friends. I googled hospitals in Scotland and found Deanhill Children's hospital. I checked Facebook to see if there was a page for it. There was and it had over 1,400 likes. I liked it from Celly's page. With more than a twinge of guilt, I friend requested some of the people who'd left comments, justifying it with my own need.

I added a link to the first blog post I'd done, but Celly's page still looked way too boring. I stuck up a few dog-on-skateboard/cat-falling-off-sofa videos and then clicked back onto my blog. Given recent developments, I thought I should put up a new post. I couldn't stomach making it too dramatic, my situation was scary enough as it was. I headed the post *So Much for a Year* and typed:

It's happening early, the separation: the little finger on my right hand has started to come apart. I hope there's someone out there who knows what to do because I have no idea.

I added the link on Celly's FB page then I friended her from my own account and had her send a friend request blast to a load of my Facebook friends. I was banking on them not checking whose request they were accepting. Her page still looked really empty, so I started adding some band likes.

"Who's that?"

I jumped out of my seat, knocking my bag on the floor.

"Ollie! What are you doing in here?" I fumbled at the keyboard trying to log off, my heart jumping in my chest.

"Maddy said you'd gone to careers."

He squished into the seat next to me, clearing his view to the computer. I felt sick.

"What's this? Whose page is that?"

I had no choice but to brazen it out.

"My cousin. She keeps threatening to frape my page, was just going to get her first."

He laughed, "Good one, what you going to write?"

I looked at the page as if she really was my cousin. "I changed my mind, I forgot she'd been in hospital."

I was weirdly annoyed at him on my made-up cousin's behalf. I hit log out and as I turned the little scrap of paper with De Montfort University written on it fluttered to the floor.

Ollie picked it up.

"University? That Madeeha's?"

He handed it to me.

"No," I said, "it's mine."

"What do you want that for? University?" He tried to dismiss it but his shoulders hunched forward, like he was protecting himself somehow. A ball of irritation squirmed inside me. I said, "Frankie gave it to me. You know, as a way of trying to get me to do some work."

An awkward little hump sat between us. He threw the piece of paper on the desk and said, "You coming up to the common room?"

I glanced back at the PC. I couldn't do any more until I got home and found those scan pictures. I nodded, sliding the name of the university into my bag before we left.

As we headed up the stairs, I stretched forward to take Ollie's hand, saw my bandaged finger and pulled back. Everything felt...wrong. How could it not? He didn't really know who I was. Worse than that – he thought I was someone else.

"Wait," I whispered, tugging his hand. I didn't know what I was going to do or say, I just knew I couldn't carry on like this. The lies were burning a hole in my chest. He smiled lazily and stepped down to me. He put his hands on the wall behind me and pressed his whole body against mine. The handrail dug into my back but his body heat energized me. I should have stepped away, but I couldn't help myself. When he bent his head to kiss me, I kissed him back.

His lips were so soft, I sank into him. For a second,

I could have cried with relief. What was I thinking? We were okay. We were good together. Then he broke away and looked deep into my eyes, searching for something. Someone. Ice crept up my spine.

I couldn't do it any more.

He deserved better. I couldn't carry on cheating him.

I looked at the floor, tears forming far too easily and trickling down my cheeks.

"Hey," he said softly, "what's up?"

I pressed my lips together. What could I say?

He brushed his lips against my tear-soaked cheek. It was such a tender thing to do, my heart swelled with pain. Then he moved his hands to my waist and heat surged through me. I wasn't strong enough to do the right thing. I wasn't.

"Ollie, I…"

The door opened above us, jerking me back to my senses. I tugged my jumper straight as heavy steps skipped towards us. It was Tommo. He high-fived Ollie as he went past then turned and, walking backwards downstairs, he said, "You still okay for lunchtime, Tee?"

Ollie stiffened in my arms and my heart juddered. All I could do was give a small nod. As Tommo disappeared round the bottom of the stairs, Ollie stepped away from me.

Seventeen

In two strides he was at the top of the stairs, leaving me cold to the core.

"Ollie, wait."

As I went after him, the door to the common room swung back and banged against my bandaged finger. I gasped at the dart of pain but followed him in. He marched to the other side of the room, his back to me, his arms folded. I knew he'd react like that, I knew it, why had I said I'd help Tommo? I'd made everything worse.

Ollie turned round but he was looking at the floor as if he couldn't stomach looking at me. He said, "This is what I was saying last night. It used to be you and me against the world, but it's like you've got other stuff going on that I don't even know about. Now, I guess I know why."

I glanced round the common room. Kristal Mitchell was watching from the window ledge.

"It's not like that."

"Then what is it like? You're doing my head in. I have no idea what you're up to half the time."

"I'm sorry," I said as quietly as I could. "The thing with Tommo, it's not what you think, it's just…school stuff, that's all, I promise."

"Secret meetings?"

"It's not secret!"

"Well, *I* didn't know about it."

"He only asked me this morning."

"Nice. Fast worker as it's only nine o'clock. Got a private line, has he?"

"Ollie, stop it, please. He just asked if I could help him with…" I couldn't say it. He'd be so mad if he knew I was helping Tommo with his English. What a mess. This was all wrong. I needed to sort things out but not like this.

He tucked his hands deep under his armpits, his jaw so tight I could see his teeth grinding under the skin. Kristal slipped to her feet, pulling her skin-tight jeans down over her stupidly high boots, ready to pounce.

"Well?" Ollie said. "I'm listening. Help him with what?"

What could I say? What possible way was there to sort this out? Fifteen had described me as a caretaker, but Ollie didn't belong to her and he didn't belong to me. None of this was fair on him. It just wasn't. I had to let him go. I whispered, "English."

Ollie nodded.

"Found yourself another little pupil then? He comes up to your exacting standards, does he?"

I fought back tears, I didn't want him to feel like he wasn't good enough. He'd tried so hard but he had no idea what he was dealing with. I shook my head. "No, it's not like that. It's just a trade, Ollie. He's going to help with my textiles coursework, Frankie thinks I could do really well and Tommo's nearly got his project finished."

"Very nice. Very cosy. You scratch his back, he scratches yours?"

I tried to swallow. Tried to hold in the tears. What right had I to cry? I'd cheated him, cheated Fifteen...Ollie pushed his fingers into his hair and took a deep breath, I could feel his anger like heat.

"And I bet your back isn't the only thing he's been scratching."

That was it, the tears spilled out. "That's not fair! It isn't like that."

He turned away, strode across the room and punched his fist into one of the lockers. In that second, I was blind to everything else. I'd caused him this pain: if I hadn't taken her life, Fifteen would be here, and they'd still be okay. I followed him, put my hand on his arm. He snatched it away.

"Please, Ollie, it's not like that, I promise."

He leaned his head against the dented locker, lifted it, then banged it against the metal. I pleaded with him, "Please, don't..."

He stormed past me, out of the common room. I followed him down the stairs and he stopped. In a low voice he said, "You're not stupid, Tee. You know when a boy is after you.

Do you want it? Is that it?"

"No! Ollie, no, I'd never…"

"I'm not good enough, am I?" he said. "I never have been."

"No. It's me. It's all me. I wish…" I trailed off.

My body was screaming to touch him but it was like all the rules had changed. He sank down, sat sideways on the stairs looking up at me, his beautiful brown eyes glistening. He looked so…defeated. My heart cracked in two.

It was over. If there'd ever been anything between us, anything that had been truly ours, it was gone and I knew it.

"I'm so sorry," I said.

I scratched at my elbows and the damp bandage loosened around my finger. I did my best to pull it tight again and yanked my sleeve over my hand, revolted by my own body. I scrabbled for something to say but I'd run out of words.

"I don't know you any more, Tee. Everything's just so hard. One minute you're like your old self, the next…" He stood up, his face ugly with sorrow and determination. He slapped the wall and said, "Meet who you like. I don't care any more."

I sucked my bottom lip hard but there was no stopping the tears. I forced the words out, needing to be clear. "Are we breaking up?"

He stared at his hand, flat against the wall and nodded: small, sharp, tight.

My chest clenched, like someone was pushing down on my lungs. There were no more words. The ones he needed to hear, the ones that would explain everything, were locked down inside me. Maybe, if I could sort things, there'd be a chance for him and Fifteen – maybe. The thought of them together pinched inside me but I squashed it down. If I ever got a chance to put things right, I would, I owed them that.

I lifted a hand towards him, accidentally bringing my bandaged finger right in front of my face. I hastily pulled it away again and he nodded once more, gave a tiny shrug and went back up the stairs.

I sank down. It was as if a stake had been driven right through the middle of me, pinning me to the floor. I knew ending it was the right thing to do, but knowing it and feeling it are not the same. He marked out my days.

The bell went for first lesson. People tumbled out of the common room, down the stairs, knocking my bag into my side. I saw Kristal's high heels clip clop past me, hesitate and then skip on. Part of me couldn't believe it. Had we really broken up? Shakily, I pulled my phone out. There we were, our two faces pressed together. We'd been happy that day. Hadn't we? I touched the screen gently.

I sat there, flicking the cover off and on my phone. My bum went numb. I lost track of time. I was churning everything over: what had happened with Ollie, my hand, the file under Mum's bed – my father's name… A whole lesson must have passed because the bell went again and I was vaguely aware of footsteps coming towards me. I stood up, my legs cramping after so long sitting hunched on the stairs. I hesitated, not sure whether to go down or up – either way there were too many people. Oh god, the school gossips were going to have a field day.

I made a snap decision and ran down, bumping past bodies as they came up, vaguely aware of people grumbling at me. My head was in turmoil. I needed Maddy to calm me down. I'd call her from the Quiet Area. I yanked the outside door open and ran straight into a broad chest, a deep woody scent and a pair of arms up in surrender.

"Oh my god, will you just stop flinging yourself at me, Teva."

Tommo.

I backed away.

"Woah. What's the matter? You look awful."

I shook my head, my bottom lip trembling. I didn't want Tommo to see me cry but the weight of everything was too much.

I made a horrible animal noise and ran past him. I don't know where I thought I was going. It was tipping down but I blundered on, tears mingling with the rain, day-old mascara running into my eyes, blinding me. I was sobbing openly. My heart hurt, my finger hurt. I felt helpless and hopeless. I ended up in the porch of the Portakabin where the chess geeks met at lunchtimes. I tugged on the door. It wouldn't move so I hit it with my fist and caught my little finger painfully in the frame around the door's window. I pressed my forehead against it and cried and cried.

Everything in me seemed to droop and I thought I was going to collapse in the doorway but Tommo's warm hand caught me under the elbow and turned me round.

I wouldn't look at him. I kept my head bowed and turned away. I was soaked; he was soaked. He reached a hand past me and opened the chess club door. It opened inwards. Even the door had it in for me.

"Come on, in," he said and when I didn't move, he pressed his hand on my back and pushed me through. I stumbled inside and he let the door close behind us.

Half-played chess games covered lots of tiny tables.

"Bloody hell, Tee, what was all that about? You look shit by the way."

"Thanks," I sniffed.

"Didn't want you to think I'd pushed you in here to ravage you. Soaking wet with panda eyes isn't really a look I go for."

A tiny half-smile twitched at the corner of my mouth and was gone. I started to shiver. Tommo looked around and found a switch for the over-door heater. It whirred into life and pumped hot air over me. He grabbed a chair and put it behind me, knocking it into the back of my knees. I fell into it with a thump. He placed another next to me and we sat next to each other in silence, our wet thighs almost touching, the warm air gently steaming us dry.

He didn't say a word, just sat with his palms together between his knees, waiting. Eventually, I felt I had to speak. I couldn't tell him about Fifteen or the new Teva ripping my finger apart, but there was something I could talk to him about: "Me and Ollie broke up."

Tommo nodded slowly. "What a dick."

I pulled my cuff over my knuckles and wiped my face.

"It's not his fault. He thought I had a thing going on with you."

"Me?" said Tommo, genuinely surprised.

I nodded. "Secret English lessons."

Tommo sat upright, trying to put some distance between us. Bit too late really.

"Shit, Tee, I am so sorry. I had no idea he'd be like that."

I shrugged.

"It's not your fault either. It's me. He says I've changed. He's more right than he knows."

Tommo shrugged. "We all change, don't we? I used to love endless reruns of *Top Gear* but now…actually no, I still love endless reruns of *Top Gear*. But seriously, we grow up, don't we? Who wants to be fifteen for ever? Unthinkable. Spots. Mood swings. Maths homework."

I turned my face away, trying to hide the fresh tears that sprang to my eyes, and managed to mutter, "Don't say that, please, just don't."

He slipped an arm round me and I let myself sink against his shoulder and cry. Stuck. Forever Fifteen. Like I'd be forever Sixteen. My tears were soft and silent, not just for me, for Ollie, but for all of us. Even Fifteen.

eighteen

Tommo sat patiently and let me cry. I think I might have stayed there all day if embarrassment hadn't got the better of me. Anyway, I had things to do, and no idea how much time I had left to do them in.

I straightened up, wiped my face on my wet sleeve and said, "Thanks, Tommo. I'll be okay now. Actually, I think I'd like to be on my own for a bit."

"You sure that's a good idea?"

I nodded. "Thanks though."

"Will you call me if you need anything?"

"Yeah."

He smiled gently, pulled his collar up against the foul weather, and dived out of the door.

Once he'd gone, I fished out my phone. Seven missed calls. My heart leaped with the habit of hope, but they were all from Maddy. Still sniffling, I listened to the messages. Maddy sounded panicky:

"I've seen Ollie, where are you?"

And:

"Tee, where the hell are you?"

And:

"Teva, please, I've looked everywhere, call me back."

I dialled her number and it barely rang before she answered in a hushed voice.

"Where are you? Oh my god, Tee, what happened?"

I heard her teacher in the background.

"Maddy? Are you on your phone?"

"Hang on a sec, Tee." She spoke to her teacher. "Sorry, Miss, it's urgent, sorry…I know, I'll catch up later, I've got to go."

There was a bit of rummaging around and then she said, "Right, where are you?"

"Chess club. Can you come?"

"Already on my way. Don't go anywhere, Tee, okay?"

I nodded. "Okay."

I clicked off the call and swiped to my home screen. I had Facebook notifications. I clicked on them without much thought and then sat up. *Mandy Belle has accepted Celly Heart's friend request as you suggested…Emily Roberts has accepted…*and on and on. Twenty-four people had friended her…my heart raced – the blog? Had they seen the blog? Pulse throbbing, I tried to log in, the connection was slow but finally up it came, and there were comments waiting for approval.

I stared at my phone. They'd be my Facebook friends.

Would they have guessed? Would they know it was me? As I tapped the screen to open the first comment, the door to the chess club burst open, and a chilly swirl of damp wind sent sweet wrappers scuttling like giant beetles. Maddy's face was pale and wet. I shoved my phone in my pocket.

"Oh, Tee, oh my god, I can't believe it."

She sat heavily in the empty chair Tommo had left next to me, gripped my arm then pulled me into a hug.

"He's such a shit! How could he? You're too good for him anyway, he's an idiot."

I shook my head, my hair sticking to her wet coat. I opened my mouth to make excuses for him, to defend him, but instead I said, "I think it's been coming a while."

"I bet he's been seeing someone else."

"Mads, don't. We've just grown apart, that's all."

"You don't think him and Kristal…?"

"No! No."

"How can you be sure? I mean, this has come out of nowhere, hasn't it? You guys were so perfect for each other."

My eyes filled with tears again. It was killing me not to tell her everything but, god, if she was this shocked over me and Ollie breaking up, how would she cope with the rest of it?

She rubbed my back. "Oh, Tee, this is awful."

I looked at the floor. Rain peppered the roof – it was kind of comforting.

Mads looked at her watch. "Come on, it's nearly lunchtime, the chess geeks will be here soon and you know how hard it'll be for me to resist challenging one of them to a game to the death."

I pressed my lips together in a sorry attempt at a smile. "I can't eat anything, Mads. I can't see anyone."

"Yes you can. You are not hiding from him, I won't let you. You're worth more than that. You're worth ten of him."

I tried to smile but a sudden shot of pain bolted up my arm. I pulled it into my stomach, gasping. Maddy stood up. "What…what's the matter? Teva? You've gone white."

"My arm," I said through clenched teeth, trying to hold it gently, the whole limb was bitten through with pain.

"What have you done? Is it a trapped nerve?"

I was panting, open-mouthed. I forced myself to get a grip. "Yeah," I breathed, "must be…arghhh!"

I jerked in my seat as another shot of pain twisted up my arm, feeding a greedy path across my shoulders, my neck, my back.

"Tee, what can I do? What is it?"

I forced myself steady, cramping waves rolling up and down my arm.

"I must have slept funny or something." I gasped again, blowing air between my teeth.

"Are you okay?"

I nodded, as slowly, slowly the pain gave way to numbness. Holding my own arm was like holding a dead thing.

"Mads, I think I need to go home."

"Maybe it's an infection from your burn? If you cut it too, I mean…" I saw her struggling to square the unlikeliness of

160

that in her head. She actually gave herself a shake as if to settle her thoughts before she said, "Give me your phone. I'll ring your mum. She'll come and get you after the morning you've had."

I gave a sharp shake of my head.

"No car, remember. I'll walk. It'll be fine."

"You will not walk. I'll get one of the boys to drive you. Tommo's got his dad's car today, he'll take you."

"No. Ollie will hate that, I…"

She cut me off. "It's none of Ollie's business. You broke up, remember? I'm calling Tommo."

nineteen

The three of us drove to my house. I gave whispered directions through a fog of pain. Despite everything, that old feeling of being different – that I didn't have friends to tea like normal kids – burrowed away at me. What was I going to do when we got there? Could I just invite them in? Did I want to? Into the chaos. In to meet my family, trapped in the house, trapped in our life. I glanced down at my betraying arm. I'd soon be just as trapped as the rest of them. Fresh pain twisted through me.

As we got near the gates, Tommo said, "That's where you live? We used to call it the Witch's House. How do you even sleep in there?"

I looked at it through the rainy windscreen. You could see the top floor and the attic rooms over the high wall. It was pretty grim looking. Dark ivy gripped the grey stone walls and crept over the slate roof – it was all a bit Tim Burton. The windows were dark shining holes hiding their dark shining secrets. I shuddered and tried to dispel the creepiness.

"It's just a house. Thanks for dropping me home, Tommo. You can leave me here."

"Don't you want us to come in?" Maddy asked. "Explain to your mum what happened?"

I shook my head. I just didn't have the strength for all the explanations. And if the other Teva was coming, I didn't want my friends to see it happen.

"No," I said softly. "I'll be fine from here. Thanks."

"Oh go on," said Tommo. "I'd love a look around Spooky Towers."

"I'm not really feeling up to it right now. Sorry."

"Another time then?" Maddy cut in. "It is weird I've never been in your house, Tee; I am your best friend."

"You've not been in there?" Tommo said, shocked. "Really?"

"I've stood in the hallway. Once."

One of Fifteen's memories popped up. It was true; she'd brought Maddy back with her one night. Mum soon saw her off. Told her the house had fleas and the fumigators were about to come in.

I rolled out the usual excuse: "Mum's funny about people coming in. It stresses her out."

Tommo looked from Maddy to me. I clutched my bag and opened the car door.

"So my mum's a nutter. Sorry. We can't all have perfect families."

I got out, ignoring Maddy's defensive mumbling.

"Thanks for the lift," I said.

"Any time," said Tommo. "You take care, okay?"

I nodded through the spattering rain.

"Go on," said Tommo, "before you get soaked again."

"I'll call you later," Maddy said as I shut the car door. They waited while I punched in the gate code with my left hand. Feeling was beginning to come back to my right arm but the wet and the cold made my fingers clumsy. Finally the little green light came on and I bolted in, shivering; grateful to hear the gate creak shut behind me, and Tommo's car splosh off up the road.

I unlocked our heavy front door and leaned against it as it clunked shut. I was glad to be home. Glad to see Six picking at the wallpaper on the stairs. Glad to see the backs of the teen heads sitting on the sofa watching rubbish TV. Glad to hear Mum bustling about in the kitchen. Glad to be somewhere I could be myself.

I hung up my wet coat and trudged upstairs to get into dry clothes. Mum had hung my trackies and a sweatshirt over the radiator in my room. I pulled them on, warm and soft. Thoughts of Ollie danced at the edges of my brain and I kept them there, forcing myself not to think about him. I resisted the urge to check my phone for texts. I went back downstairs to find Mum and tell her about the pain in my arm.

She was typing at the kitchen table while Eva mashed a banana into a little plastic teapot. Mum looked up, slowly emerging from whatever world she was creating on her laptop.

"Hey," I said.

"Hello. What's happened?" she said, looking intently at my face.

I shrugged, trying not to cry. "I had a…my arm…"

I held out my aching limb. Mum took it in both hands; she gently peeled the bandage from my finger. I winced.

"Painful?"

I nodded.

"Oh, Teva. I did say it wasn't a good idea to go in today."

I curled my other hand around my phone.

"I can't just stay home and wait for it to happen, Mum. I can't."

Her face stiffened but I had a head full of questions and I didn't want to dance around them any more. I needed answers. Still, I surprised myself with the first thing that came out of my mouth.

"Why has Dad got a different name to us?"

She lifted her chin and said, "How do you know that? Have you been going through my papers?"

A hot flush crept into my cheeks but I hadn't been spying. It was *my* medical record not *her* papers.

"No. I saw my file on your floor."

"Teva, those papers are private."

"They're about me. You won't talk to me. How else am I

supposed to understand what's happening if you won't tell me anything?"

I could see her battling inside herself. I stood a little taller and said, "For all I know I could be dying."

She froze but she didn't deny it.

"Is that it? *Am* I dying? Is this going to kill me?"

Time stopped for what seemed like minutes. Eva was quiet, Mum didn't move.

"Mum? Please? Am I dying?"

She gave the tiniest shake of her head and the world started moving again. I sat at the table, unable to hold myself up. My legs felt like marshmallow.

Mum made tea, put it in front of me and sat down. She pushed her laptop to one side and said, "I changed our name."

Was she really going to talk to me? Properly?

"Why?"

"I didn't want the same name as your father. He left us, Teva, I didn't want any part of him. He…he wasn't kind."

I flipped the case off my phone. "I don't remember."

She sighed. "Sometimes I think it's better that you don't. There was a time, before you were born – and for a while afterwards – when he was lovely. So attentive. He made me feel beautiful."

I looked at her.

"I know," she said, "fat little me."

"Mum…"

"Well it's true, no one had ever looked twice at me. Short,

fat, plain. My friends couldn't believe it when I started dating the gorgeous Dr Tarrant."

"He *was* a doctor then?"

She nodded.

"So why didn't he help us?"

Mum took a slurp of tea, her eyes firmly on the table.

I carried on. "Why did he leave? Why doesn't he even keep in touch?"

She shrugged. "I suppose he just woke up and realized he was married to a fat boring woman when he could be with someone young and beautiful."

She looked so sad, so defeated. Part of me knew I should back off but I had no choice, I had to ask.

"Mum, if he's a doctor, surely he could help us. Couldn't he?"

She flinched. "I can't make him be a good dad to you. I'm sorry, Teva, but I can't. I tried, I really did."

"Maybe he deserves another chance?"

Mum gave a hollow little laugh. I needed more than that. Whatever had happened between him and her, he was still my father. My dad the doctor. Suddenly, I knew what I wanted to do.

"I want to contact him."

Mum stood up so violently she spilled hot tea all down her front.

"Ow, god, ow, *ow*."

I tried to help as she hopped about pulling wet fabric away from her, tearing her sweatshirt over her head, pulling off her trackies, throwing them to the floor.

"Cold water," she said and ran out of the room. I followed her dimply, white legs as she heaved herself up the stairs as fast as she could. She headed to the shower in her room and shut the door behind her. I listened to her shriek at the cold water hitting her skin, then I sank down on her bed.

My medical folder called to me. As if she was reading my mind, Mum yelled through the bathroom door, "Don't look for that file, Teva. Do you hear me?"

I heard her. But she was in the shower and all I had to do was look under the bed. I could slide out those pictures for the blog and maybe, maybe I could find my dad from the records.

twenty

I dropped to my knees and felt for the file.

It wasn't there. I pulled out the suitcase; the file wasn't underneath it. I rummaged inside; the smell of musty clothes wafted around me, but there was no sign of the file. I peered under the bed. It was gone. She'd moved it. She must have seen it was disturbed and known I was going to ask about him.

The shower door slid open and I shoved the clothes back in the case, pushing it back under the bed, shouting, "You alright, Mum?"

"Yes, yes, I'll be fine."

I was wondering where to look next when Fifteen appeared in the doorway holding my laptop.

I was across the room in a stride. "Why can't you leave my stuff alone?"

Her face was set in a grim line.

"Ollie dumped you."

The words landed heavily. I said, "Not exactly."

"What do you mean?"

"I mean, we both agreed it wasn't working out."

"You were meant to look after him. That's all you had to do. Just for a tiny bit longer."

"How did you know?"

She turned my laptop round. She was on Ollie's Facebook page. He'd changed his relationship status to "single". A dart of sorrow lodged in my heart. The page was full of people saying how sorry they were, how they couldn't believe it. God, even Kristal bloody Mitchell, the lying cow. Gossip fodder, just like I thought.

Fifteen said, "He broke up with you because he's still in love with me, didn't he?"

That was the last thing I needed to hear. I clenched my teeth and said, "It doesn't matter, does it? Mum has locked the ladder in the garage. No more little excursions for you." She flinched at that and for half a second I was sorry. But I burned inside, at the unfairness of our lives, and I took it out on her. I snatched my laptop back.

She glared at me. "Do you think I'm going to stay in this prison for ever? Do you really think I'm going to roll over like the others and do what Mum says until I'm dead? I'm not Fourteen – too afraid of the world to live. What gives Mum the right to decide who knows about us and who doesn't? I've had it. *Had it.*"

I looked deep into her dark blue eyes and she looked right back. We wanted the same thing. Surely, if we worked together…?

"Look, I know how you feel…"

"No. No, you don't. You never loved Ollie. You loved being his girlfriend. You loved how it made other people see you. You used him to make you feel good. That's not love."

I shook my head but I had a horrible feeling she was right. Well, about eighty per cent right. I hadn't even been talking about Ollie. I was talking about our life. Our non-life.

It was then she spotted my little finger curling round my laptop. Her eyes actually lit up – I thought that was a thing that only happened in books.

"Well," she said, "bad luck on you, sister. Welcome to my world."

She spun round and waltzed out of the room. Stress danced on my skin and I fought the urge to scratch. The lock twitched on Mum's bathroom door and I hovered. The laptop in my arms called me to check on the blog but I was finally getting somewhere with Mum, wasn't I? I waited for her.

She came out wrapped in her bathrobe, rubbing her hair with a towel.

"You okay?"

"Yes, thanks, love, what a silly thing to do."

I bit the bullet.

"So, I want to contact Dad. If he's a doctor, surely he'd want to help us."

She hid her face in the towel for a second, then said, "Your dad doesn't want to see you, Teva. I'm sorry, but that's the truth."

"But it's been years, maybe…"

"That's an end to it. Please don't mention his name again."

Disappointment burrowed an ugly path right to my core. Fine. I went to my room, shoved a chair against the door and sat on it.

I opened my laptop. Ignoring all the fake break-up sympathy on my own Facebook page, I went to Celly's. The blog had been shared four times. I clicked through to the admin site.

Twenty-four comments waiting for approval. Twenty-four! I went down the list.

There were a few on the theme of *OMG that's so weird/ terrible/disgusting* and a few more that said *Bullshit*, or worse. I deleted those. Two were from people who said they had cancer – they must have connected through the children's hospital – and knew what I was going through. Their comments sent a chill right through me. I replied saying how sorry I was, how much I wished I could help. I deleted the comments telling me where to get Viagra.

In all, there were thirteen comments from genuine people, but not one word from anyone who could actually help. I had to do something to get more hits. I had to step things up – be brave. If anyone was going to set a bomb off under all this, it was going to be me, not Fifteen trying to patch things up with Ollie.

I knew the kind of stuff everyone shared on Facebook and as I wasn't a piano-playing cat or a skateboarding donkey, I had to take another route. I needed to shock people into sharing my posts. I had to turn Celly into a freak show.

Something painful grew in my chest, but I made myself look at my finger. I flinched from its solid evidence. I had to toughen up. I. Had. To. Face. It...

Her.

I touched the nail. Felt the dip in the skin where the two fingers joined. A shiver rolled across my back. I thought for a minute it was me shuddering with disgust, but those hot waves wriggling under my skin were her. Again.

"Sod off," I whispered. "It's my life and you're not having it."

My skin tightened. Blood pounded in my ears and I sat rigid until it passed. She was getting stronger. The need to find a fix strengthened in me. I picked up my phone and awkwardly took a picture of my splitting finger with my left hand.

I uploaded the picture to the blog. My head throbbed with tension as I wrote underneath, *This is how it begins. I don't know how much time I have left. If anyone out there can help me, please, please, send me a message.*

I posted it, not sure how I felt. No. That's not true. Through all the sadness over Ollie, all the confusion of trying to live a normal life on top of my actual crazy reality, one thing scented the fat tear that rolled off my cheek onto my laptop:

Fear.

twenty-one

I struggled to get out of bed again the next day. All night I'd been waiting for something to happen, hyper alert to any tiny change in my body. But in the morning, there I still was, more or less in one piece.

I sat on the edge of my bed for a bit, dread weighing me down. On top of that, like a heavy cloak of evil, I knew school was going to be horrible. Everyone would be asking about me and Ollie. Kristal would be gloating her head off.

What even was the point of going in? I gave myself a telling-off. It got me out of the house while I still could. It made me feel like I was still alive.

Come on, Tee, get some breakfast, you'll feel better then.

The kitchen was unusually quiet. Mum was pottering about and the others were reading or colouring or eating. I think Mum may have told them not to stress me out. It made me squirm; I didn't want to be treated like a thing that was about

174

to break. I wanted some real actual help to get through this.

Mum noted my uniform.

"You're not going in again?" She took my hand, stroked the back of it, carefully avoiding my fingers. "Why don't I call in sick for you?"

"Good plan," I said. "We can go to the doctor."

She dropped my hand.

"Don't start, Teva."

"Don't start? Why not?"

"You know why not. No one will believe you."

"They will if Fifteen comes with me."

Mum's face went white. "Don't, please don't. You don't understand…"

"No. You are so right, I don't understand. How you can let this happen to us over and over and do nothing, nothing at all to stop it? Sometimes," I said, "I feel like it can't be real, that I'm going just a little bit mad."

A warm tear splashed off Mum's cheek onto my hand. For half a crazy second I thought of the phoenix in Harry Potter, thought her tears would cure me. But no, this was real life. My ugly, splitting finger stayed exactly the same. Her tears helped nobody.

She wiped the wet gleam from her pink cheeks and turned away. So much for being a team.

My phone bleeped a text message. I glared at Mum for a second then I checked my phone. My heart leaped. It was from Ollie:

Maybe we just need some time. x

What? Was that a question? I scrolled up and saw a line of texts. Texts I hadn't sent. Fifteen. She'd sent him pictures of them together, before me, having fun. Super subtle, not. Oh god. How had the sneaky cow even got hold of my phone? This I didn't need. I read his text again.

Time, eh, Ollie?

Well, that's a luxury for you and all the other normal people. Not for the likes of me. I was debating whether to text back when my phone rang in my hand and Tommo's name flashed up.

My thumb hovered. Talking to Tommo would only make things more complicated. Still, almost of its own accord, my thumb pressed green and the call connected. I put it to my ear and headed back to my room.

"Hey."

"Hey. How you doing?"

"Yeah, I'm alright."

"Look, I know the timing isn't great, but I really could do with some help before my English resit. If you can't do it just say, I'll ask someone else. I just didn't want to, you know, when we'd already talked about it."

I didn't answer and after a beat he said, "Teva, you don't have to hide away, none of this is your doing."

He was right, but for all the wrong reasons.

An image of him settled in my mind, so quiet and still, sitting next to me in the Portakabin, his wet thigh next to mine. He'd been so patient. Kind. I seemed to defrost on autopilot.

I found myself saying, "Okay, shall we try lunchtime again?"

"Fantastic. You are officially an angel."

"I'm really not. I only said yes so I could copy all your coursework for textiles."

Tommo laughed a big bear chuckle and I smiled a tiny, tiny smile.

He said, "I shall prepare to have my work ravaged."

"You do that."

"Right, better go, I'll see you later. Thanks, Tee."

"You're welcome."

"Bye then.

"Yep, bye."

"Well, hang up then," he said.

"I can't," I said. "You hang up – I have a phobia of being rude."

He laughed again and the phone clicked off. The little smile on my face stayed there, right up until I returned to the home screen. Ollie and me. Our happy windswept faces smiling. I touched his beautiful cheek and all the sadness I'd pushed away leaked back in.

I changed the picture to one of me and Maddy wearing matching cat ears, physically shook myself and stood up. I didn't have time to waste moping about. I flipped my laptop open and tugged my uniform on as I scrolled through to Celly's blog. I didn't bother checking Facebook – I was already running late and I needed to see the blog stats.

The page loaded and I couldn't believe what I saw. I froze, my sweatshirt halfway on, halfway off. I squeezed my eyes shut and open again. The number stayed the same. I pulled my sweatshirt on and logged out and back in again in case there'd been a mistake. The number actually went up in that short space of time. I'd had over seven thousand hits. Seven thousand! And there were comments, dozens of them.

"Oh my god, this could work, this could actually work."

I started reading through the comments, flinching at the foul ones and the ones calling me a fucking freak. Mum was right about that then. I started deleting them, then I thought, no, I'll approve them, let the world see what people could be like. I recognized some names from school, but there were a lot of anonymous comments and loads of people I didn't know. When I got to the first one from a Dr Feelgood my heart lifted. It didn't last though. The suggested remedy of that particular "doctor" was bicarbonate of soda and an early night. It didn't take me long to realize that anyone could call themselves a doctor on the internet.

It was going to take me all day to go through all this. I took my laptop to the bathroom and carried on scrolling through as I cleaned my teeth and put a fresh bandage on my hand. It had obviously been the picture of my finger that had got the blog so many shares. I didn't want anyone to see it for real and realize the freak finger was mine – not yet anyway. I switched from the laptop to my phone and worked through the comments as I walked downstairs, ruffling Six's hair as I passed her. I didn't notice Mum in the hall until she said, "Teva, don't you think you should stay at home?"

"Nope."

I pulled my coat on, still checking comments as I headed for the door.

"Well at least have some breakfast."

"I'll get something at Mads'."

It was freezing outside. The frost bit my fingers but my touchscreen didn't work with gloves. I crunched down our drive, my nose reddening, speed reading and approving comments as I went. The internet slowed down as I moved away from our house and so did my feet.

A comment came up from a Mr Fixer – a stupid name but what he'd written warmed me through. I stopped walking as I read: *Celly, just because there are more of you doesn't mean you are any less. You don't have to hide away. You've done nothing wrong. You don't have to be ashamed.*

I read it again, trying to figure out why it felt so familiar and then I twigged. *You don't have to hide away.*

Exactly the words Tommo had used on the phone.

Mr Fixer. Could it be him?

I typed a reply – after all, he didn't know who Celly was, did he?

That's so sweet but not everyone thinks like you. Take a look at the rest of the comments, quite a lot think I'm a freak...

I stood while the comment loaded and then walked on, the signal flickered but it was enough to keep approving comments. By the time I got to Mads' house, I was not nearly as depressed as I should have been.

twenty-two

Maddy was leaning out of the door looking for me, her arms wrapped tightly round her body against the cold. When she saw me, her face cracked into a smile and she raised a hand. I half ran the last bit and she hugged me in through the door.

"I was worried you weren't coming in today."

"So was I."

"Is your back okay?"

I frowned, trying to think what she was on about.

"My back?"

"Yeah, your trapped nerve."

"Oh that." My finger throbbed inside new wrappings. "Yeah, sort of."

"I tried to call you earlier, your mobile was engaged."

"Tommo rang about his English."

Maddy pulled back and looked me in the face, her eyebrows raised. "You could do a lot worse, Ms Webb.

My god, that boy is fit, if he looked my way I don't think I'd say no…"

"Too soon, Madeeha, way too soon. It was nice to talk to him though."

"I bet it was. Mum was going to drive but shall we walk in so we can chat? You had breakfast?"

"Not hungry to be honest. Heartbreak diet. Yeah, let's walk."

And then I knew; it was time to talk to her. There might not be another chance and I wanted to try and explain. I didn't want to risk her finding out some other way, not now the blog was out there. My heart pounded but I stiffened my shoulders. It was time to tell Maddy the truth.

Mrs Ranjha appeared with little Jay on her hip. She slipped a warm wrap of tinfoil into my pocket adding, "I'm not saying anything, my dear, just don't go hungry for any young man."

Maddy and I headed up the road arm in arm. I said, "I can't believe you told your mum."

"Yes, you can."

"Yeah, I can."

We walked on and I tried to find the words to tell her. In all my imaginings, I'd never come up with a simple way to explain my life.

Maddy said, "It makes me so angry when I think about how unhappy he's made you."

My little finger twinged. I slowed down, I just had to come out with it, there was no easy way.

"I'm not unhappy just because of Ollie, Mads. There's other stuff that made it…complicated."

"Oh, Tee, come here." She pulled me into a hug, her long hair blowing into my face.

I said, "There's something I need to tell you. I don't really know where to start. I don't know what you're going to think."

God it was so hard.

She held my elbows in the palms of her gloved hands,

"You can tell me anything, Tee, you know that. I know what everyone thinks, but look, just because my family are from Pakistan, it doesn't mean I'm an idiot. I do know about sex…"

"It's not about sex, Mads."

"You're not pregnant then?"

"No. I'm not bloody pregnant – oh my god, do I look pregnant?" I opened my coat, checking out my stomach.

Maddy caught her arm through mine and started walking again.

"You don't look pregnant – just what can possibly be so hard to tell me? We're best mates, aren't we? We know each other's secrets – that's how it's supposed to be. You're the only person in the world who knows I cheated in that Year Seven spelling test."

I let a stream of air out through my pursed lips. Maddy had no idea, changing an *o* to an *a* when marking your own spelling test was not a world-shattering secret. I tried again to find the words, my stomach balling up so tight I was glad

I hadn't had any breakfast – it might well have been on its way back up.

"It's not easy to explain; it sounds so weird and Mum has this thing about nobody knowing."

"I'm listening."

"I'm...different to other people."

"Okay..."

"In a way I'm not surprised at what happened with me and Ollie. It all got so complicated because, well, I..."

Maddy's walking slowed next to me. "I think I know what it is, Tee."

"You do?"

"Yeah."

How could she possibly know – unless she'd read Celly's blog. She might have – she was a bright girl, Maddy, she might have put two and two together. Something like relief lifted me until she carried on.

"And it's totally cool. It's the twenty-first century, Tee, not 1984. I couldn't care less if you're gay, straight, bisexual or anything else."

"What? No, Mads, no."

"The thing is, oh god, how can I put this..."

"What?"

"I don't want it to come between us, I mean, in case you were thinking...which you're probably not, but you know..."

"What are you on about?"

"I just don't want there to be any confusion...I love you, you know that, but just not in that way..."

"Maddy, I'm not telling you I fancy you. Seriously? How is this suddenly about you?"

"I'm sorry. I just thought, you know..."

I couldn't believe it. It was hard enough trying to find the right words without Maddy filling in all the wrong ones.

The nerves that had been zipping through me exploded in a starburst of anger – at life, at my own pathetic inability to tell my best friend what was going on; I couldn't stand it.

I had to get away before it all erupted out of me.

"I'm sorry, I've got to go," I said. "There's something I need to sort out."

I sprinted away from her.

"Teva! Wait!"

"Sorry, I can't...I need to do something."

I heard her make an attempt to run after me but her shouts dropped away pretty quickly. I just ran, forcing myself on, cold air scorching the back of my throat as I sucked in oxygen. Running was not a thing any of us had ever been any good at but the effort of it made me feel better. A bit, anyway.

A stitch stabbed into my right-hand side and I slowed down as school came into view.

"Stuff you," I muttered. "Not today." I sped up again and ran right past the gate. I had no idea where I was going except that it wasn't school.

I ended up in town. It was grey and miserable; the only bright spots were big red fifty per cent off notices in most of the shop windows. I kept walking and found myself in front of the library. The door opened automatically and a waft of warm, book-filled air circled round me. It tugged me inside and before I knew what I was doing I was at the desk asking for the Wi-Fi code, setting up camp in the reference section and opening Celly's blog on my phone.

I started a new post:

So today I tried to tell my best mate about my condition. Want to know what she said?

I let all my frustration spill out, then I sat back and stared at the words. I couldn't post it. If Maddy read it she would know it was me. I couldn't do that to her, not like this.

I tapped my fingers on the desk while I tried to decide how to change it. A man on the desk opposite coughed and I looked up. He nodded towards my drumming fingers. I curled them into my palm. Something wasn't right. I looked at my fingers already knowing what I was going to see. My throat filled with sponge. There, next to my bandaged little finger, the ring finger was sporting two nails. Nausea swirled through me

I squeezed my eyes shut. It took a minute before the world steadied again. I let go of the bad air inside me and reread the blog post through blurry eyes. I deleted the bit about her thinking I fancied her and just said she didn't listen, then I added this to the end:

Another nail is coming through. I'm not ready. It hasn't even been a year. And there's something else odd too. Normally the separation is quick, over in a night, not this slow peeling away.

Something feels wrong, if anything about this is right. Please, if anyone can help, contact me.

I pressed publish and slumped in my seat. If this was a battle with the shit life throws at you, I was losing pretty badly.

twenty-three

I sat in the library for a bit, flicking the cover on and off my phone, ignoring the man now openly tutting at me. I checked my watch. Ten thirty. Get me. I had officially bunked off school.

I'd ignored four calls from Maddy and three texts:

I'm sorry, I'm an arse.

I'm sorry, I'm a double arse.

I'm sorry, I'm a triple fat arse with cherries on the top.

What was I supposed to say? I knew it was unfair, but the thing was it had taken so much courage to try and tell her and then she'd made it into something about herself and I couldn't help feeling a bit let down. Another text popped up:

Tee, please, I'm sorry, what else can I say?

I sighed. I'd lost my boyfriend, I didn't want to lose my best mate as well.

I texted:

You don't need to be sorry. I'm fine. I'll text you later. Just need a bit of time out.

Oh, Tee, thank god, I thought you were never going to speak to me again…

I sent her back a picture of a kitten blowing a kiss and left it at that. I'd speak to her later. I sent a quick text to Tommo asking him to meet me in the town library if he still wanted to go over his English and then I got out a notepad and got to work on a Google search. A search for my father, Dr Tarrant.

Thousands of results popped up. Millions. 8.3 million to be exact. How would I know which of them was anything to do with my dad? I refined the search, Dr Tarrant Medical UK – the number came down to half a million. Half a million? How was that even possible? I was going to need more information. I flicked over to Celly's blog.

Mr Fixer had commented again:

I can't believe what you're going through. I wish I could help – sounds like you need a better friend. Keep your heart open, stay strong, Celly x

I smiled to myself. If nothing else, the blog made me feel less alone. I skimmed over the usual batch of freak screamers. They had a new twist – it was amazing how many ways people could write a vomit sound. Then I came across something else.

Hi, I write for Chatter Magazine *and read your story with great interest. We'd love to feature you. If you're under eighteen we'd need parental permission, but we can do the interview wherever you like. We even send along our own photographer!*

Sadly, I'm not a doctor, so I can't help in any other way but you'd get paid £250 and it would certainly raise the profile of your cause. If you're interested, contact me at jan@chatter.com, Jan x

My heart thumped. *Chatter* was just the kind of trashy magazine that left me cold. It was freak show central. Yet what did I think I was doing with the blog? I needed this kind of publicity, didn't I? *Chatter* was huge; it was everywhere. Even in hospital waiting rooms…

I didn't approve the comment but I opened up my Hotmail account – for once glad of the stupid name I'd chosen when I set it up. Newgirl16 typed back:

Thanks for your message. You're right, this might really help me…

I stopped. The blog wasn't about me; it was about Celly. I couldn't hide behind it if they came to photograph me. And Mum would never give permission. My heart slowed and I finished the email:

But my mum would never agree. She doesn't even know about my blog. She'd go mad if she knew. Thanks for trying to help, Celly.

I pressed send.

People were finding me. The blog might really work. For once my heart was hammering away for the right reasons. My phone buzzed in my hand. I smiled at a text from Tommo:

Fantastic, you superstar. Stay strong, Tee.

Stay strong? I flicked back up to the comments and there was the same comment from Mr Fixer – *stay strong*.

It had to be him, didn't it? He was one of the first to

comment, so it had to be one of my Facebook friends. Mr Fixer was Tommo. Could he be any lovelier?

An email flashed up. Jan from *Chatter* had mailed me back already:

Hey, don't worry, that's totally understandable. If your mum would feel better about it we don't need to use your face, we can just shoot your hands and any other parts that would be of interest to our readers.

A frown bit my forehead – Mum really was right, wasn't she? *Any other parts?* To people like Jan, I was practically the elephant man – all the world would be interested in was the weird things about me. I read on: *Of course if you're eighteen, your mum doesn't need to be involved at all, we could meet somewhere. Jan x*

She was giving me a chance to sneak behind Mum's back! For a minute I was shocked an adult would behave like that and then I mailed her back: *Okay, let me think about it.*

I stretched my back for a second and another email pinged in.

Hey Teva,

Sorry you're not in today. If you feel up to it, why not have a look at De Montfort Uni? I checked with careers, they said you didn't see them yesterday. It would be such a great fit for you, but you'll need to get your portfolio sorted – for both textiles and art. We can talk about it when you're back at school.

Hope you feel better soon, Miss Francis

Frankie.

Bloody hell. She didn't give up. Even when I was off sick

– sort of. I rubbed my face and then found myself googling the uni. Given the mess of my life, I knew it was pointless but I couldn't help it. I scrolled through the pictures of students' work – the contour fashion was beautiful but there was sportswear too – and weird, sculptural things that didn't even look like clothes. I'd only need three Cs if my portfolio was good enough and if I got the apprenticeship in the summer… For about ten minutes I went into a little fantasy world – I thought: *I could do that, I could get those grades.* It was like I genuinely forgot for a moment. Then I caught sight of my fingers.

There was no future. Not unless I found a way… I emailed Jan:

Hi. I've thought about it. When can we meet? Can you come to me? Celly.

She messaged me straight back:

Sure, that's great. So you're eighteen, right? Send me your address and phone number and we'll get things moving straight away. I just need to check when the photographer is free. J x

Yes, I'm eighteen, I typed back, confirming the lie she was clearly quite happy for me to tell. *I don't want to meet at home, you can phone my mobile though.*

I sent her my number.

The address is just for the contract. You can give it to me when we meet up if you like? Is there a hotel near you? We can meet there.

Contract? A tiny worm of worry niggled at me. I shrugged it off. I had to do this to have any chance at a future. I mailed her back: *I'll look into it and get back to you ASAP.*

A shadow fell across the table and I looked up. Tommo stood over me, a big toothy grin on his face. He was wearing tight jeans and a white T-shirt with the sleeves rolled up so the world could see his muscles. A faded, childish picture of a cock was visible on his forearm.

"Tattoo?" I said.

"Nice, isn't it? Courtesy of Jake and Ed. Can't bloody wash it off, the sods."

"Aren't you cold?" I said.

"No, baby, I am smokin'."

"You're a walking cliché."

"I try."

He slid into the seat next to me, and the man opposite huffed, closed his book loudly, and moved away.

"There goes another one – jealous," said Tommo, "a trail of envy wherever I go."

I couldn't help but smile even as I pulled on my gloves to hide my disgusting hands.

"You can touch me without gloves on, you know? I'm not that precious."

I tipped my head to one side, waggled my covered fingers and said, "Cold. Why would I want to touch you anyway?"

"Everyone does eventually. I'm irresistible."

"Incorrigible."

"Probs," he said. "Whatever that means."

He pulled a notebook and a copy of a war poets' revision guide out of his bag.

"I am all yours," he whispered, leaning close. "Do with me what you will."

I nudged him in the ribs and flicked over the pages until we got to Wilfred Owen, which wasn't easy wearing gloves.

For the next hour we talked about poetry – imagery and rhythm, emotion and storytelling and I honestly didn't think about anything else. Tommo paid attention. He scribbled notes the whole time. He didn't make stupid jokes about how fit he was and, even though I was hotly aware of how close he was sitting, I didn't think about it either. We were talking about sarcasm and irony in one of Wilfred Owen's poems and he said, "I get that. Lads do it all the time when they think they've been cheated. Say after a rugby game, if the ref's been a bit crap, you'd never shake his hand and say, *You were crap*, but you might say, *Excellent refereeing, Sir –* and everyone would know you didn't mean it."

"Yeah," I said. "It's exactly that sort of feeling only…"

"Worse," we said together.

I smiled.

He said, "There's another poem like that, isn't there? By the posh guy – what's his name?"

"Sassoon?" I said, excited that he was so engaged. "Yes, he writes a bit like that but he puts this kind of cheerful rhythm in his work that contradicts what he's saying. Hang on, I'll find it."

I felt normal. So normal that when my hands got too

warm, I pulled off my gloves to flick through the book and point out the poem. I froze. My distorted fingertip was clearly visible – to both of us. I looked at Tommo, waited for him to comment. He said, "Had enough? Want a coffee?"

He didn't glance at my hands, didn't see me turn into a 1930s freakshow. I curled my fingers into my palm and said, "Coffee?"

"Yeah. Shall we go to Swallows?"

"Coffee?" I asked again, having trouble processing the simple question.

"I'll pay," he said. "As a thank you."

My brain caught up and I shook my head. "You're supposed to help me with my portfolio."

"Oh come on, I think I can stretch to coffee too."

Tommo pulled his school sweatshirt out of his backpack and put it on. I packed my stuff up and followed him outside, part of me thinking, *What am I doing?* The sky was grey and heavy. I looked up, feeling the weight of it above me. Tommo snatched at something in the air and grinned: "Snow!"

He held his hand out for me to inspect the tiny spot of water on his palms.

"You melted it."

"That's something I do," he said. "Can't help it when you're this hot."

He slipped his arm around my shoulder and squeezed me quickly before hopping in front.

"Come on," he said, "let's get takeout and go sit on the green."

194

I couldn't figure out if he was really flirting with me or if it was the usual Tommo banter, but you know what? I didn't care. It was like I was taking a day off from my life and trying out another one. And I liked it. Tommo tipped his head back and stuck out his tongue, darting around trying to catch snowflakes in his mouth. A few became a few more, until snow was floating all around us, swirling in little eddies, settling on our shoulders, melting in Tommo's hair. He jogged to the coffee shop and I ran to keep up.

An old-fashioned bell pinged as we stepped inside and were surrounded by soft chatter and sweet-smelling steam.

"Latte? Cappuccino?" he asked.

"Actually, can I have tea? Strong, milky, no sugar."

I stood back until he handed me the hot paper cup and we headed back outside. I curled my hands round the warm tea, watching the snow land on it and melt away. We walked back towards the cathedral, snowflakes falling heavily.

"We could build a snowman," Tommo said, like he was still a kid.

"I'm not sure there's enough for a snowman yet," I said, the chill beginning to seep through my coat. "It's got to settle first."

"Yeah, maybe you're right. Shall we head back to school?"

I shook my head.

"You go; I've got some stuff to finish in town."

He stopped, took a sip of his coffee and said, "Don't avoid him, Tee. It'll be easier when you've got the first day out the way, honestly. Come back to school. We'll work on your portfolio."

My heart swelled a bit. He was so kind, he really was. He said, "Frankie told me you're thinking of applying for De Montfort. You could do it, Teva – your portfolio will need to be amazing though, everyone wants to go there."

Did they? How did he know this stuff when I had no clue? And there I went again, forgetting that it was all pretend, that I didn't have a future. Not yet.

"Seriously, Tommo, I've got stuff to do. I'm not hiding. I will be working, I promise."

"Sure?"

"Sure. You can help me tomorrow."

There was a slightly awkward moment of parting, smoothed over by Tommo tapping my cup with his and saying, "Okay. Don't pretend you've got snowed into the library because I will come and find you, Teva Webb."

I laughed and watched him run off down the road, smiling to myself.

It was weird. I felt lighter, like being with him had lifted me a bit. It wasn't like with me and Ollie. When Ollie left me it had always felt like a part of me was being ripped away.

Ollie. I sighed.

Sorrow stirred like sludge in my stomach. Or maybe it was guilt. Ollie felt like a different part of my life. The truth was, I had more important things to worry about. Snow settled on the end of my nose, melted in the warm steam from my tea. I trudged back to the library.

The reference section was quiet as death. I pulled out my notepad and my phone and took off my gloves. The new nail didn't look any worse than it had earlier. I felt it, trying to get used to the weird new shape. There was something oddly tactile about the groove between the fingertips – I could see why people would be fascinated. I was kind of fascinated myself.

I brought up the blog and posted:

Sometimes I imagine what it would be like to have a future and then I remember. I'm breaking apart. It makes it hard to talk to people, to carry on like everything's okay. Things aren't okay and I'm not sure they ever will be.

Within seconds Mr Fixer had replied. He'd made it back to school fast.

There's always a way to move forward. I wish I could help you find a future.

Could he know it was me? It was like he was talking right to me. I replied: *Sadly, that's not as easy as it sounds. Thanks for cheering me up though.*

Straight back came: *We could try. Where do you live?*

I messaged back: *Nice try, Mr Fixer, my mum warned me about people like you.*

He sent back a smiley face and it kind of infected me. A tiny smile crept onto my own face.

A little grey-haired lady whispered to a librarian who was slipping books onto a shelf. She had a rolled-up tube and was gesturing to a noticeboard. The librarian nodded and I watched the old lady pin up a notice for a support group for quitting smoking.

She smiled at me when she was done and whispered, "All welcome, every Tuesday at St Mary's Hospital."

"Oh, I don't smoke," I said.

She patted my shoulder and meandered off saying, "Good girl, that's the way."

I stared at the poster.

The hospital.

Something in my brain went click. My splitting fingers would show them the truth. I didn't need the others to come with me – I had my very own *other* bursting to get out. I'd find myself a doctor at the hospital.

I stood up, stuffing my notebook into my bag.

It was a ten-minute walk to Accident and Emergency. I felt energized. Finally, I was doing something real.

twenty-four

I walked so fast I was sweating by the time I got to A&E. I looked up at the big white letters over the door and took a deep breath. As I stepped forward to go in, the door slid aside with a giant shhhhh…

The waiting area was crammed with pale, miserable people clutching at limbs or sick bowls. They glanced at me with a brief flicker of interest before turning back to their own pain and the super-quiet telly above them. On the far side of the room, two women sat behind a high desk topped with a thick sheet of glass and a couple of narrow gaps to talk through.

I walked forward, my mouth getting steadily drier and my armpits steadily damper. There was a big red box drawn on the floor in front of the desk. I looked about for some clue as to what this meant. Were you not supposed to cross it in case you gave the receptionists germs? I hovered a foot experimentally over the line and was nearly knocked over by an angry young mum dragging a small boy with a saucepan jammed on his head.

"Don't look at me like that," she said to the receptionist. "Not my fault he can't keep his hands to himself, is it?"

The mother took a clipboard from the woman, scribbled on it and handed it back. Then she hauled the little boy by the shoulder of his coat to a seat. I watched them, thinking, for all Mum's faults, she would never treat any of us like that.

"Can I help you? Excuse me?"

I turned round; the receptionist was talking to me. Stepping forward into the box I croaked, "I need to see a doctor."

She handed me a clipboard with a form on it. "Fill this in; a nurse will see you shortly."

I shook my head. "I need a doctor."

She smiled, a one-size-fits-all smile. "The triage nurse will assess you first. Just fill in your details."

I looked at the details they wanted, not sure this was such a good idea after all. I hesitated over writing my name and in the end put Celly's name and Maddy's address. I flipped the cover off my phone as I read through the rest and worked out what year I'd have been born if I was eighteen, just in case you were supposed to have parental consent.

The woman took the clipboard back and tapped at her keyboard.

"Is this a thirty-two?" she said, pointing at the house number. I nodded and she tutted at the screen. I wondered if

Maddy's mum had the house registered here already. Of course she would, little Jay was born here. I chewed the inside of my cheek, ready to bolt from the room, but the woman just said, "Alright, take a seat. Someone will be with you shortly."

I sat as far away from Saucepan Boy and Scary Mother as I could and checked my phone. A notification was waiting – another comment on Celly's blog.

Anonymous had written: *Have you seen the film* A Beautiful Mind *...just saying*.

I googled it.

Ice cracked over my skin.

The film was about a man, John Nash, who saw people. People who existed only in his imagination. One of them was a little girl who never got old. Years would pass and she never changed. Like little Eva. Six. Fifteen. My stomach lurched. That wasn't me. I couldn't have imagined an entire houseful of people. They were real – Ollie had seen Fifteen. She'd been round his house. Hadn't she? Or had I invented that whole thing to make sense of why we broke up?

No. No, that was crazy. Mum knew they were there – she looked after us all. We talked about the others all the time. Only we didn't, did we? She did everything she could *not* to talk about them. Was it possible? I looked at the groove in my fingers, touched it. It was real; it had to be. I read more about Nash. He had a whole crazy life going on, all in his brain...it wasn't just people, he imagined whole places existed, whole jobs...the room spun around me, sweat burned my skin then froze it.

Had I done that? Imagined it all? God knows there'd been enough times when I'd felt I was going mad. The world felt unsure beneath me. Was that the real reason nobody else was allowed to know? Because Mum knew they'd lock me up and throw away the key if they realized how nuts I was? My stomach lurched. I looked around for a loo and ran. I banged open the cubicle and leaned over the toilet, wretching.

It all made sense. Why Mum wouldn't take me to a doctor. Why she wouldn't talk about the others. Why Tommo hadn't passed a single comment about my splitting fingers when my hand had been right in front of his face.

I'd blamed Mum for hiding us away, but what if there was no "us". What if it was just me…my brain?

Breathless, I grabbed a bunch of tissues and wiped my mouth. I had to get outside – I needed cold, fresh oxygen. I blindly aimed for the exit; the overhead heaters gushed with hot, suffocating air. A voice behind me said, "Sally Webb?"

Why wasn't the door opening? It was automatic, wasn't it?

Someone said, "You got to press the button, love."

"What button?" I couldn't see a button. Heat poured over me, drowning me, making the world swim. The voice said again, "Sally? Sally Webb?"

He meant Celly. Me. I hesitated. What did they do with mad people? I couldn't process it, I needed time, I had to work out what to do. Someone stood up and smacked a large silver button by the side of the door – it slid open. Cold air poured in and I plunged into it.

I had to think. I braced my legs, trying not to slip on the icy pavement, and walked as fast as I could. I pulled my hand out of my pocket. I could see the newly emerging finger as clearly as I could see my own knuckles. I traced the dip between the separating digits. I could feel them – feel them touching and being touched. I slid the fingers of my good hand protectively around the fingers of the bad and held them tight. My grip on the world was as light as a cobweb.

Could I really have imagined them all? Was it possible? I could hear someone breathing heavily near me. I looked up, snapped my head left and right, behind me – fear sent pinprick traces of panic dancing over my skin. There was no one there. It was me; the heavy breather was me.

Was I mad? Was that it? Was that why I had a counsellor, not a doctor? Choking on a ragged breath I dug my phone from my pocket. I needed evidence. Real or not real. I scrolled through looking for the texts Fifteen had sent me. How would I know? They looked like they were from her but they'd been sent from Mum's phone.

Oh god.

And then, from under nausea's green blanket of horror, came another thought. If I was mad, if I was imagining all this, if the separations weren't real, I still had a life ahead of me. A twisted, weird kind of life, but it was mine, all mine. I slowed down. If it wasn't real, what was the worst thing that could happen?

What *did* they do with mad people? Did they really lock them up? Tie them in straitjackets and fling away the key?

Surely they couldn't do that any more? Which was worse, being mad or being a freak? I didn't know any crazy people. Did I? Or maybe I did. Maybe they were just really, really good at hiding it?

The bitter cold air chilled my lungs. I didn't know where to go. Wind drove snow into my face. I drifted back towards town, past the hippy shop that scented the street with warm clouds of sandalwood. Past the camera shop that had been closing down for years. I stopped outside Swallows.

Condensation trickled down the inside of the windows. I stood outside for a second then pushed open the door. I bought tea and a toffee muffin and found a squishy leather armchair.

I sat and shivered for a bit – I had no idea what to do next.

I checked my messages. Jan from *Chatter* had mailed me again: *Any thoughts on where we could meet?*

I shuddered. If I was crazy, I really didn't want to be outed by the likes of her.

My shivering hit new heights. I was having my own private earthquake. My phone trembled in my hand. I reached for the muffin and took a bite. A cloying, doughy lump stuck to the roof of my mouth. I swilled it down with too-hot tea.

Could it be true? I thought of all the time I'd spent trying to find other people like me on the internet and discovered nothing. All the blog comments that had turned up nothing like my condition. Until the one about Nash in *A Beautiful Mind*.

If it was real, it wasn't possible for me to be the only person in the world who had it, was it? There must be someone else surely? And if there was, if they existed, they'd be online. Everything was online.

The more I thought about it, the more it seemed to fit.

So what was I supposed to do? What did mad people do? How did they get on with their lives? Did they just fake being normal? Pretend everything was okay?

Could I do that? I did drama. I was supposed to be a pretty good actor according to Miss Davison. In a way it wasn't any different to the pretending I'd done all my life.

I could do it.

I *would* do it.

Full of resolve, I set to work. If none of it was real, I didn't need to find a cure, did I? I logged onto Facebook. I meant to delete Celly's account but I wasn't quite ready for that – there was just the chance I was wrong, that it *was* real, and I'd still need it. I suspended it instead. I messaged Jan, though, I was cutting her off whatever: *I'm sorry, I've changed my mind, I don't think this is a good idea.*

Already I felt a weight lifting but I needed to do more, something positive. I needed to build on the things that could make my life…what…? Normal. Sane. School things. Things that kids did all the time.

I texted Maddy.

When's the next fashion show thing?

If all the other kids were doing it, then so would I. My fingers throbbed. I ignored them. I ate my muffin, bit by torturous doughy bit. I finished my tea, buttoned up my coat and my phone pinged a text.

I'm so pleased!!! Meeting now. Can you come? You're going to love it, I swear. M xxxxx

It was almost three o'clock already. With a tiny blip of worry that I'd be in trouble if any teacher saw me rehearsing when I'd not been in school all day, I texted, *On my way.*

Maddy texted back, *Yay!!! I'm so sorry about earlier. I love you. BTW, if anyone mentions dentist just go along with it. It's your cover for the meetings you missed. x*

I shook my head. She may not have been perfect when I tried to talk to her, but Maddy had my back. Always. As I walked, I made up little conversations in my head. How to seem sane if I bumped into Ollie, for example: "Hi, you okay? Can't stop, meeting someone."

I practised my *I'm fine* face.

I ran through scenarios with Tommo – those were easy, he did all the talking – all I needed to do was keep him at arm's length and that wouldn't be hard. He probably only flirted with me because that's what he did – look how he was with Celly and he didn't even know her.

The hardest was Maddy. I wanted so much to *really* talk to her, to share with her, but that hadn't gone so well and now…could Maddy cope with a nutter for a best mate? Which was worse, a friend who was a circus freak or one who was crazy? I walked faster as my mind raced and I realized I was muttering pretend conversations with myself. *Stop it, you mental case, just stop it.*

I got to the school gates as the bell went for the end of the day. A wave of grey and blue washed towards me, parted around me and flowed on. I hitched my bag on my shoulder and powered through, heading for the gym.

There was a handwritten note on the door: *Fashion Show Rehearsals, Top Secret, Y12 & Y13 Only.* I took a deep breath. It had to be better than going home and facing up to whatever was there – real or not real. Proof that I was mad or proof that I was falling apart.

twenty-five

I hovered outside the gym, nerves fluttering like a bunch of pixies having a disco in my stomach. I lifted my chin.

Come on, Tee, you can do this.

A shot of adrenaline pulsed through me. I had a future; if I was mad I had a future. A crazy one maybe but… *One step at a time, Teva.*

I pushed open the gym door. A damp smell of sweaty feet and hairspray fogged around me. It wasn't just us meeting in there, at least another six groups were scattered round the room. Dancey people were stretching, sitting on the floor tipping their heads onto their knees, folding themselves in two just to show everyone they could. Shy people stood around the edges of the room chewing their lips, arms folded, ponytails pulled high and tight. All the cool people were sitting smack in the middle of the room, laughing too loudly at each other's jokes.

I looked for Maddy and stumbled forward as she hugged

me from behind. She pulled me round and put a serious face on.

"I'm so sorry about earlier. We'll talk later, yeah? I promise I'll listen."

I stuck a half smile on my face, not trusting any words that might come out of my mouth. She beamed back and took my hand.

"I am literally so glad you came. I cannot tell you. It's so much fun. We've got about halfway through the planning already. Come on, the others are over there."

She tucked her arm in mine and hopped over outstretched legs and abandoned bags to a scattering of girls sitting in a circle with their bare feet all pointing to the middle.

A wave of oh-poor-you-you've-been-dumped pity was rising from them. I could smell it oozing from their sad, upturned faces.

"This is us!" said Maddy, spreading her palms out to indicate the ragtag gathering. Lola and Barnet were there and some girls from Maddy's maths class. We were undeniably one of the nerd groups with a light dusting of weirds. Ollie would think it was hilarious – and not in a good way. I forced a smile.

Barnet flicked back her pink hair and, putting a hand on my ankle, said, "You've got to show him life goes on. No boy is worth the heartache, okay? Not one."

Lola, watching Barnet's every movement with big doe-eyes, nodded and said, "She's *so* right."

I forced a smile, secretly burning inside that they didn't

just *know* about me and Ollie, they had opinions about it too.

Worse than that, it looked like Maddy had primed them all to be nice. I wanted to tell them it was fine, Ollie was genuinely the least of my worries, but that would have opened up a can of worms I really wanted to avoid.

"Do you need to get changed?" Maddy asked, grinning like an over-keen cheerleader, as she effortlessly knotted her hair into a loose bun on top of her head. I looked down at my wet coat. I wasn't exactly dressed for a dance rehearsal.

"I thought we were doing shoes?"

"Yeah, but Tee, you know how this works, right? It's not like modelling. It's a laugh – we do a crazy dance thing."

"Er…"

"Don't you remember last year's show?"

I quickly found Fifteen's memory of it. Then I thought, if Fifteen didn't exist, this was my memory, so why did it have that slight cloudiness that settled over all my former selves' memories. Was that what everyone's memories were like? My brain hurt trying to figure it out.

Maddy went on, "Someone filmed the fancy-dress-shop routine – Darth Vader, two sumo wrestlers and a pantomime cow doing the Macarena! It was hilarious. It got about a billion hits on YouTube. Come on. Just take your coat off and we'll show you what we've done so far. All you need to know is, the more people laugh, the more money they put in the charity bucket, okay?"

I nodded. "Okay."

They got to their feet and we shoved a few bags to one

side to clear enough room to practise. There was a sporty group next to us – half boys with gelled-up hair and half girls with super-neat French plaits. They were all ready to go, with their skintight trackies and neon gym vests. One of them was locking an iPod into a docking station.

The sporty group fired up a skippy dance track and the whole group bent over with their hands on their knees, before launching themselves into an insanely energetic aerobic routine – legs flying everywhere.

"Mads, how are we all going to practise in here?"

Maddy reached in her bag and pulled out her dad's prized Bose speakers.

"Let them try and drown out these babies."

Lola handed her phone to Barnet. Their hands lingered over the exchange, their eyes locking in the way couples' do. I had a brief pang for Ollie but it fluttered away as Maddy flicked to the right track. "Monster Mash", a song I remembered from Halloween parties at primary school, boomed out. It was so loud, the sporty group stopped mid-leapfrog to glare at us. Maddy gave them a big grin.

"Sorry! We booked this time slot; we'll only be half an hour-*ish*."

Then she turned her back on them. She was pretty cool sometimes. They sat down grumbling as Maddy took control.

"Right, let's show Tee what we've got so far."

They lined up in front of me with a space between Alice and Janey. Maddy pointed to the gap. "That's where you'll go."

"It's proper easy," said Barnet. "Just join in when you've got it."

Maddy flicked the remote back to the beginning of the track and they started a kind of zombie, heel-toe line dance. When they got to a bit that went "*Wa-ooooo,*" they rushed forward and back again like a wave, zombie arms outstretched. It was all the same thing repeated over and over but it was really quite funny. When they stopped, I clapped.

They smiled shyly, pleased, and Maddy put her hands on her hips as if she needed to catch her breath.

"That's the bit we've done so far," she said. "Let's do it again and you just try and follow."

We played it over and over with me trying to pick up the steps, self-conscious at first, aware of all the other groups watching, waiting for us to finish. I kept turning the wrong way, bumping into Alice one minute and Janey the next, until it got so ridiculous we were all laughing.

"Oh," said Maddy, "I've just had a brilliant idea. You could, like, pretend to be getting it wrong. We could stage it so you swing your arms out at the wrong time and you just keep missing, hitting someone. Like if Alice ducks there and you swing out your arm..."

"I can't do that! I'll never get the timing right. Look what a pig's ear I'm making trying to do it right."

"No, you will. Look, let's try it, every time I shout *swing*, you put your arms out and Alice ducks."

We did it. It was really funny until Maddy shouted "Duck" instead of "Swing" and I ducked and swung and smacked Alice in the back of her legs so she fell onto all fours.

"Oh my god, I'm so sorry, I'm such an idiot."

I went to help her up but Alice rolled onto her back and said, "It's…no…good…I'm…dead…" And lolled her head to one side. For one horrified second everything stopped and then Alice cackled with laughter. Pretty soon we were all giggling helplessly on the floor next to her, repeating her words and flopping our own heads to the side.

"This is genius," said Maddy through her laughter, "this is how we'll finish it, one zombie clouting another until we're all dead!"

We lay there, clutching our ribs, letting the laughter subside for a minute, until Mads said, "Come on, one last time and we can let the others have their music on."

We ran through it again, getting more confident in our clowning. The sporty kids looked at us like we were *all* a bit mental. I smiled at the irony of that but I really didn't care what they thought. I hadn't had fun like this since, well, since ever.

twenty-six

When we finished rehearsing, I threw my arms around Maddy.

"Thank you for making me be a zombie. It's brilliant. You're brilliant."

She hugged me back, fiercely, trying to prove how much I meant to her, and something in me strengthened. Good thing too, because the next thing she said was, "You need to do two dances though. Frankie had a word in registration – she really, really wants you to show off your corset."

I gave her a pleading look but before I'd even had a chance to ask her if she'd be my model, Maddy said, "Oh no. No."

"Maddy, please, it's really important. You know how nervous I was about even doing the boots dance. And you'd look fab, you'd really show off the contours, you've got boobs and everything, pleeeease."

I wished I could tell her how important it was – that suddenly I had a shot at a future, at the apprenticeship and I wanted to grasp it all.

She shook her head. "My dad would go mental. But if you really don't want to, I've had an idea."

"Go on."

"You might not like it," she warned, "but I think it could work."

"Okay."

"Well, it was something Tommo said about how he'd happily model his own work, you know what he's like. He was joking, I know, but I thought you could do a sort of Rocky Horror thing and get the boys to model your stuff."

"What boys – Tommo excepted – would prance about on stage in corsets?" I said.

"Are you kidding me?" Maddy said. "The boys' rugby team love wearing women's clothes – any chance to drag up and they're there. And it's for charity – I'm sure they'll do it."

"You think? Will they look awful though? Corsets are designed for girls, Mads, they won't look right on boys."

"They might not look exactly right but, hey, if your corsets can even give some of the boys a waistline, well, doesn't that make them really good at what they're meant to do?"

I thought about it for a second. It might work – and it would mean I didn't have to model mine. However much I wanted to embrace life, I had to draw a line somewhere and not displaying my scratched-up skin to the rest of the school was definitely it.

I said, "Do you think Frankie will go for it?"

Maddy shrugged. "She might, if we sell it right. As long as she doesn't think we're taking the mick."

"Ollie's not in the rugby team." I don't know why he'd popped into my head just then – habit, I suppose.

Maddy brushed it aside saying, "No, he isn't, so you don't need to worry about that, do you?"

I smiled. It was a pretty cool idea.

"Okay. Let's go and see if Frankie's still about."

And let's put off going home for as long as possible.

I let Maddy do all the persuading. After a few frowning questions, Frankie caved in.

"Okay, okay, as long as your work looks alright and the boys are up for it, I'll talk to Mr Winchester tonight."

Maddy joked, "Poor you, Miss, that'll be a hardship."

Frankie actually blushed. Mr Winchester, the boys' rugby coach, had muscles on his muscles. He was possibly even fitter than Tommo.

Deflecting our raised eyebrows, Frankie said, "How's your portfolio, Teva?"

"Deft change of subject there, Miss," I said, but I decided to be honest. "It's not great, actually, but Tommo is going to help me. I'm going to try and get it together so I can apply for that uni."

I surprised myself with that last bit. Was I really going to do that?

Frankie's face lit up. "That's great, Teva. Really great. Wow. Well done. Now you just need to get to work on your buddy here. Tell her she really needs to think about Oxbridge."

I grinned at Maddy. Something weird was happening inside me. It felt so good to be talking positively, to feel motivated. I didn't care if it was pretend, for a few minutes a pretend future was better than… I pulled myself up with a jolt. If it wasn't real – the separations – then it was okay for me to plan. *If* everything was just in my head, planning a future was exactly what I should be doing. My knees went soft, and I had to lean against the desk so I didn't fall over.

"I'm so glad you're feeling better, Teva." Miss Francis squeezed my arm. "Maybe a day in town was good for you?"

She knew I'd skived off then. All I could say was, "Sorry."

"Look, it really might have done you some good but next time you feel like running away, come and see me, okay? Right," said Frankie, "I'll go and find Mr Winchester."

We followed her out of the classroom and I panicked at the thought of going home, of having to make sense of whatever was there. I said, "Can I come back to yours, Mads?"

"Course you can, my darlink."

I slipped my hand through her arm and pulled her to my side.

"Thanks. And seriously, thanks for forcing me to do zombie dancing. It really was fun."

She pushed open the door to the outside. Both of us shivered and stopped to do our coats up tight. Maddy said, "Would you hate me if I did apply to Cambridge?"

"Do you want to?"

"See. I knew it. Everyone will think I'm a stuck-up cow, totally full of myself."

"No. No, Mads, I'm honestly asking – do you want to? You've always been so anti the idea." I glanced at her face: she was chewing on the side of her bottom lip, the age-old sign of *Yeah, I said that, but...*

"You said it was full of public school kids, that you'd hate it, that kids like us didn't go to places like that?"

"Yeah."

"You said they'd all be way too clever for their own good and not able to tie a shoelace between them."

"Yeah. I know."

"But you still want to try?"

She nodded.

"Then you should. It doesn't matter what other people think. If it's in your gut, you've got to give it a go."

"That's what I think," she said, starting to walk, "and if I don't get in, well it wasn't meant to be, was it?" She turned and looked me in the eye. "Are you really going to try for the knicker course?"

I elbowed her in the ribs.

"I'll need to get my portfolio properly sorted. I'll need some modelling shots of someone in my corset. Not in a jokey way – it can't be a boy. I need to take some arty shots."

"Ha. Well I think Kate Moss might be a *leetle beeet* out of your league."

"What about you?"

"Oh, come on! What is it about you trying to get me in my underwear?" There was an uncomfortable second when we both remembered she'd thought I'd fancied her about twelve hours earlier. Maddy brushed it away saying, "No. Sorry. I love you but no. Can't you put it on the model thing in the textiles classroom?"

"I suppose."

"Anyway, I thought you said it was made to fit *you*?"

"Yeah."

"So the best way for you to show it off, is if you do the modelling, isn't it?"

"I guess." Me or someone like me, I thought, wondering if Fifteen would do it. A familiar swirling started up in my stomach. Fifteen, real or not real? I changed the subject.

"So what do you have to do to get into Brainbox School then, genius?"

She opened her mouth and I sank gratefully into her chatter.

Unfortunately, when we got to Maddy's, her mum was having a sale thing in the front room. There were saris everywhere and so many women you couldn't move.

"Uh oh," said Mads, "sorry, hon, you'll have to go. Even I'm not welcome when she's doing her market trader bit. I'll see you in the morning, yeah?"

I swallowed the disappointment.

"Yeah," I said. "No worries."

I hitched my bag over my shoulder and headed down the road, flicking the cover off and on my phone where it nestled in my pocket.

At our gate, the keypad glowed sickly green in the gloom. I turned my back on it and leaned against the concrete pillar that flanked our scruffy gateway. I got my phone out. No messages from anyone. Including Fifteen. Was that because my brain could no longer conjure her up, because I'd figured out she and all the others weren't real? I turned round and looked up at the house. A figure stood in the window of the room I thought of as Fifteen's. She was watching the gate. If it wasn't Fifteen, who was it? Not my chubby mother that's for sure. I stared up at the window and a dead weight settled in my stomach.

I took a deep breath and punched in the gate code. Time to find out if I was crazy or if I was about to be ripped in two and thrown aside like an old biscuit wrapper. I didn't like either of the options much but on the whole, I favoured crazy.

twenty-seven

Six was sitting on the stairs, picking at the wallpaper. I pressed my fingers to my eyes, opened them and looked again. Yep. She was still there, looking at me a bit oddly after the eye pressing. I raised a hand and she raised one, feebly, back. She looked so real, could my brain really be inventing her? I stood for a minute trying to decide what to do next. My stomach rumbled giving me the answer. How could I be hungry in the midst of my crazy life? I've no idea, but there you go, I was. I headed to the kitchen.

Eva was standing on a chair, playing in the sink, while Mum pushed garlic butter into a sliced baguette. My mouth watered.

"You're late," she said.

"Nice to see you too."

"It is nice to see you, Teva, it's just quite late. I was worried. Are you…okay?"

"I was rehearsing," I said.

She crunched tinfoil round the baguette and put it in the oven. I touched the back of Eva's dress. She felt real to me.

"Everything's been alright then?" said Mum as I made a cup of tea.

I wanted to say something but I didn't know how to start... *Okay, Mum, I get it now, the reason you won't take me to the doctor is because I'm actually a bit mental and there's not much that can be done to unmental me.*

Yeah. I didn't fancy saying those words out loud. Instead I just said, "Fine. Everything's been fine."

I took my tea and went upstairs, trying Fifteen's door as I went past. It scuffed against something – the old chair trick, no doubt. *Real or not real?*

"Go away," she said.

How could that be a figment of my imagination? I tried the door again. Something hit the floor behind it, letting the door open a fraction.

Fifteen yanked it fully open, making me spill hot tea all over my hand. She glared at me in a cold fury.

"What?"

"I just..." I willed myself to see through any tricks my mind was playing. I reached out to touch her. She snatched her arm back, saying, "Get off me, you weirdo."

Then she slammed the door in my face with so much force it made a small hurricane in the hall.

How could that not be real? My fingers throbbed. I felt like I was at a crossroads. I had to do something but I just didn't know what. The blog seemed a bit stupid now. Worse.

If I was crazy, trying to find a cure for something that didn't exist was like waving a red flag over my head while playing loud trumpets and singing, "I'm mad as a squirrel, lock me up, please."

I shut myself in my room. Were the others real but not who I thought they were – not my other selves? How could they be explained? Were they sisters? Sisters who'd miraculously appeared despite no father being around for forever and a day. Sisters who'd appeared in the wrong order – me being the newest of them when I should be the oldest. Sisters who never left the house; who nobody else knew existed… I sipped my tea. It wasn't doing the job I expected of it. Quite frankly, that cup of tea did not have the power to make everything okay.

But maybe I did?

I didn't know what was wrong with me. I didn't know if the others in my house were in my mind or if they really were younger versions of me. I knew if I tried to tell anyone about them, they'd think I was mad. Maybe I was. Maybe I really was. I did know one thing though: when we'd been rehearsing for the fashion show I'd hardly thought about my condition, whatever it was. Or wasn't. If I was crazy, maybe, if I just kept myself busy, I could *make* myself normal?

I got my portfolio out. I started making design notes for my corset and I didn't stop. I worked and worked until Mum called me down for tea. I ate it swiftly, not engaging with anyone else. Then I went straight back upstairs and worked some more. And that was just the start.

Over the next few days I made myself busier than I'd ever been in my life. I did everything I was invited to do. Work with Tommo on his English? Of course. Knuckle down to coursework with Frankie? Yes please. Fashion show rehearsals? I zombie-stomped with the best of them. Maddy was right, too – seven of the boys' rugby team agreed to model our corsets. Tommo was wearing mine and one of his mates was wearing the bunny outfit. I helped choreograph a fantastic dance for them – well, I say dance, it was mostly hip-wiggling around the stage, doing a sort of cancan. I wasn't a hundred per cent sure it would get past the censors – i.e. the Head – but it was funny.

Maddy kept saying how proud she was of how I was dealing with the whole Ollie thing. The truth was, I was burying everything. Everything. And Ollie was right at the bottom of the pile. I felt guilty accepting her sympathy for that but I figured, if she knew the rest of it, I'd have had that sympathy anyway.

When anything odd happened, like the horrible wriggling under my skin, I put it down to being cold. It couldn't be a separation or it would have happened by now, wouldn't it? That's how I convinced myself, that and by bandaging up my splitting fingers and refusing to look at them. I avoided the others, especially Fifteen, as much as I could. That wasn't hard seeing as I was staying away from home for as long as I dared. When my appointment with Elliepants came round, I didn't go.

I took routes round school that kept me away from Ollie

– it wasn't that I couldn't cope with seeing him, just, when I did, he was a bit weird. Once, I caught his eye, and he shook his head at me. What was that about? He made me feel even crazier. So I stayed in the gym, the library, Frankie's classroom, Maddy's house. I did everything to avoid facing the things that haunted me. I encouraged Maddy to talk about college. We discussed Cambridge so often that I started to feel like it was one of our friends. I was grateful for it.

After two weeks I was exhausted. I'd tried so hard to stay away from the dark tunnel of thought that led to everything I was trying to ignore but, like a whirlpool, the pull of it was endless and the closer I got, the harder it was to resist. Fighting all the time was so tiring. I may have hidden my two splitting fingers under a wad of bandage, but they throbbed incessantly, calling to me. The urge to check them was unbearable. I kept thinking maybe, if I looked, I'd just see normal fingers under those bandages, proof that the others weren't real. *Maybe, maybe, maybe…*

I kept fighting until, eventually, the last fashion show practice before the dress rehearsal came around. We were pretty much perfect with our swings and ducks and by the time we left the gym we were all smiling. I felt okay. Then my phone buzzed in my bag and I took it out without really thinking.

I can't wait for ever. Ollie needs me.

Fifteen.

I deleted it and whispered to myself, "You're not real, you're not."

It started to rain as we left school. I said to Mads, "Can I come back to yours?"

"Again?"

"Well if it's a bother..."

"I didn't mean that, Tee, it's just you've hardly been home recently. It's a bit odd that's all. Is everything okay?"

I had to physically clench my gut to keep the panic down. *Don't make me go home, Fifteen might be waiting.*

I said, "Mum's got a book deadline – she likes the peace and quiet. I thought maybe I could sleep over?"

Maddy shrugged and said, "Okay, Mum won't mind. She loves having you round. Hey, did I tell you about Maaz? He asked me if I wanted to watch him cage fighting. He's hilarious, pretty clever too. He's applied to Homerton – it's really sporty..."

I could have cried with gratitude as she talked endlessly about yet another boy.

When we got to hers we worked, we gossiped, we watched crap TV, but the snake of worry I'd buried inside me was uncoiling. I encouraged Maddy to talk and talk, even when we went up to bed. She had the future all sorted in her head. She'd even been on Google maps to see how far De Montfort was from Cambridge. My fingers throbbed. I tucked them underneath me, asked her about Maaz, about her personal statement – anything to keep her talking.

"Not now, Tee, go to sleep, it's nearly two."

Her breathing changed as she slipped into sleep. I lay on the fold-out bed, dark thoughts gathering in my mind, pain beginning to pulse up my arm. The bubble of worry in me grew and grew. I was going to burst if I didn't do something. I had to check my fingers. If they were okay, maybe I was okay? I couldn't fight it any more.

It took everything I had, every ounce of willpower in me to hold it together until morning. The thought of having a crying fit like I had on our bathroom floor when I first saw my fingers…I couldn't do that at Maddy's and I couldn't trust myself not to, if I looked at my fingers and things were worse.

As soon as the sun was up, so was I. I gently shook Maddy awake.

"I'm sorry, Mads, I've got to get home. I forgot, I've got drama homework."

Maddy looked at me but her deep brown eyes didn't focus.

"Did you hear me, Mads? I've got to go."

"Mmmm," she murmured, pulling the duvet over her head and turning away. I grabbed a sheet of paper out of the printer on her desk and wrote a note:

See you at school, might be a bit late.

I unhooked the stair gate and tiptoed downstairs, praying Maddy's mum and dad weren't already up. I was in luck. As quietly as I could, I slipped out. A sharp, bitter wind was stirring. I stuffed my hands in my pockets and paced my way home, my cloudy breath warm in front of me as it flowed over my cheeks. All the way I tried to persuade myself not to do what I was planning to do.

It was pointless. My sensible self was never going to win a battle with the boiling madness inside me. It was wearing me out.

I clunked our heavy front door shut and took a deep breath. Six was sitting on the stairs; it was getting to the stage when Mum would have to redecorate. Again. I don't know why she didn't just paint it, then Six would have nothing to pick at. I gave myself a shake. It was all *so real*. I went up past her and squeezed her skinny shoulder. She felt warm and solid under my hand and I nodded to myself.

The rest of the house was quiet. I pushed open my bedroom door. It was just as I'd left it, except my T-shirt drawer wasn't fully closed – a bunch of white fabric ballooned out of it. I was pretty untidy but Fifteen was way worse than me and she never, ever closed anything she'd opened. From cereal packets, to cupboards, contents would be left sprawling everywhere. I pulled out the drawer, straightened my shirts and tucked it back in again. Then I stopped for a second – how imaginary was a messy drawer? Why on earth would my brain conjure that up?

I held my bandaged fingers close. I knew I was going to look at them. I knew I'd run out of the strength I needed not to. Still, I held off as long as I could. I felt a bit sick. A bit disgusted with myself – like I was giving up. Like I was making a decision that wasn't going to be good for me.

I was running on automatic now, my heart rate rising,

my lungs seeming to shrink as my breathing became shallower, faster. A million tiny prickles danced over my skin. I unwrapped the bandage.

My little finger had an almost complete replica joined along the top of it. I swallowed down the rising bile in my throat and put my hands on my knees. I nodded to myself, my mouth a grim line, my eyes hot and wet. How could I tell if I was imagining it? How could I tell what lay ahead of me? And then I knew.

I would cut off the new bit. I had super sharp embroidery scissors. If it wasn't real, one of the fingertips wouldn't hurt, would it? And if it *was* real, I'd be getting rid of her before she got rid of me. I'd take her out, piece by piece, until there was nothing left. A hot spasm jerked through my veins, stiffened every limb, like she, the new Teva, was fighting me. I held on, controlled every muscle. Something in me remembered Fifteen. Remembered the last time this happened to us. A weird kind of strength heated my blood. I could feel it pulsing through me, a determination to be the one who'd win.

Tension knotted my neck, my back. With huge effort I spread my hands out; both fingers responded to my instructions. I hunched and released my shoulders, rolled my head on my neck and forced my body to relax. Slowly, slowly, my muscles softened, aching, poisoned with adrenaline.

I took a deep breath, dragged my computer onto my knee and logged onto my blog. For a weird minute I forgot Celly was me and expected to see a new post, something about how good she'd been over the last couple of weeks, getting on with life, being normal. There wasn't of course, but there were comments, lots of comments.

Hey Celly, how you doing?

Where are you?

Tell us what's going on?

And:

Celly, I'm worried about you, Mr Fixer.

Oh, Tommo. He was so sweet. I felt bad about deceiving him. I messaged him back: *I'm okay, just got a lot on my mind – on my two minds.*

Straight away a message pinged back:

Seriously, could we meet up? I could help you.

I didn't stop to wonder why he was up so early, I just pictured his face as he realized Celly was me. Shock turning to confusion turning to...what? Disgust? I messaged him back:

I don't think so. I'm taking matters into my own hands anyway.

I smiled at my own stupid joke.

I took a snap of the scissors and posted: *Time to see how deep this goes, don't you think?*

twenty-eight

I opened the scissors and pressed the point into the finger that lay on top. I pushed hard and a dull pain bore into me. I did the same thing to the finger underneath and got exactly the same feeling. I placed the tip between my fingers and scored a cold valley. I gasped but I hadn't even broken the skin. The pain was so vivid both fingers had to be real.

And if they were both real, she had to go.

As I thought the words, I felt her wriggling under my skin. She was struggling inside me, but she couldn't do anything, not yet. I had all the power and I was going to get rid of her. She seized me again, stiffening my body. I forced myself to loosen up, then I held the scissors to the point where the fingers joined at the bottom. The top one was the one that was breaking away so that had to be her, didn't it?

I screwed my eyes shut and pressed and pressed. Sweat pricked my forehead and I gasped, barely believing what I was doing, but seeing no other way. I held the point of the scissors in place, sucked in a breath, and drew it up towards the tip of the finger, growling at the tearing pain, trying to ignore the blood. I adjusted my grip, a thudding in my ears blocking out the world. I pressed my lips together and dragged the scissors back down. Under the hot agony, blood bloomed. I winced back sobbing gulps, thinking, *This is what I look like inside. This is what everyone looks like. I'm just full of blood, nothing else, there's no other person waiting to come out.*

What I'd done was...

Crazy.

There was so much pressure in my head it was blinding me. What did it mean? I could see the other finger, I could see it, I was cutting a groove between the two fingers, one on top of the other. How could that not be real? I couldn't make sense of it...

What was I doing?

I had to stop it. Stop the blood. I grabbed my pyjama top and wound it round my hand. Tears streamed down my face from pain and anger and I don't even know what. Blood was everywhere. Mum was going to go ballistic.

I needed to clean up the mess. I stood up and as I did I knocked my laptop to the floor. The screen came alive and I saw comment after comment from Mr Fixer – Tommo...

Whatever you're thinking, don't do it.

Celly, please, don't.

Celly! Answer me, please.

Call me, text me, I'll send you my number.

As I struggled to calm down another message pinged up:

I want to help you.

My whole arm hurt. I clumsily typed with my left hand.

You have helped, I said, *more than you'll ever know.*

I liked Tommo, I mean I *really* liked Tommo. Rightly or wrongly, he'd helped fill the Ollie-shaped hole in my life, I could see that now. I had Maddy but maybe I was like a wonky bike and I'd always need two stabilizers. And I felt like Tommo liked *me*, the real me, the one who could sew and do English and…my laptop pinged a new message: *Meet up with me.*

I hesitated, then typed back: *I don't think so, you don't know what you're asking. You don't know who I am.*

He said: *I think I know exactly who you are. Blonde hair, deep blue eyes?*

God. He did know. He'd guessed. And he still wanted to help. I typed back with my awkward left hand: *How did you find out?*

Back pinged, *Just a guess. Things you said.*

I stared at the screen. He knew and he wasn't running a mile. He didn't even seem all that shocked. I typed again. *I think I'm nuts.*

You're not nuts, you're just dealing with a lot of stuff. Tell me where I can meet you.

I said, *Not school?*

He said, *With everyone else around? Maybe we should keep this to ourselves for a bit? Until you feel more settled? What about a cafe?*

My cheeks flushed. That was so thoughtful. I could feel

myself calming down just messaging him. I said, *Okay. What about Swallows?*

Swallows? Which one is that? What road?

Short memory, Mr Fixer! At the end of West Street, by the old cattle market – the one we went to for coffee in the snow?

Oh yeah! Sorry, need a brain satnav…

Ha! West Street, Tiechester, Yorkshire, The World, The Universe, Space…that help?

Funny girl. I'll get back to you with a time – don't do anything crazy.

Too late. Still, the thought of sharing with someone what I was going through, of finally having someone to talk to, it both terrified me and gave me hope. I said, *I'll try not to.*

I took a deep breath and closed my laptop with my pyjama-wrapped fingers. I felt weirdly settled. Sore but calm. I went to the bathroom to clean up the mess I'd made of my hand.

Rusty clouds swirled down the sink, revealing the ragged skin where I'd hacked at myself. I shuddered, not quite believing I'd done it.

I took my hand from the water and a rich red line filled the rip. I put it back under the tap and opened the bathroom cupboard. My whole body was trembling.

I found Steri-Strips in the cupboard and stuck them over the wound, pulling the gap closed. It was still bleeding, but I just about managed. I tore a fresh bandage open with my teeth, pressed some tissue against the wound and bound it up tightly.

I cleaned up the mess, hiding my bloodstained PJs at the bottom of the laundry basket. I'd deal with those another time. I felt calmer but my hand hurt so much. There was pain in both fingers. At least I thought there was – what did that mean? I had no idea.

Trying to cut your finger off though? That was crazy.

I sat on the edge of the bath and listened to the creaking of the radiator pipes as the house began to wake up. I tried to make sense of it all, but how did you make sense of something that you can't begin to get a fix on? There was no one else like us, no one else who had even seen the others; the only sensible answer was that I had made it all up. Besides, what I'd just done was crazy so *I* had to be crazy, didn't I? Normal people didn't see two fingers on their hand and try to cut one of them off. How was I supposed to know?

The bathroom door opened and Twelve came in.

"Oh, sorry," she said, rubbing her eyes, "didn't realize you were in here."

I looked at her hard, tried to see some shimmer around the edges, some pale patch where my mind hadn't quite filled in the detail.

"Do you feel real?" I asked her.

She said, "I need a pee, can't you go sit somewhere else?"

I left her to it. In the stillness, after what I'd done, I felt strangely okay. Able to put the coat of pretence back on. I still had no idea what was real and what wasn't, but in some ways it didn't make any difference. I just had to get on with life.

Elliepants always said I should live in the moment.

In the moment.

Fine.

So. School.

I looked at my hand. The bandage looked ridiculously huge. Mrs Ranjha would ask a lot of questions. I texted Mads, *Running late, see you in reg.*

It was dress-rehearsal day. I got my make-up out. I needed warpaint.

twenty-nine

A watery sun was doing its best to defrost the chilly streets. Ice dripped and melted into glittering pools on the pavement.

I felt...lighter, I don't know why. I'd reached a new low that morning and yet something was driving me forward. I felt like I had hope. Don't get me wrong, I knew things weren't okay. I was brittle and twitchy, hot with nerves but, against all odds, that flicker of some kind of future just would not die.

I was late for school. Classes had already started; I sensed the quiet hush of industry behind the closed classroom doors. I went straight for the textiles room and stuck my head round the door.

Frankie beckoned me in. A bunch of tiny Year Sevens looked at me with bored expectation.

"This is Teva," Frankie said, "one of my best students. If you've got tickets for the fashion show you'll see her work tomorrow night. Now, get on with your hat designs, I'll be back in two minutes."

A gentle chatter rose as they got down to work and Frankie came over. She put her hand on my arm.

"You okay? You look white as a sheet."

I swallowed. "Yeah, no, I'm fine. Can I work in here for a bit?"

She nodded and pointed to a table at the back. I got my portfolio out with my stupid, fat, bandaged hand.

"That bandage gets bigger every time I see it, Teva."

"Oh yeah," I said, "that burn, it got infected."

"Well no wonder you're looking so pale. Don't overdo it."

A twist of guilt tightened my throat. She believed me so easily. I smiled and nodded and got out my corset. I had to thread a longer lace through the eyes and attach the last poppy before Tommo could wear it. Bless him. It was a right fiddle trying to do anything with my mutton of a hand but I worked solidly for that whole lesson and, when the bell went, I was snipping the stray threads of a finished piece of work. I held it up. As the Year Sevens left the room I saw a couple of the girls look at it admiringly and saw it through their eyes; I'd made something pretty cool. The Union Jack lining was vivid against the army green of the corset – and the poppies added drama and emotion to the whole piece.

A hand touched my shoulder. It was Frankie.

"Teva, it looks great. If the supporting written work in your portfolio comes anywhere near the standard of your garment, you'll easily get an A this year. I'm so pleased you've knuckled down. Here," she slid a folded green slip across the table towards me, "this was in the register for you."

An appointment with Elliepants.

I stared at it.

"It won't open itself, Teva," she said, smiling gently.

I tried to laugh, failed, picked up the paper and flipped it open.

Sorry you couldn't make Monday. I've scheduled a space for you at 2 p.m. this afternoon.

2 p.m. – right in the middle of the dress rehearsal. I wouldn't be able to go. What a shame!

As I stuffed the note in my pocket and packed my bag, Frankie said, "I'm really impressed with you, Teva. I heard you and Ollie broke up. It's great how you've stayed on track. Keep it up."

A group of Year Nines barged in. Frankie snapped at them, "Line up outside. *I* will tell you when you can come in."

They straggled back out again and she winked at me. "Seriously, I'm really pleased you seem to be on top of everything, but if you need to talk, you know where I am."

She made me feel like I mattered and it warmed me through. I managed to say, "Thanks," before I battled through the crowd of kids waiting in the corridor.

I had drama before lunch and I paid proper attention all the way through. Erin kept bossing me around, telling me to do things I was already doing.

The fifth time she tried to direct me, saying, "Teva, this is where you reach for Matt's hand," Miss Davison came to my rescue.

"Erin, you're interrupting the flow of the piece. Teva knows exactly what she's got to do and she's doing it very well."

It felt good to be right and I couldn't suppress a slightly smug smile. Erin looked like she'd been slapped.

As Miss Davison dismissed us she said, "Good luck with your dress rehearsal, fashionistas."

Erin said, "Thanks, Miss, I've tried to bring in a Brechtian element to the whole thing but I'm not sure everyone else will carry it off."

Miss Davison said, "Good grief, I should think not, Erin, the fashion show is meant to be fun. I hear your textiles group has something fabulous up their sleeves, Teva? I can't wait to see that. Miss Francis is so proud of you all."

In that moment I was actually happy. I was humming as I left the room to go and find Mads and humming as I rummaged in my bag for my phone, and humming as I walked straight into Ollie's chest.

"Hey," he said, and my betraying legs turned to liquid. For a beat, we made eye contact and, in that moment, I stopped breathing. I tore my eyes away and looked at the floor, the walls, anywhere but at Ollie. It was the familiarity of him that overwhelmed me, seeing him so close for the first time since we broke up, my body reacted on autopilot. All the organs in my chest seemed to grow hard angles. I managed to croak, "Hi."

"Are you okay?" he asked, like he really meant it. I forced myself to nod. He put a finger under my chin and lifted my face so I was looking at him. Seconds ago I'd been actually happy but now a huge hole had opened up in front of me and I wanted to step in it and disappear. My chin wobbled. Why was I responding like this? I was genuinely fine. I was over it. I really was. I would not cry, I would not.

"Good," he said, and I struggled to work out what was good, until I realized he meant me being okay. It wasn't fair. How could one person have the power to swing your emotions round their head like a ball on a string? I pulled my head away from his touch.

He dropped his hand and said, "I've been thinking about what you said. Do you want to have lunch?"

What I said? My forehead went into full crinkle mode and he gave his lopsided smile followed by a little shoulder shrug.

His voice dropped an octave and he said, "Thanks. For the messages, it means a lot. We've got a lot of history, you and me."

Messages? God, Fifteen! But there was no Fifteen – she was in my imagination, wasn't she? Which meant I must have written to Ollie. How could I have been messaging him without knowing it? How? My brain couldn't make sense of it. I felt like I was on a tiny boat being pitched about on a wild sea and I just had to cling onto the sides and not let go.

"So," he said, "lunch?"

A little pulse beat in my temple and I almost, almost said yes. Words formed in my mouth and I prayed someone would come and save me: Maddy, Tommo, anyone. I was going to say yes. I was going to give in and say yes and follow him like a puppy to the canteen. I opened my mouth and even as I thought the words, even as I knew I was going to say them, I didn't. It was like some stronger, more mature me took over. I shook my head and stepped away from him.

"No," I said, with a confidence I didn't believe. "You're alright. I'm meeting Maddy."

His face fell and guilt flooded through me. None of this was his fault. I softened the rejection with, "Maybe I'll see you later? At the dress rehearsal?"

And I walked away.

My arm tingled and I thought, *This is how things are supposed to be*. Me growing up in a normal way. Not an inner me escaping, but both of us, growing up, moving forward. I could feel us working together. If it was real, if there was another me waiting for her moment, maybe she wouldn't come out, maybe I'd just gradually morph into her like other people did. It felt possible. Maybe that was why the separation was so slow this time, because we were nearly there, nearly fully grown. I shook my head. I was doing it again, building up reasons why things happened when they weren't even real. But I was coping, wasn't I? I was dealing with things like a normal person. Maybe I should cut myself some slack.

I called Maddy. She picked up straight away.

"We're in the courtyard," she said through a mouthful of food. "I've got paninis. Come and sit in the sun, it's beautiful out here."

I ran all the way there. Someone had pulled a couple of picnic benches together and a crowd sat around in coats and scarves, basking in the weak sunshine. Maddy's bag was on the bench next to her and when she saw me she yelled, "Over here, Tee," and lifted it up, freeing the space she'd saved for me. She handed me the panini she'd bought and I sat next to her.

"I just ran into Ollie," I said, still unable to believe I'd walked away, "literally."

She stopped chewing for a second then swallowed her mouthful. "Okay. So how did that go?"

I looked up at her. "I dunno, I felt a bit sorry for him. He asked me to lunch and I said no. You'd have been totally proud of me."

Her smile nearly split her face in two and she put an arm round me. "That's my girl. I've got something that'll cheer you up too." She pulled a baby oil bottle out of her bag and leaned close to whisper, "This was Tommo's idea – I think he's hoping you might help him put it on his delicious muscly chest. I was thinking we could do it together? You really should share with me – we are best friends."

I blushed scarlet and nudged her in the ribs.

"No baby oil is going anywhere near my corset! It'll ruin it."

"Shame," Maddy said. "I was looking forward to it."

I shook my head. "Honestly, how vain is that boy?"

Maddy smiled. "I think it's a defence mechanism."

"What?"

"You know, after being such a weedy little kid. Ed told me he was really picked on in primary. I must have told you."

"No, Maddington, you did not."

"He had leukaemia when he was tiny, lost all his hair and everything."

My mouth dropped open.

"I thought everyone knew?"

"No, they didn't. I didn't know. Wow."

No wonder he was so understanding with Celly; he'd kind of been there himself.

I looked around to see if Tommo was in the courtyard. He was a couple of tables away, watching me. I raised my hand to him and he smiled broadly, then mouthed, "What about the baby oil?"

I mouthed back, "No way."

He laughed and held his hands out, palms up. I felt a silent connection between us, remembering our secret plan to meet up. It felt so good to have someone on my side who understood, even if we couldn't talk about it at school.

I turned back to my table, listening happily to the banter. My face started to ache and it took me a little while to realize why. I was smiling more than I had in weeks.

thirty

The gym had been turned into a dressing room for the rehearsal. The Year Thirteens who were organizing things had collected the loaned clothes from the shops that were supporting the show. Rails of outfits were laid out to try and give a bit of privacy to each group as they got changed. Whilst most people were taking full advantage of the hidden corners, there were a fair few fake-tanned bodies on display for all to see. I looked about for the textiles rail to hang up my corset. Tommo was already there, stripped down to a pair of cycling shorts. He waved his hands down his body. "Will I do, Madam?"

I could feel the heat from his bare skin.

I said, "You are literally so vain."

He looked at me seriously.

"What?" I said. "You're going to tell me it's in the contract of being a god or something?"

He gave me a cheeky smile, and shrugged, his head tipped

to one side. Without warning, he stumbled forward, colliding into me, as Jack, one of the rugby lads, leaped on his back saying, "Come on, cowboy, let's ride."

"Get off me, you arse, I'm talking to Teva."

What is it with boys? The moment descended into a bit of a tussle between the two of them and I left them to it. As I picked my way back to our group, though, I was smiling from the inside out. My fellow stompers were already half covered in zombie make-up. I got out a mirror and patted white goo on my face before patching in my eye sockets with purple. We backcombed our hair, spraying so much hairspray that Alice nearly had an asthma attack. Hiding behind Maddy, I climbed into my jeans and check shirt, fumbling the buttons with my bad fingers.

"What've you done to your hand, Tee?" Alice asked.

I batted the question away. "Just a burn, it's fine. Is the running order sorted now?"

"Yep," said Maddy, reaching into her bag to pull out a laminated sheet and a roll of tape to stick it on the wall. "I printed it off. We're on third and the boys in corsets are on last. Plenty of time to get back and help them change."

She threw the bottle of baby oil at me.

"No!" I said. "No matter how tempting, this'll ruin my corset. I can't get grease all over it."

"Oh, Tee, you spoilsport, just thinking about massaging that into Tommo's pecs was helping get me through maths."

She pouted as she pulled the laces up tight on her walking boots.

"What about glitter powder?" said Alice, holding up a tub. "He'll look like a gorgeous vampire."

I smiled at her *Twilight* reference and said, "Glitter is a genius idea. Can I borrow it? Are you sure?"

She nodded and handed it to me with a happy sigh. I plonked my booted feet in front of Mads and said, "Do me a favour, tie my laces?"

She did and we made our way through the various bodies towards Tommo and the rest of the rugby boys who'd volunteered to don corsets. We were halfway there, about parallel with the gym door, when Kristal and her cronies burst in. They were doing the opening dance routine. Their hair was sleek and glossy, their eye make-up dark and smoky. They had black leggings on with the neon pink T-shirts designed especially for the fashion show helpers. Not that there was much left of the actual T-shirts – they'd slashed them, cropped them and tied the hems tight to their skinny waists. All eyes were upon them, until a gap parted in the middle of them and Ollie came through. The pink T-shirt suited him. I'd managed to avoid seeing his breakdance thing but apparently it was so good they'd put it in the opening routine. Nothing to do with Kristal being in charge of that particular number of course. She put a hand on his shoulder and he slipped an arm around her skinny waist.

Maddy whispered, "Some people are so desperate."

I waited for the knee-weakening wave to ripple through me. It didn't come. I just thought, *Fine, if that makes you feel better, fine.*

He was looking right at me, his eyebrows half raised, like he wanted me to say something. The only thing I could think of was, *Don't let that bitch get her claws in you*, but I could hardly say that. I smiled at him, hoping I looked friendly, hoping it was a look that said *I'm sorry*.

Erin busied her way through the huddle of dancers and Ollie. She was stage-managing and loving every second. Wearing her fashion show T-shirt like a baggy dress, she had a set of headphones round her neck that she insisted on calling "cans". She announced, "Beginners, please, ladies and gentlemen."

When everyone looked at her blankly, she said, "We're about to start the rehearsal – can the first people onstage get ready?" and flounced out again.

Maddy and I bore down on the rugby boys who were modelling workwear before they moved onto the corsets. High-vis jackets over naked chests that were just crying out for glitter.

"Surprise, boys! Who's first?"

You'd think they'd hate it, wouldn't you, those rufty tufty rugby lads? Not a bit of it, they queued up for us to sprinkle magic dust over them, banter flying:

"Can't say no to a zombie."

"Yeah, you might bite us."

"If we're lucky."

"Jack, have you drawn yourself a six pack?" Maddy asked as she smoothed the glittery powder across his chest. He shrugged his shoulders.

"You have, you little tart, honestly."

"Me next," said Tommo, presenting himself in front of me. I smiled up at him and there was that connection again. I had to look away so I dipped my fingers in the glitter pot. I put it on his chest with my good hand.

"God, your hand is freezing!" he said, catching hold of my wrist.

"Sorry," I said. He held my hand to his skin.

My heart fluttered.

"Okay, it's warmed up now," he said, letting me go. Using the tips of my fingers I traced warrior patterns across his skin until one of the other boys barged between us and said, "Alright, Teva Webb, you perv, my turn, I think."

As they lined up to go onstage in their jeans and yellow jackets, chests glittering, Maddy and I high-fived each other. Erin called round the door, "Workwear, take your places, please. Fancy Dress, three minutes, Walking Boots, six minutes to stage right."

I know it was only the dress rehearsal but a shiver of excitement tripped through me as we made our way to the edge of the stage. In some ways, I preferred dress rehearsals – all the fun, none of the stress. We watched the end of the fancy-dress-shop dance – three giant chickens doing the Bolero with three sumo wrestlers.

"Look," whispered Maddy, "they're dancing chick to chick." She started waggling her elbows around, singing, "Dance with me, I want my wings about you." I couldn't help laughing.

Erin came hurrying over. "Will you two please respect your fellow artistes and restrain yourselves."

I honestly tried to be quiet but Maddy mimed laying an egg and when Erin glared at her, she said, "Sorry, I thought you said strain yourselves."

I snorted with laughter.

It got worse when the first chicken came offstage, and removed its head to reveal a sweaty, bright-red girl from chess club.

"Boiled Egg Head?" Maddy whispered. And that was it. By the time we were lined up onstage I was struggling to control myself. The lighting switched to a dim green glow and the music began, Maddy and me still shaking with suppressed giggles. The opening stompy bit was fine but when we started "woooo-ing" at the smattering of people watching the rehearsal, I was crying with laughter and so was she. We stumbled off at the end, breathless with stomping effort and hilarity, back to the changing room where we collapsed, panting, on the floor.

Maddy said, "Oh my god, that was so funny! I don't think I've laughed so much in my whole life."

Alice said, "I didn't realize you were laughing, I thought you were doing a zombie shimmy."

And we were off again. Actual tears were running down my face. Eventually, stutteringly, it stopped. I took a tissue that someone was holding out to me and mopped up the tears. The rest of the girls from textiles were already helping the boys get into the corsets. We'd made them puffy skirts

250

out of black bin liners and Tommo was lacing up his mate, Jed, into his bunny-girl corset. There were some half-blown-up balloons on the floor and Tommo pushed two of them into Jed's top.

"Where are my ears?" said Jed.

"Keep your tail on," Tommo said, reaching behind the balloon pile and plonking a pair of black and pink bunny ears on Jed's head. There were way too many of us in the tight space and someone fell onto the balloon pile with a loud POP.

"Those were my boobs!" said Tommo.

"How very dare you burst my appendages?" said another boy. It was descending into chaos.

"Right, come on, let's get you laced up," I said, wrapping my corset around Tommo's waist. As my arms curled round him, he kept very still. Heat flowed between us; the nearness of him flustered me. I could feel my cheeks burning and I was glad to slip behind him to tighten the laces.

"You can do it tighter if you like, just let me get my balloons in first...okay, I'm ready."

I pulled in the laces and one of the balloons popped out and flew up in the air. He caught it in one hand.

"I hate it when my breasts escape," he said and I was giggling again.

"There," I said, "you are done."

Maddy said, "Come on, boys, let's have a photo."

Lined up, they looked amazing, like a steam-punk bunch of cross-dressers.

Erin stuck her head round the door.

"Corsets, places, please."

I said, "Good luck and thanks, guys."

Tommo stopped in front me, his eyes the softest yellow brown, like burned butter. There's a name for it but I couldn't think what it was. I felt something drawing me towards him. I was sure he felt it too but then Jed caught up his hand and started swinging it, saying, "Come along, Tomina, 'tis time to play."

"Teva. Hello, Teva, are you listening?" Maddy waved a hand in front of my face and I shook my head.

"Sorry, what?"

"Do you think we can sneak round the front to watch the boys do the corset dance?"

I smiled. "Yeah, come on, let's time it for when Erin is by the stage."

We tiptoed to the gym door, checking Erin wasn't about, then slid up the corridor, out into the playground and ran round to the front of school to sneak into the hall. As we opened the door to come back in, we remembered, we weren't supposed to wear the boots outside, as the shop wanted them back.

"Oh well," said Maddy, "that's shoe business."

And we were laughing again. We hooked our arms together and quietly pushed open the hall door. One of the charity shop routines was on before the boys and it was great. Funny, loud and the lighting was awesome – there were lasers and everything – the tech geeks had excelled themselves.

A few teachers had sneaked in to watch. The place was buzzing. Then I spotted my straggly-haired counsellor.

"Oh no," I muttered.

"What's up?" Maddy whispered.

"Nothing. I think I might go back though."

"What? Why?"

"No reason, I just…"

Too late. Elliepants had turned round to see who was talking and clocked me. She smiled at me and reached into her bag for something.

"Who's that?" said Mads. "Is she your LS teacher?"

"Mmm, I gotta go, sorry." I turned and bolted out of the room. As soon as we were in the corridor, out of sight of everyone, Elliepants caught up with me.

"Teva, wait, hold on." I tried to speed up but when she caught my arm, good manners just wouldn't let me ignore her.

"Here," she smiled, handing me a white scarf covered in black skulls, "I know I shouldn't speak to you out of room seven but as long as no one sees, hey? I thought you'd want this back."

She pressed the scarf into my hands and scooted off.

I recognized it, but it wasn't mine.

It was Fifteen's.

thirty-one

My mouth went as dry as unbuttered toast. If *Elliepants* had seen Fifteen – and who else could it be? – then she *had* to be real. Didn't she? And she must have been here, in school, again. I twisted the soft weight of the scarf between my fingers. The hope I'd had, the hope *I'd built*, that it had all been in my head, sputtered like a dying flame.

I had to be sure she hadn't made a mistake. I raced after Elliepants and caught up with her before she went back in the hall.

"Where did you get this?" I said, holding up the scarf.

"You left it in my room earlier."

"Today?"

"Yes, this afternoon."

"I didn't see you this afternoon," I whispered. "I was rehearsing all afternoon, you must have got it wrong."

"Well, I don't think that's possible, is it?"

I licked my lips, my brain running at a zillion miles

an hour. I couldn't have been in two places at once. Even *I* couldn't conjure that up.

I closed my eyes for a second then said, "The person you saw – are you sure it was me? She wasn't a bit smaller, a bit paler...? Like me, but not me?"

Elliepants brow creased with concentration.

"I'm not sure what you're saying, Teva."

I said carefully, "Could she have been someone who looked like me – only younger?"

"Like a sister?"

"Yes, yes, like a younger sister?"

"Well, I suppose it's possible. But you don't have any sisters, Teva. I have your full family history and there's just you and your mum at home."

The world spun. No sisters, but she'd seen Fifteen. I looked down at my bandaged hand, where I'd hacked at it... Hot, prickling sweat burned my skin. Was this proof then, that it was all real?

I looked up at my counsellor and suddenly a spasm shot through my body, rocking me so fiercely, it threw me backwards. My head cracked against the floor. I was rigid with pain.

A chill swept over me and that was it. I remembered nothing more until a warm hand cupped my shoulder. Through a dim fog I heard voices murmuring. I felt so far away, grounded only by the tiny fibres of the carpet I could see when I opened my eyes. When I closed them there was only blue – shades of blue and grey and a kind of humming thickness.

I knew the world was still there, but it was like I'd been wrapped in cotton wool. I sank into it. Hid in it. More voices came.

"Teva, can you hear me? My name's Tanya, I'm a paramedic, we're just going to get you into our chair, okay?"

Her voice tinkled like a wind chime through the fog and I think I nodded; every bit of me felt thick and sleepy.

Pictures came in snapshots whenever I dragged my eyes open. Green uniforms. White faces. Blue sweatshirts. Hands lifted me, sat me, tucked me, wrapped me, wheeled me out of the warm, into the cold and into the ambulance. Maddy came, held my hand.

"Oh my god, Tee! What's wrong with her? She's my best mate, I have to go with her…"

I tried to lift a heavy arm towards her but it was trapped under a blanket, strapped close to me. I couldn't move and I didn't really want to. Maybe that was the point of straitjackets. They held you together when you couldn't do it yourself. My head was all jumbled. I couldn't think clearly. The ambulance door closed and I shut my eyes and kept them shut as we drove away.

Eventually, we bumped to a stop. There was a flurry of movement; the medics slid me from the chair to a bed. A white light burned through my eyelids and I turned my head away.

Another voice. Male. Urgent.

"Teva? Teva, can you hear me?"

Fingers tapped my cheek, a hand lifted mine, pinched the

end of my finger, held my wrist, put it down. Still I didn't open my eyes.

A man's voice again.

"Her sats are settling... Teva? Can you hear me?"

This was what I'd wanted: help. So why were tears trickling from my closed lids?

"Have you managed to get hold of someone at home yet?" the voice asked.

"The mum's on her way."

A gentle hand picked up my bandaged fingers and started to peel away the wrappings. A burst of shame exploded in me and I pulled my hand to my chest and blinked against the too bright light.

"Ah, hello there, Teva. I'm Dr Williams. My colleague just wants to take a look at your hand."

I shook my head, my jaw seemed to have locked itself shut. It was the oddest feeling, being there, acutely aware of every noise – the light, the heavy air – and yet not be able to get any words out. Had they drugged me? A nurse tried to take hold of my hand.

"Please," I managed, "don't."

She placed my hand back down saying, "Alright, lovely, when you're ready. Might need a stitch or two though, bit of blood's seeped through your bandage. Not a bad job with that by the way, done a first-aid course, have you?"

Her matter-of-fact tone helped ground me. I inched closer to consciousness and whispered, "My mum showed me."

"She showed you well."

A bleeper went off and Dr Williams said, "Teva, another patient needs me now but I'll pop back and we'll have a little chat about what we're going to do. Your mum will be here soon, okay?"

I'd been so happy. We'd been having so much fun. It wasn't fair that this should happen now; it wasn't fair.

"I'm meant to be at school," I mumbled, "we're doing our dress rehearsal."

"Ahhh, the zombie make-up explained then. Well, I'm sorry but I think they might have to manage with one less member of the living dead. We're pretty sure it's nothing to worry about but Ms Fenton was a little concerned. We need to make sure there's nothing seriously wrong before we let you loose again. Okay?"

A nurse handed me a pack of wet wipes. "Do you want to give your face a clean? Don't want to scare the other patients, do we?"

As I wiped my make-up off, I wondered what Elliepants had told them. They didn't seem to know I was a freak. Or mad.

Not yet.

My mind tipped back and forth – fight or flight? Run or stay? I struggled for breath.

"Calm down there, Teva, just breathe steady, nice and slow." The nurse held something over my face, a paper bag. I fought against it but she held it firm, saying, "Steady now, in and out, in and out, that's it, keep it calm. Think of something nice."

Tommo's eyes. Amber. That was the colour. Amber. Big, solid, funny, silly Tommo with amber eyes. Some deep-seated loyalty made me try and replace thoughts of him with thoughts of Ollie, but they wouldn't stick. I just kept seeing Ollie's head tipped towards Fifteen's. I gave in, letting Tommo steady me.

Slowly, my breathing returned to normal and the dizziness passed. The nurse said, "Just a little panic attack. Nothing to worry about. Right. I'm going to see if your mum's arrived. Okay? I won't be a tick. If you start to panic again just hold the bag over your nose and mouth and breathe."

I watched her pull the curtain round me, sealing me off behind its flimsy defence. I was making it all worse. Panic attacks on top of everything else. I searched my pockets for my phone and was comforted by the picture of me and Maddy on the screen. There was no signal, though. Not a single bar.

I lay back, cut off from everything. Everyone. Then the curtain flicked open and the doctor stepped back in with the nurse close behind.

"The cavalry has arrived, young lady. Mum's in reception. Now we really need to have a look under that bandage, if that's okay?"

My spine stiffened. There was something about the intensity of his concentration; it reminded me of something. I shrank into the bed. He said, "You're running quite a temperature. I suspect what you're hiding under there might be infected."

I pulled my hand into my chest, covered it with my other one. The machine by my shoulder registered my climbing heart rate. Why didn't I just show him? I'd wanted help and here it was. Why couldn't I just take it? I was swamped with an awful, creeping anxiety I didn't understand. It welled up from deep inside me – it was all I could do not to wail like a frightened toddler.

The curtain twitched back again. I jerked with panic but Mum appeared, red-faced and bewildered.

"Ah! Mum, is it?"

She nodded.

"Excellent," said the doctor. His pager bleeped again – he read it and said, "Foiled again, eh? I'll be back as soon as I can. Some time with Mum will do you the world of good."

The nurse followed him out.

Mum came straight to me, burrowed her arms around my shoulders and gathered me into a hug.

"My poor baby, I'm so sorry. What you've been through…"

For a minute I disappeared into the comfort of her hug – until the heat of her, so close, started to make me feel dizzy again. I wriggled backwards, forced myself to breathe steadily.

"I'm okay. They think I had a panic attack."

"Oh, sweetie, don't worry, we'll get you out of here as quickly as possible."

I shook my head. "Mum, I think I should stay. I think it was her – the other Teva." I covered my face with my hands;

I couldn't stop the tears. It took me a minute before I could say, "Mum, is it actually happening? Am I mad? Is all this" – I held up my bandaged hand, my voice cracking – "is it...is it in my head? Are the others real?"

Her mouth dropped open. "Are they *real*?"

I nodded.

She took hold of my arms and looked deep into my eyes. Shaking her head, she said, "Teva, I'm so sorry. I'm so, so sorry. I didn't realize you thought... I never imagined..."

"Am I mad?" I whispered. "What's wrong with me?"

I waited, screwing up the bed sheet in my fist, willing her to give me some answers. Finally, finally she pinched the bridge of her nose and said, "Okay."

I swallowed.

She spoke so quietly I could barely hear.

"You're not mad."

Which meant...*she* really was coming.

Mum tried to unpick my fingers from the sheet but I was frozen. I wasn't mad. The wriggling under my skin, the pain that had jolted through me, that had knocked me to the floor, it was *her*. I started to shake.

Mum said, "I never meant to make this worse for you."

A silent tear slid down her face. My heart hardened a little bit. This wasn't her tragedy. I said, "Just tell me everything you know."

She bit her lip. "Not here, let's get you home. I'll tell you everything there."

Rage simmered inside me. It was real; I was going to be

ripped in two. And my loving mum was going to try and lock me away with the others.

"No, no you don't. I know what you'll do, you'll make excuses, you'll say we'll talk and then you'll find a reason not to."

She stood up and turned away.

"Mum, if you don't tell me what's happening to me, I will scream the place down, so help me god. You *will* tell me. You will."

She opened the curtain and I opened my mouth to make good on my promise but she checked outside, then sat in the chair by the bed, as close to me as she could get. In a voice still so quiet and fragile I strained to hear her, she said, "Alright."

"All of it – I mean it, or I'll tell everyone here."

She looked at me, her face white, and then she seemed to collapse a little bit. With a soft sigh, she started talking. It was a like a dam breaking – a slow trickle, then the words just poured from her.

"When it happened first, to Eva, I was so frightened, Teva. I thought she was dying, she screamed so much. I knew something was badly wrong. The hospital was about thirty miles away, but your father's clinic was just a ten-minute drive. I bundled her...you...into the car and rushed there. They stopped me at the gate but as soon as they heard Eva screaming, someone got your father. He took Eva from me. He held her so tenderly, I was so relieved, but then he said it was better if I didn't come in with her. I'd had a bad cold and he used that as an excuse to keep me away from her. I tried to stay with her; I followed them right up to the door of the isolation ward. He shut me out. Locked the door. I was terrified. I could hear Eva screaming inside the room and I could do nothing to help."

Mum blew out through her mouth like she was letting go a decade of bad air.

"It was three weeks before Eva came home. I spent most of that time in that corridor, sleeping on the floor, eating out of vending machines. When she was through it, your father brought her out of the ward like he was some kind of saint. He handed her back to me with a smile – as if he hadn't kept me locked out for all that time. I took her home, just glad to have her back and well again. I had no idea what had happened, no idea about..." She tailed off.

"What? No idea about what?"

She swallowed and said, "I didn't know what had happened. He told me it was a kind of cancer but I'd seen cancer...and you didn't cure cancer in three weeks."

She stopped, pressed her hands to her eyes. She had to steady herself before beginning again. "I was grateful to have her home but, over time, it became obvious that Eva wasn't developing like she should; it was like she'd just stopped growing. Your dad said it was to be expected after the trauma of her illness; he even persuaded me she should be home-schooled so she wasn't exposed to germs. For a while, I accepted it, but after two years, when she still hadn't grown, he said he'd take her back to the facility, to run some tests.

I had no reason to say no. I thought he'd saved her life that first time. This time, though, I insisted on going with her. I don't know why he allowed it. I think he must have been so confident in his security…he was always so sure of himself. Anyway, he let me stay with her. We had our own room and I never let her out of my sight. I didn't suspect what was going on – I mean, how could I even begin to guess? I don't think I would ever have found out if one of his lab assistants hadn't told me. I guess you can't safeguard against other people's morals. Angus, his name was, he told me everything and as soon as he got a chance, he took me to Six."

Mum pressed her podgy fingertips to her eyelids. I pushed her gently. "Six?"

Mum nodded. "She was at the clinic. I knew she was mine straight away. That Angus was telling the truth. She had the same fluffy blonde hair, the same dark blue eyes as Eva but she was strapped to a bed, barely able to move."

Mum's shoulders shook with sobs. When, at last, she managed to look up, her face was wet with tears. "Teva, I am so sorry. But how could I tell you this – about your own father? I thought it was better you didn't know."

"Didn't know what? What had he done?"

She sat up a bit straighter and carried on. "When the first separation happened, he kept the child. She would have been Four. And then again, when Five appeared, he kept her too." Mum smiled gently but her chin was trembling. She shook her head. "I had no idea. How could I imagine such a thing?"

She rested her hand on my arm, stroked it with her thumb. "We left that night, me, Eva and Six – Teva as I called her then. Angus helped us escape. Our house had belonged to his parents, he was incredibly good to us. I changed our name and we hid. I didn't know there'd be more of you – I started Teva...Six...at school. I thought it would help her get over the trauma of what had happened to her. I didn't know it would keep happening, that you'd have to share the name each time one of you took the place of another at school."

"What happened to Four and Five?"

Mum's whole body trembled with the effort of not giving into the tears pooling in her eyes. She breathed, "They didn't survive your father's...*experiments*."

A chill spiked the hairs on my arms, across the back of my neck. I pictured little Six, frail and frightened, not knowing who Mum was that night, only knowing the hospital, being whisked away. What had she seen? What had happened to her? No wonder she had buried those memories. No wonder all that was left was a deep gut feeling of terror. I wondered if she'd known Four and Five. If she remembered them. Worse than that – I wondered if she'd seen what had happened to them.

The curtain twitched open and Mum's head snapped up. The doctor bumbled in.

Mum pressed herself back against the bed, guarding me. She might have been short but she was wide and I was well hidden behind her. She pulled her shoulders back, like she was ready to launch herself at Dr Williams. I saw in her the anger that Fifteen carried. That we all carried. It surprised me. She'd always been so gentle and contained.

My mother was a lioness protecting her young.

thirty-two

I placed a hand on Mum's and said, "Mum, it's okay."

Dr Williams said, "Ah, hello again, Mrs Webb. We think Teva's had a bit of a panic attack, that's all, but we are a little concerned about her temperature. And we need to have a look under that bandage – she's been a bit reluctant to take it off. Perhaps you can persuade her?"

For a good ten seconds Mum didn't budge and she didn't speak. I knew, though, the hiding had to end. I was so tired, and I wanted to lean on someone who knew what they were doing. I wanted Dr Williams to help me.

I unwrapped my finger and said to him, "It's a bit more complicated than an infection."

I held out my hand. Mum gasped when she saw what I'd done, the jagged cut vivid and ugly against my pale skin. Shame rippled through me. The doctor wiped at the wound with something sharp-smelling and sting-y. Then he gently turned my fingers this way and that before lifting his head to look at me.

"How did this happen?"

"Scissors," I said.

"It's quite inflamed," he said, nodding. "But this…" He ran his finger over my nails and, with a sickening flush, I saw the telltale signs of another tip emerging – the tiny uplift of the top nail.

"Hmm," he said, interest lightening his voice, "polydactyly, I think." He knew what it was! He knew what I had. Relief surged through me – all that searching the internet and I really only needed one doctor to give me the name of it.

"Polydactyly?"

"Mmm, I think so," he said. He uncoiled his stethoscope from round his neck and held it up with a quick smile. "May I?"

I nodded.

He pressed the cool round disc to my chest and moved it from place to place, listening, a deep frown grooving his forehead. Eventually he stood upright.

"Okay – things don't sound so great in there."

I mumbled, "No shit, Sherlock!"

He gave a wry smile.

"First things first, is Teva allergic to penicillin, Mrs Webb? Tetanus shot up to date?"

Mum shook her head and he ducked out of the curtain saying, "One minute."

As soon as he was gone Mum's whole attitude changed. She stood up and said, "Your colour looks better, Teva."

She placed the back of her hand on my forehead and said,

"Your temperature doesn't seem too bad either. How are you feeling?"

"Erm, better than I did, I suppose." I was conscious for a start.

"That's what I thought. You know, it would be such a shame if you missed your show."

She sighed and shook her head slightly, showing just how sad she'd be, then she said, "I just wondered, as you're feeling so much better, if you wanted to come home now? There's so much pressure on beds in hospitals. Someone else might really need this one. Do you feel well enough to leave?"

I didn't feel great. And there were other things. I wasn't sure I could trust Mum for one – would she just go back to hiding us when I got home? As for the fashion show, though I did want to do it – it had been so much fun – and I didn't want to let the others down, I couldn't help but think I needed to just concentrate on the coming separation. A hard knot tightened in my chest. The truth was, I was afraid things were going wrong. What if *she* couldn't get out and we got stuck, half and half? We couldn't survive like that. We'd need medical help.

I said, "I don't know. If I stay, they can help me, Mum."

"I know, I know. I suppose I just don't want to leave you on your own and I can't leave the others all night, can I?"

"Oh. I suppose not."

I pictured Six on the stairs – little Eva being looked after by a reluctant Fifteen. If Fifteen was even there. The last I knew she'd been in school with Elliepants.

"I know you need help, Tee, but you seem fine for now. What can they even do until it actually happens? You could have your injections, then we could come back if things changed, couldn't we?"

"Back?" said the doctor, suddenly reappearing.

Mum smiled. "She's got something important on at school. She's been working so hard at it. I'm quite keen to get her home."

The doctor wiped a patch on my arm, said, "Sharp scratch!" and jabbed a needle in. He put the used syringe in a small yellow bin, repeated the process with a different syringe and then stood in front of me with his arms folded.

"Hmmm. Okay, well the immediate problem does seem to have been resolved. I would like to make an appointment for you to see the cardiologist though, Teva, and you'll need some antibiotics." He scribbled out a prescription and gave it to Mum. "Any spike in that temperature, Mrs Webb, just bring her straight back, okay?"

Mum nodded.

Then he said, "Just one other thing. We don't seem to have a medical record for Teva, not even the name of a GP?"

"Yes," said Mum, "we moved here from abroad and never got round to it. She's not needed a doctor before."

"Lucky girl."

The speed of the outrageous lie astonished me.

The doctor picked up my hand again. "We need to get a clean dressing on this though. Bit too late to stitch it.

I'm afraid you're going to be left with a bit of a scar."

I couldn't help it; a laugh escaped me.

"You know," he pointed to the extra fingers, "if these really bother you, Teva, there are other ways to deal with them. Home surgery really isn't the best option. We can arrange for you to see a specialist, if you'd like that?"

I nodded. "God, yes. That would be great."

"Okay, I'll see to that as well then. What's the thing you're doing at school?"

A nurse came in and redressed my hand while he was talking. He was going to help me. He really was going to help me. I was so grateful I nearly cried.

"Fashion show," I mumbled, my chin wobbling. "I want to do textiles at college."

"Ahhh, probably a bit of stage fright that set off all this then – that with the infection, bound to make you a bit unsteady. Any other worries, you can call the hospital or just come straight back. Have you got our number?"

I shook my head and he pulled a card out of his pocket. Mum snatched it from him.

A little taken aback, the doctor said, "Right, well I'll leave you with the nurse."

Things were happening too quickly. Any minute now and we'd be out of the hospital. Before the doctor got through the door, I said, "Can I ask you a couple of questions?"

He checked his watch but said, "Yes. Of course."

"Why is it different this time? Why is it taking so long? Do you think it's okay? What if she gets stuck?"

His brow furrowed and he looked at Mum for help. She gave me a pitying look and said, "She's seeing a counsellor."

He nodded and the penny dropped.

I didn't know what polywhatsit was, but suddenly I was pretty sure that wasn't what was wrong with me. It couldn't be. There was no way he'd just let me go if it was. He didn't understand at all. He thought I'd cut myself because I couldn't cope with my ugly fingers. And Mum was encouraging him to think I was crazy. Fear fluttered through me.

"Wait," I said, "my fingers haven't always been like this, it's recent, they're splitting off from me. It's the new me trying to get out."

Mum pressed her mouth into a sad line and put her hand on my shoulder.

"Mum! Don't do this, I need his help."

I swung my legs over the bed and stood up. My knees were like jelly. Mum had to put a hand under my arm to steady me.

"There you go – she's feeling much better, aren't you, Tee love? You just need to relax a bit, have some fun with your friends."

"No. Please." I grabbed at the doctor's coat. Mum pulled my hand away.

"Teva, don't do that… Come on now."

Dr Williams' face tensed with concern. He said to Mum, "I could get someone to contact the mental health team more urgently."

"No! No. We're fine," Mum said. "I can look after her."

I slumped back down on the bed, my jaw slack.

"Okay, well, we'll be in touch about those appointments."

He swooshed out of the cubicle: gone. Mum snapped her head towards me.

"Didn't I tell you what they'd be like? Right, we're getting out of here."

"You did that, you made him think I was mad," I said, barely able to believe it, hope collapsing inside me. I couldn't think what I could say or do to prove I wasn't crazy. I was drained. Utterly drained.

Within minutes Mum had me discharged and outside A&E. She waved down a cab. Once we were inside it, I sat as far away from her as I could. She'd snatched away my chance of getting help, and now she was so on edge it made me nervous – it was like sitting next to a bomb. I hardly dared speak in case she exploded. She wouldn't even look at me; instead she stared stonily ahead as she gave the driver our address.

I pulled out my phone to see if I could get some signal to text Maddy. Mum grabbed it off me.

"What are you doing? That's my phone."

She didn't answer. I spoke calmly and firmly: "Mum? Can I please have my phone back? Maddy will want to know how I am."

She shoved it in her bag. Short of wrestling with her in the back of the cab, I was stuffed.

The taxi drew up outside our gates and Mum handed the driver ten quid, before practically dragging me out of the car. As she punched the gate numbers in, her head was flicking from side to side like she was nervous someone could be watching. She marched me up the path. As soon as we were inside she yelled, "Kids, here now, please!"

The others drifted to the hall and we stood around in a puzzled circle, our fluffy blonde heads all at different heights, our body language ranging from bouncy to saggy to brittle and uptight. I looked at them; how did I ever think they were in my mind? They were so...solid.

Mum said, "Pack one bag each. We're leaving."

Our collective jaws dropped. Fifteen went white.

"What?"

"You're kidding?"

"Why?"

"We can't just leave!"

"Don't argue. You older ones help the youngest. And no phone calls to anyone."

"I'm not going," Fifteen said, her voice dry.

"Yes you are. We're a family. We stick together," Mum said.

Fifteen said, "I'm not going and you can't make me."

Something inside me clicked. I went and stood next to Fifteen.

"I'm not going either. I'm staying with my...my... sister." The word sounded strange, felt strange, but what else was she?

Fifteen looked at me, confused. I gave her a grim smile back. She was part of me and I wouldn't leave her. No matter what she thought of me, we needed each other.

thirty-three

I felt for Fifteen's hand. It was cold and stiff but she let me take it and as I held it, it warmed and softened. Mum was flapping her arms but I wasn't listening to her ranting, I was just acutely aware of my sister. All my focus was on the place where we joined together. How could I have forgotten just how much she was a part of me? I squeezed her hand and she squeezed back. I had to force my attention back on Mum, who was pulling stuff out the drawer in the hall table, looking for something.

"Get up stairs and pack a bag, or don't. It's up to you, you can come with nothing but you are coming, make no mistake."

"We're staying here," we said again.

She pulled something from the drawer triumphantly and spun around pointing a big bunch of keys at us.

"You have no idea what he's capable of doing. Of course you aren't staying, don't be ridiculous."

Fifteen shrugged her hand from mine and said, "What who's capable of?"

I looked at Mum and her panic made complete sense. She was reliving the horror of the night she'd escaped with Eva and Six.

"Our father," I said softly.

"Dad? Our dad?"

I heard a tiny sniffling cry from behind me and looked round. Six was scratching and scratching at the wall. Smears of blood spattered the plaster from her tattered fingertips. Mum held her hand up to silence us and went to Six. She cradled her gently, kissing the top of her head.

"Shhh, he's not coming back, it's okay, it's going to be okay."

Mum glared at us, like we'd upset Six. And she was upset. She was truly terrified. Watching her made my gut writhe like a barrelful of eels.

Six was remembering something we had all forgotten. She'd protected us from her memories by burying them as deep as she could.

"What's wrong with her?" Fifteen said. "She's always whining."

"Don't," I said. "She's been through stuff we've no idea about."

Fifteen stormed upstairs, past Mum and Six, spitting as she went, "No one ever tells me what's going on."

Mum held Six's upturned face between her palms and spoke gently to her. Six nodded at whatever she said and Mum kissed her nose.

In that moment of tenderness, I knew, really knew, that whatever Mum had done, it was out of love. And fear. For us. It all made sense, why she'd kept us hidden, why there could only ever be one of us at school – so no one would know. So Dad couldn't find us and do to the rest of us whatever he'd done to Six. With a sickening lurch I fitted Four and Five into my family picture. They were gone because of him. That's why we'd left our father. Mum had hidden us and now she thought the only way to protect us was to hide us again.

I closed my eyes and took a deep breath.

"Mum, we need five minutes. Can I talk to you in the kitchen?"

Seven pulled at me. "Don't shout at Mummy."

"I won't, I promise, I just need to clear some things up."

Mum nodded and said to the little ones, "Make sure you've got Peepee. Off you go."

I followed her to the kitchen.

"Don't ask me too many questions, please, Teva. I can't bear it and there isn't time. You just have to trust me."

"I do."

I saw her visibly relax and felt bad for what I was going to say next.

"But I can't leave. And I won't."

Her face paled.

"Tee, please… They might have taken a blood sample before I got to the hospital. Before you were conscious. They'll find out. He'll find out, I know he will. He'll find us."

"Even if he does, it's not going to happen in the next

278

ten minutes. Just slow down, let's think this through."

She sank into one of the kitchen chairs, her head bowed.

I said, "I'll help you get the others sorted but I have to stay. When this separation is over, I'll have a life here and I'm going to live it."

"You won't be safe – he'll find you."

The gate bell rang, splitting the air between us. Mum spun round to check the CCTV. It was Maddy. Wonderful Maddy. An idea formed in my head. If other people knew about us, knew the truth, my father could do nothing. As long as we tried to hide, nobody would miss us, but if we became visible, public, he wouldn't be able to hurt us – too many people would know. We'd been going about this all the wrong way.

The bell rang again.

"I need to speak to Maddy, Mum. Please give me my phone."

"Don't tell her, don't!"

"It's time, Mum. We can't keep running away. Other people will help keep us safe."

"You don't understand."

"Look, if everyone knows about us, what can he do? He can't sneak us off to a secret lab, can he? You can't just kidnap people with no consequences."

"Oh, Teva, please, please just listen to me. You don't understand the reasons why you're like this, it might…you…"

She was white as a sheet and the words just stopped in her mouth. I could see there was something she wasn't telling me but I was so caught up in my idea I pressed on. "I might not understand all of it but I know enough. I'm making my own decisions from now on. I'm staying; Fifteen too. We'll stay with Maddy if we have to."

My phone rang in Mum's bag; her face pinched. I reached for it and she tugged it away.

"I know you're trying to keep us safe but this can't go on, Mum, it can't."

I took the bag. She let go reluctantly and I answered the phone. I watched Maddy on the security video, staring up at the house.

"Mads, give me a minute and I'll be down."

"Tee, are you okay? Where are you?"

"I'm fine, I'm home, just give me a sec. And I'll open the gate."

"I've been in a right state. They wouldn't tell me anything at the hospital. Tommo's here too. He drove me."

I noticed the car parked behind her. My heart leaped into my throat.

"Let us in. Please."

I looked at Mum.

"They're going to find out."

"No."

I said, "Give me two minutes, Mads." Then I clicked off the phone.

I pushed my fingers in my hair and my thick, bandaged hand reminded me of quite how bad things were.

"Mum, I'm going to tell them."

"No! Teva, please. Okay. Just listen, please, then you can decide."

Eva pushed open the kitchen door and climbed up on Mum's knee. She twirled her little hand into Mum's short pale curls. Pain squeezed my heart at the thought of not being with them.

"Okay," I sighed, "talk."

"Your father, he didn't just try and…understand your… this condition, Teva…"

She took a deep breath and squeezed her eyes shut, like she had to force herself to speak. She looked at me and said, "He made you like this."

"What?"

She clutched her own throat with her hand, like she was choking on the words.

"He was working in genetics when we got together. I was such a fool. I honestly thought he loved me but, looking back, I think he just needed a *vessel* to carry the…child… he wanted to create."

"Create?"

"Don't think I'm sorry, Teva, I'm not. I hate what he did to you, but I'm not sorry I'm your mother and I never will be."

"I don't understand."

She wouldn't look at me. She said, "You weren't conceived in the, you know, normal way. He told me he couldn't, that there was something wrong with him." She gave a tired laugh. "I believed him. I actually felt sorry for him. Whenever we tried to…well, that doesn't matter. The point is you were artificially put into my womb."

"What does that even mean?"

"He made you and then put your embryos inside me."

"Embryos?"

Mum nodded. "There were four. You were the only one that survived."

My brain was struggling to keep up.

"Are you my actual, biological mum?"

She paled but nodded. "I think so; I hope so. We look a bit alike, don't we?"

She touched a hand to my hair and smiled sadly.

When I tried to speak, my voice had gone all high-pitched and dry. "What went wrong?"

"I don't know that anything went wrong. I think he meant for you to be like this. He was…odd. How do I tell you this? His 'clinic' wasn't a proper clinic. It was a research lab for gene therapy."

The gate bell shrilled through the house again, followed by my phone bleeping. I texted Maddy, stalling her: *5 more mins. x*

"Just tell me everything you know."

"He added something to your genetic code. Something that shouldn't have been there."

She bit her lip and looked at me with glassy eyes. "He added a gene normally found in insects."

thirty-four

Cold horror washed over me, misted my eyes and landed with a sickening drop in my stomach. Hot waves of nausea followed and I bolted to the sink and vomited.

I mumbled, "Break it to me gently why don't you?"

"I am so sorry, Teva."

I filled a glass with cold water, gulped it down.

"So, what am I, like half bug or something? Jesus. What a cock-up he made of that then – I don't even get wings just some shitty way of splitting off from myself?"

"I think it was an aphid."

"Christ. That's just brilliant, I'm half greenfly!"

"I don't think it works like that."

"Why? Why would anyone do that? My dad...my own father? Why would you do that to your own child? That's so fucking freaky."

"Don't swear, Teva."

"Don't swear? Are you kidding me?"

My phone rang again. I answered it.

"Two seconds, Mads. I'm sorry. I will get to you. I promise."

I turned back to Mum. "When did you find out?"

"Please don't be angry with me, Teva, I didn't know, I swear..."

"I'm not angry with you, I just, honestly, you've just told me I'm barely human and..."

"I didn't say you were barely human; a tiny, tiny bit of your DNA was altered."

"When did you know? Did you try and stop him?"

She shook her head. "I swear, I didn't know until Angus told me, and then what could I do except get you away from him? I think he had plans to keep us all in that lab, me included. I think he still would."

She looked up at me, her eyes begging for some kindness. I slumped against the sink, biting my lip. Did this make a difference? Could I still tell Maddy? I stood up. There were no other options, the new Teva was coming and I wasn't hiding away for the rest of my life.

I said, "Mum, it's okay. I know you did your best. But it ends here. We're not running from him any more. *He's* in the wrong, not us. He can't do anything worse than he's done already, can he?"

I lifted my head and walked out of the kitchen. Fifteen was behind the door. Her eyes like saucers.

"We're made of fly?" she said, sounding small and frightened and so like Six.

I stopped for a second. Trying to remember why she

always made me so mad. Trying to put in place the reason I'd always mistrusted her. Ollie. It seemed so stupid. He seemed so removed from me. I hugged her, hard and fast, muttering, "I'm sorry, I should have thought about you more..." I thought of Ollie and Kristal at the rehearsal. It wasn't even his fault; he'd had two Tevas to deal with. I said, "I'll do whatever I can. I'll help you get him back."

I hugged her again before heading for the remote keypad that would release the gate lock. The world had been kept out for far too long.

Mum pulled at my sleeve.

"Teva, wait. What will they say? Think it through."

I didn't care. I'd had enough. I keyed in the number to let my friends in and spoke to the intercom: "Come up the drive, Mads."

I turned back to Mum.

"I'm not running away, like I have something to be ashamed of."

A violent shudder rippled under my skin. It was so strong I had to brace myself by the door. When it passed I said, "He might have made us like this but I'm not going to let it ruin our lives any more. It stops here, Mum. I'm going to make myself a life and I'm going to help the others do the same."

"But they'll never grow up, they'll never move on like others their age. It can't work, how can it work? They can't grow."

"We might not get bigger, we might have to deal with some pretty weird stuff but all of us *can* move on. All of us can learn stuff. So what if Eva is technically always three; she'd be the best-educated three-year-old on the planet if she went to playschool. She could be Queen of Colouring In. More than that. Who knows what she could do if we stopped treating her like a baby? The others need to go back to school. And I'm going to college."

"How? You can't, nobody will…"

"Nobody will what? Accept me? We'll see, shall we? I'm going for that apprenticeship; I'm going to do everything I can to give myself a future."

Again, I felt the electric bite of the new Teva inside me but I pushed past it. Past her.

The doorbell rang loudly through the hall, jolting us all for a second. I nodded sharply at Mum and then opened the door. Maddy and Tommo stood on the step. My best friend threw her arms around my neck, nearly squeezing the life out of me. She stood back and examined my face, then looked around for my mum and saw Fifteen. It would have been funny if I wasn't so frightened of what she'd think. Her mouth dropped open and went from me to Fifteen, like she was watching a tennis match. Eventually Tommo said, "You've got a twin?"

And Maddy said, "You've got…a sister?"

I shook my head and said, "Come in."

I led them into the front room, for the first time conscious of how it might look to other people. The old-fashioned deep leather sofa, sun-bleached and cracked, the armchairs with stuffing erupting from their pale striped arms; the coffee table heaped with magazines of holidays we'd never taken.

Seven, Eight, Twelve and Thirteen were already in there. Maddy and Tommo watched astonished as the rest of them filtered in like some weird version of *The Sound of Music*. Finally Mum waddled in with Eva on her hip.

Fifteen hung back by the door, her sleeve pulled over her fist like a snake-puppet hand. She used it to angrily brush away tears. I guessed why. She hadn't seen Maddy for so long, she must have dreamed of a reunion, and Maddy didn't realize who she was. Twelve and Thirteen sat cross-legged on the sofa, mildly curious, but that was all. The Maddy they had known had been quite different. They had each other – theirs had been an amicable separation. Hardly a separation, to be honest – they were always together.

Fifteen said, "Welcome to the Freak Family."

Mum slipped her spare arm round Fifteen's waist. For once, Fifteen didn't push her away but sank into the embrace.

Maddy said, "There are so many of you. You always said you wanted a little brother but you have all these sisters, you never said. Where, why, I…?"

Tommo shifted uneasily from foot to foot. I took a deep breath.

"These aren't my sisters. Not exactly."

"But you all look so alike." Her gaze went from face to face, taking us all in.

"We look alike because we are alike." I bit my lip, I think I was kind of on autopilot. I'd dreamed of how it would be, telling Maddy – the nerves, the hugs, the relief – but my imaginings had been nothing like this. I just felt sort of battered. Numb.

I said, "There's no easy way to explain this. I'm not the same as you. I don't have sisters in the normal sense of it. These," I waved a hand around the room, "are all my former selves."

I tried to smile but Maddy just shook her head.

"What?" she said, looking at Mum to see if I was joking. Tommo stood with his hands pushed into his hair, just staring with his mouth open. I wanted to say to him, *You knew, though, you've seen the blog.*

Maddy gave a lopsided kind of laugh and said, "Stop taking the piss, Tee."

I said, "I'm really not. It's messed up, I know. I'm sorry I couldn't tell you, it's…complicated. Basically…"

"Basically," Fifteen interrupted, "*she* stole my life, like the parasite she is." The poison in her voice physically hurt. I thought we'd crossed a line, that things were better between us, but clearly she still hated me.

Maddy looked from her to me and back to Fifteen. "I don't get it."

"It's simple enough," Fifteen said. "She kicked me out of my own body, stole my life, my best friend and my boyfriend and you, by the way, never even noticed."

Maddy's cheeks flushed.

I tried to defend her. "Maddy, you couldn't have known, Fifteen is just…angry."

Fifteen turned away from us and pushed her back against

the door frame with a thud. "I'm not called Fifteen. My name is Teva. You stole it, remember? And I think I've got good reason to be angry, don't you?"

Maddy was still playing Teva tennis and eventually said, "So you're both Teva?"

"Yep," we said together.

"That's not possible. Not...how? Like clones? Why?"

I took a deep breath and explained as simply as I could:

"There's something wrong with me. All my cells replicate and make a new version that sort of splits away from the existing one – Tommo, you know, you've seen the blog."

He looked up, his face white and confused.

Mum sighed and said, "Why don't I make us all some tea?"

Maddy had her hand pressed to her open mouth. She was clearly having trouble taking it all in. She pointed at Twelve and Thirteen.

"You look like Teva when we were in Year Nine, when we set up Boy Watch for Valentine's Day."

Twelve raised her eyebrows. "When *I* set it up, you mean?"

Maddy sucked in a breath. "God, it's like travelling back in time, you..." She pointed at Eight. "You were the first one, the one I met at school in Year Two."

Eight shook her head and pointed out of the door. "Nope, that was Six, she's on the stairs. She's a bit weird."

"She was," Maddy muttered. "She was a bit weird."

She looked back at me. "She...*they* are all *you*?"

289

I nodded.

"I can't believe this, it's crazy."

I shrugged.

Eight stood up, her brow furrowed. "If you're Maddy, how come you've got basoomas? You look funny."

Maddy hid her chest behind her arms.

"Yeah, I guess I do. God this is so…freaky."

It was right about then that Tommo swayed sideways and crashed to the floor.

thirty-five

Mum put Eva down and went straight into nurse mode. I was quite impressed actually. I'd never really seen it when I wasn't on the receiving end and then, well, your mum is supposed to do all that stuff, isn't she? But watching her deal with Tommo, she looked like she really knew what she was doing – which was a good thing as the rest of us just stood round like gormless twits.

"It's alright, Tom, you've just fainted that's all. Lie still until you feel better."

She tucked his hand under his head, balanced his body on one side and said, "Teva, can you finish making the tea?"

I nodded and headed to the door, stepping over Tommo on the way. Maddy followed me into the kitchen.

"I can't get over this, Tee, it's so weird, I can't get my head round it."

"Welcome to my world."

"How do you cope? Why didn't you tell me? How does it happen? How do you cope?"

"You said that already."

"I know but how does it happen? How *do* you cope?"

I flicked the kettle on, turned round and shrugged.

"I've had to, haven't I? Not much choice."

"But what are you going to do? Will it happen again?"

I held up my bandaged hand. "Looks like it."

She couldn't have looked more disgusted if I'd waved dog poo in her face.

"Bloody hell, Tee. What about college? Who…? How…?"

I cut her off.

"I've been thinking about that. I don't see why I can't go. I mean I am growing up, just not in the same way as other people. It's not like sending one of the little ones out into the world to fend for themselves. Me and Fifteen, we're practically as big as we're going to get. At our age we're only a tiny bit different from adults. Physically anyway. It's different for the little ones, I know that, but I don't see why I can't just live a normal life."

"And what about the new one? What will she do? She'll be you – won't she want your place at college?"

I opened my mouth to try and explain, but pain twisted my fingers, seeped up my arm – the same dizzying shock that hit me at the fashion show sent me stumbling back against the sink.

"Tee? Are you okay?"

I pulled my arm into my body and tried to nod, but my

brain seemed to crash in my head and my vision blurred. I vaguely saw Maddy run out of the kitchen and return a minute later with Mum.

Maddy flapped about. "What should we do? What do we do?"

I struggled for enough breath to speak.

"It hurts. Mum, I'm not sure this is...aargh!"

Pain jerked through my whole body, throwing me backwards. I hit the floor with a whole new jarring agony. Tears – of anger, frustration, pain – burst from me. I thumped the floor and howled. Mum put her hand to my forehead and said, "Shhh, it'll pass, you can do this, just breathe...breathe."

Slowly the pain ebbed away and I sat shivering in a blanket someone had tucked around me. The kitchen had filled with people: Tommo, Maddy, my sisters...

"It's always a bit like this, right?" I said to Mum.

She said nothing, her face pale.

I tried to convince myself. "Fifteen, I remember, she was so angry, fighting it – that was as bad as this, wasn't it? Quicker, but as bad?"

Mum didn't answer. Instead, she picked up my wrist and checked my pulse. I watched her counting and saw her face relax a little.

"Better?" I whispered.

"A bit. Oh, Teva, love" – she pushed the hair away from my face and looked full at me – "I don't know what to do. I can't leave you here, on your own, I can't..."

She chewed her bottom lip and suddenly, as much as I

wanted to stay and live my life, I didn't want to be left without her.

"Please, Mum, just stay. We'll talk to that doctor, he seemed okay, didn't he? Give it a chance, Mum, please. People know about us now, it's not the same. We won't be on our own."

A bolt of violent energy jerked through me again and I snapped my jaw shut so fast I bit my tongue. I waited for it to pass. Breathless, I said, "She's trying to get out now, isn't she?"

Mum nodded.

"What if she can't?"

Mum shook her head. "I don't know."

We sat in silence for a bit and then Mum said, "Okay. We'll stay. We'll see how things go overnight and I'll call that doctor in the morning."

I wasn't sure I believed her. I think she was still playing for time, but I had no strength to fight. It was all I could do to let her help me upstairs. I crawled into bed, weak as a runty kitten. I didn't even hear Mum send Maddy and Tommo home but she must have done.

I slipped in and out of sleep, churning things over and over until my head hurt with it all. I knew there was no stopping it now. There had probably never been a chance – she'd been growing inside me all that time and she'd have to come out. There wasn't room for two of us.

I got up early, feeling absolutely awful, and stumbled to the bathroom. I stopped in front of the mirror. I looked terrible, like death in a dressing gown. I hadn't done a great job with the wet wipes – my face was still patched with white make-up.

As I washed it off, I tried to decide what to do. Could I cope with school? With the fashion show? Physically, I felt bloody awful but a little flame of hope was burning in me and it gave me so much strength. I had a shot at a future, I really did. I just had to take it. I wanted that apprenticeship and, ridiculous as it seemed, I was going to try and get it. Believe it or not, I was excited about the possibilities. I smiled to myself. Maybe I *was* a bit mad after all.

I ran a bath, thinking it would be easier to keep my bandaged hand dry that way than in the shower. I wanted clean hair for the afternoon… It was funny really, just a few weeks before I hadn't even wanted to do the fashion show and now I was clinging to it like a raft of normal. I tried not to think about the separation. I knew it was going to be bad but, once I was through it…well, I had a life to look forward to. I really did.

I sank into the water and lay back, and that's when I noticed the skin on my stomach. There were hundreds of red marks, like little tiny splits. I sat up, sending water sploshing to the floor. I rubbed at them, panic spreading through me. I got out of the bath like it was full of cockroaches and grabbed my dressing gown, hiding my skin underneath it. I stood shivering in the middle of the room.

What to do?

I couldn't stop the separation, I knew that. And I couldn't

tell when it was going to happen exactly. I knew that too. So, did I call the doctor? I thought maybe I should but I think I knew he wouldn't be able to help. No one could. It was too late. I just had to ride it out now.

I got dressed carefully, my skin so tender I could hardly bear my clothes touching it, and headed downstairs. Mum was already in the kitchen, nursing a cup of tea. There was one waiting for me.

She smiled. "I heard you get up. Come and sit down. We need to talk, Tee, we need to make some plans."

"Yeah, I know, I've been saying that all my life."

"I know, I'm sorry. I have honestly tried to do the right thing." She sighed. "I know you might not believe it."

"It's alright, Mum. I know. And I know there's a lot to sort out but, just today, can we forget about it? I'll do the fashion show and then we can start dealing with everything tomorrow."

She opened her mouth to say something but I cut her off.

"Please. Just one day. We're going to be okay. We are. It's not just you and the little ones any more, Mum – you've got me and Fifteen and Maddy and Tommo and maybe even Dr Williams. He seemed okay, Mum. I think he'll try to help, I really do. Okay, he can't stop the new Teva, but no one is going to let Dad lock us up; no one is going to do anything to us we don't want. You can't muck about with people's bodies without their permission. There are laws against doing what he did. If the worst comes to the worst, we could have him arrested."

"Oh, Teva, you have no idea how harsh people can be. Lord knows what they'll say about you. There might be people who think you're not…human."

The force of what she was saying stunned me for a second, but then I thought, *The world is full of people who cope with bigots every single day. Look at Kristal calling Maddy a stuck-up Paki just because she's jealous of her. You can't stop idiots being idiots, you can only hold your head up and be true to yourself.*

"Well, we'll deal with that when it happens, won't we?" I said.

"You make it sound so simple."

"It is simple."

"What's simple?" Fifteen came into the kitchen dressed for school.

I looked at Mum; she looked at Fifteen and said, "You can't go to school."

"Yes I can."

"You can't, you're not registered."

"Yes I am. I'm Teva Webb, I've been registered at that school since I was Eleven. No point waiting, is there? Everybody will know all about us by lunchtime."

"Maddy won't say anything, nor will Tommo."

"Maybe not, but I will. I'm going to get Ollie back."

She smiled and pottered about making toast, loudly slapping plates and cups onto surfaces, full of her own victory.

Upstairs, Eva started shouting, "I need a poo, Mummy. Mummy!!!"

Mum sighed and went to get her saying, "Just think about what I said."

I was done with thinking. My arm throbbed. I flexed my fingers to try and get over the cramp that gripped it. I hurt all over actually. My skin was alive with pain and every joint seemed full of a deep, throbbing ache. I knew what I wanted, though. Maybe it was stupid but I finally felt like I could be me, really me, and I didn't want to wait. I totally understood how Fifteen felt.

"You can't stop me," Fifteen said.

"I don't want to," I said. "You can walk in with me. I'll find Ollie with you, he might have a hard job believing you otherwise."

That surprised her. I smiled as I left her in the kitchen with her toast stuck halfway into her mouth, while I went up to do my teeth.

If I'm honest, going into school with Fifteen wasn't just about helping her, it was about helping me, too. For one thing, if *she* was there I wouldn't be the only freak. And for another, she gave me hope that after the separation, once the pain was over, I'd be okay.

thirty-six

Walking to school was hard. Fifteen was impatient to get there but I felt really rough. My skin hurt, my head hurt, even my lungs felt too small for my body. I tried convincing myself it was just nerves – and I *was* nervous, so nervous about what people were going to say.

By the time we got to Maddy's door, Fifteen was practically skipping, but I could barely walk. She knocked on the door with a big grin on her face and when Mrs R opened it, Fifteen flung her arms around her and dived into the house.

"I missed you, Mrs R! Got any chapattis?" She went straight to the kitchen, and we heard her say, "Oh my god, is this baby Jay? He's enormous!"

Mrs R, however, hadn't moved from the doorstep where she was staring at me with her mouth wide open. Eventually she pointed to the kitchen and then back at me. Then, thankfully, Maddy came downstairs.

"Morning," she said. "You look pretty grim."

"Thanks."

Maddy's Mum spoke at last. "Who is that? She knows me?"

"It's a long story," I said. "She…kind of thinks she's me." Let Maddy explain it. I looked at my friend. "Do you mind if we get going? I'm not feeling too great." I pointed to the kitchen. "Fifteen is here."

"Oh!"

"Yeah, oh."

I had to ask them to slow down the rest of the way, I could barely breathe. Fifteen was asking Maddy all sorts of questions, mainly about boys, it has to be said, and Maddy was laughing, answering where she could. I felt a twinge of envy at how easily they'd fallen into their old relationship. Maddy kept looking at me, though. I thought she was being sensitive to how I was feeling about her and Fifteen but eventually she said, "Are you sure you're okay, Tee? Are you sure you're up to school? You look terrible."

I nodded. I didn't have enough breath to answer properly. I think I knew something was wrong. Knew that I should be heading for the hospital, but a bigger part of me wanted to ignore what was happening to my body and relive the fun I'd had the day before – when I'd thought all of this was in my head. When I'd just been crazy Teva, with hopes and plans for the future, messing around with my friends, coping bloody brilliantly with Ollie and feeling proud of what I was doing. So I kept putting one foot in front of the other until we finally got to the school gate. Fifteen was practically running, excitement oozing from her. I couldn't let her down either, could I? She'd waited a long time for this.

I tried to be pleased for her but my head was hurting so much I just wanted to sit down. Lie down, if I was honest. But I'd said I'd talk to Ollie and I would. I owed her. She was right, I'd taken him from her and now was payback time.

Fifteen stopped and turned round, her smile as wide as a Cheshire cat's. "He'll be in the common room, won't he? Don't worry, I know where it is."

"Yeah, I know you do," I muttered. She took no notice, her mind focused on one thing only.

Maddy took my arm. "Are you okay with this? Really?"

I shrugged. "It feels like the right thing to do. He didn't really break up with her, did he? He broke up with me."

"You're shivering."

"I'm just a bit cold. I'll be fine."

"What's that on your neck?"

"What?"

"That red mark, you've cut yourself."

My hand flew to my neck.

"It's okay, it's nothing…just…it'll be nothing."

My whole body throbbed with pain.

We followed Fifteen up the stairs to the common room in silence – that suited me. Just getting up the stairs was effort enough. When I passed the spot where I'd broken up with Ollie my stomach flipped itself into a knot so tight it bent me over. I had to stop for a second, clinging to the banister.

"Hey, come on, you're doing brilliantly," Maddy said, but this had nothing to do with him. It was about *her*, the new Teva.

Fifteen beamed from the top of the stairs, waiting for her grand entrance.

I whispered, "Maddy, I don't think I can do this."

"Christ, I'm not surprised."

"You don't believe in Christ."

"Maybe I should start. Look, you don't have to, I'll go in with her."

"Come on! Hurry up, will you?" Fifteen looked about five years old standing there. I expected her to start flapping her arms about.

"I have to, Mads, I can't let her down. Help me."

And she did, she helped me climb the stairs, held onto me when I wanted to run to the loos and vomit. I think she thought I was just nervous but it was more than that. I was breaking apart.

Fifteen looked like it was Christmas. "Ready?" she said, as if we were going to give everyone the best surprise they'd ever had.

"Look," I said, "this may not go how you think. People might be a bit freaked out."

She shrugged and looked at Maddy. "You weren't bothered, were you?"

"Well, no, not bothered exactly but..."

"Well then, come on."

She pushed open the common room door and I forced

myself to stand tall. Maddy gave my arm a squeeze. There was the usual banter going on in the room but it seemed so separate from me. I realized I hadn't been in there since I'd broken up with Ollie. How things had changed in such a short time. I saw him straight away. He was playing pool, thankfully not with Kristal. Fifteen may have killed her, which wouldn't have been a good start.

It was weird, standing there next to Fifteen for the first time. It wasn't like the room went suddenly quiet, it was more like a slow turning off of conversation. Little pockets fell questioningly silent as they saw us both. I raised a hand in a sort of wave. Then Ollie looked up and saw her. His face said everything: his immediate reaction was to smile and then, as if he remembered that wasn't how things were any more, his brow dropped and his face went flat. Then he saw me and I watched revelation dance across his face as if he'd always known there were two of us. His chin dropped and he shook his head, looking from her to me. My stomach flipped and squeezed, and for a crazy second the habit of needing him surged in me. I took half a step towards him but Fifteen was already there, right in front of him, her head tipped to one side.

He said something and I watched her physically recoil – you know, like when they show someone getting hit by a gunshot in slow motion. Ollie fired some bullet at Fifteen and she took the hit clean in the chest. I hurried forward and put my hand in the palm of her back.

"A game?" she said. "You think this is a game?"

He held his palms up towards her. "What else is it? You told me you could explain, but this? Two of you? What are you, like twins? You took it in turns?" He shook his head. "That's sick."

Fifteen said, "I told you, I can explain it all and I will if you give me half a chance. She's not my twin and none of this is my fault so you better hear me out."

He backed away. I waited for Fifteen to plead with him but she stepped forward, her hands on her hips, and I remembered how sparky their relationship had been before I took over. I saw a light glimmer in his eyes and the corner of his mouth twitch into a smile. Watching them, I realized I'd let so much go, afraid to challenge things because I just wanted to keep everything safe. Yet, here was Fifteen, fronting up to him, and he didn't run. He smiled.

Should I have been jealous? I don't know. I thought how strange it was that *I* felt like the odd one out instead of Fifteen, but there was a sense of relief, too. He was hers, he always had been. I thought we were the same, her and me, but she was right, we weren't at all. I felt like I'd done a lot of growing up but I could see I'd let go of some stuff too, stuff I should maybe have held onto – fiery, angry, shouty stuff. I kind of admired her.

She was solid. Fierce. Eventually Ollie said, "Okay. Not here though. Let's find somewhere quiet."

I put my hand on Fifteen's shoulder and leaned forward to whisper, "I'll leave you to it. I think you've got this."

As I turned away I saw the rest of the common room

watching us with their mouths open. I looked at Mads and she held her hand out to me. "Come on," she said. "Let's start with Frankie, shall we?"

thirty-seven

We were late for registration thanks to the fact I was moving at the pace of a snail and we'd been slightly waylaid by some pretty enormous life events. I realized with a shock that I had textiles all morning. I hadn't thought about actual lessons – it seemed odd for normal life to carry on while nothing was at all normal. Never had been really.

Tommo was already there with his portfolio out. He held a hand up to me and I put my undamaged one into his big, capable bear paw. He squeezed gently before letting me go. Maddy was speaking to Frankie – I hoped to god she was explaining, so I didn't have to. Frankie was nodding, her face all concern. She glanced up at me and gave a half smile.

They came over and Maddy said, "I explained you've had some serious family issues and that your mum will be coming in to talk to the school."

I nodded, not trusting myself to speak without crying. Frankie said, "I wish I'd known, Teva, no wonder you've been finding things so challenging. You can speak to me, you know, I'm not easily shocked: there's not much I haven't heard before."

I gave Maddy a pained look. I doubted Frankie would have heard anything like my story. I said, "Thanks, Miss. I know, but I think I'll leave it to Mum."

Frankie said, "Alright, sweetheart, whatever you feel is best."

She rubbed her hand up and down my arm. I flinched away like she'd burned me.

"Sorry, Teva, have you hurt yourself?"

The pain made my eyes smart. I swallowed it down and said, "No, it's fine. I'm fine."

Frankie said, "Okay, well, sit down before you fall down, you look shattered. Take it easy today."

Maddy said, "Do you mind if I go to maths?"

I looked around the room – no one was taking any real notice of me. They were all busy with portfolios or checking their corsets were perfect for the show later that day. Word wasn't out yet.

I shook my head. "No. You go. I'll be fine. I'll see you at lunch."

Somehow, I got through the morning. I couldn't help thinking that, for a new beginning, it was a bit of a shame I was feeling so terrible. Tommo was really quiet all lesson so, while I was working on my portfolio, I distracted myself by thinking about my personal statement. It didn't really work. I stumbled over everything that I'd done before I emerged – were those things me? Did they count? My head throbbed, but sitting still for a bit gave me time to recover. I wasn't feeling quite so exhausted when the bell went.

I asked Tommo if he was going to the canteen and he said, "Sorry, Tee, I'm meeting some of the lads, we're going to the gym."

He didn't quite meet my eyes and I said, "Really?"

"Got to buff up before the show tonight."

He smiled but I got the definite feeling he wanted to avoid me. I thought of Fifteen challenging Ollie and I said, "This has freaked you out, hasn't it?"

He shrugged but didn't say anything so I said, "But I thought you knew? All your comments on my blog."

"What blog?"

"Celly's blog: it was on my Facebook; I thought you were Mr Fixer?"

"Sorry," he said. "I didn't read any blog."

"But I thought you'd guessed. We were going to meet for coffee."

"Er, no we weren't, Tee. I'm sorry but that wasn't me."

Little crawly insects of worry crept up my arms. Mr Fixer wasn't Tommo? I racked my brains trying to remember what I'd said to a complete internet stranger. What a total idiot I'd been.

Tommo said, "I'll see you later, yeah? Don't forget the glitter."

I could see he was trying to be light-hearted but it was like trying to inflate a cannonball. I disgusted him and he could barely hide it. My heart sat heavy in my chest. Thank god Maddy had stuck by me.

Just walking the short distance to the canteen left me breathless. I leaned against a wall outside the hall to rest. I got a few weird looks but no one shouted freak. Then I saw Fifteen and Ollie, holding hands, laughing. He said something and she went to slap him. He caught up her hand and pulled her close, hooking his arm around her neck. She looked up at him adoringly and tipped her head onto his shoulder. I saw how they seemed to fit where I'd always felt slightly uncomfortable. I always got a neck ache when we walked along like that. I guess I was a tiny bit taller than Fifteen, just enough to be out of kilter. Ollie looked like he'd found something he'd lost.

For a moment, I couldn't take my eyes off them. I won't lie, I did have a twinge of jealousy, but it wasn't for Ollie. It was for what they had, the ease of it.

They saw me looking and Ollie flicked his gaze away almost immediately. Fifteen gave me a tiny half smile. She wasn't gloating, not exactly, but there was a hint of victory about her and you know what? I didn't even mind. I smiled back and gave her a little nod. I was happy for her, and a little bit proud that I'd helped give her a future. Because I had. I'd done that, despite everything.

Maddy appeared. "There you are. How are you doing? God, you look awful, are you feeling alright?"

"I've got a bit of a headache." That was the throbbing, pounding understatement of the century.

"Maybe you're hungry. The other Teva had your chapatti this morning."

I knew what she was doing, she was trying to make it all ordinary. I wanted that more than anything and tried to pick up her tone. "Yeah, and you wondered where I got my greedy chapatti habit from."

"I've got some paracetamol, they might help?"

We headed for the counter and I washed the tablets down with a plastic cup of water. Armed with a couple of giant cookies and two teas, we found a table in a corner and sat down.

Maddy said, "I'm so excited about tonight; my whole family are coming. Do you think your mum will make it?"

"I don't know, maybe. It's so cold in here. I wish those bloody Year Nines wouldn't keep leaving the door open."

"I keep remembering how many of you there are. It's mind-blowing. This was the thing you tried to tell me, wasn't it?"

I nodded.

She looked down and then back up at me, her eyes brimming with tears. "I'm so sorry, I should have shut up for five minutes and let you talk."

"Your talking has kept all of us sane over the years, me especially. Don't ever be sorry, Mads." I shook my head. "I probably wouldn't have told you anyway. Mum so drilled into us that people would hate us if they found out. I guess I never wanted to risk it."

"I can't believe she did that."

I lifted my biscuit to take a bite and Maddy said, "Wait, Tee, there's a fly on your cookie."

She swatted at it and it buzzed off.

My twisted imagination whispered, *Hello, cousin.* I laid the biscuit on the table, reaching instead for my tea, a tidal wave of fish flip-flopping inside me.

Maddy said, "Hey, there's Tommo. Tom! Over here."

He was standing at the counter on his own. *So much for going to the gym then, Tommo.* I said, "Don't call him, Mads."

"Don't be silly."

"Seriously, don't, Mads."

Everything had changed. Everything. But Maddy hadn't quite realized it. She yelled, "Tom, you deaf whatsit!"

"Leave it, Mads, please. I don't think he wants to sit with us. With me."

"Don't be an idiot, Tee, he's not like that."

I think you'll find he is… I thought but didn't say. I couldn't blame him. I freaked *myself* out, why wouldn't he find me totally revolting?

Maddy shut up though. She didn't actually want to put Tommo to the test.

"Are you going home before the show?" she said.

I wrinkled my nose. I was supposed to have drama in the afternoon. After that there wasn't much point in going home. We had to be back for five.

"I don't think so. They're keeping the cafe open, aren't they? I think I'll stay here."

I didn't add that I wasn't sure I'd make the walk home. Instead I said, "I think I'll work on my sketchbook."

"Good plan. Why don't we hang out in the library?"

I nodded. I felt like I'd cheated her. She'd spent so long persuading me to do the fashion show and now I'd managed to suck all the fun out of it by being in such a state. The paracetamol were helping though: my head was clearing and I felt a bit less wobbly.

"That's a plan then, Stan," I said and she squeezed my arm.

thirty-eight

The gym was buzzing again and it was catching. The performance was due to start in less than an hour. The fluttering in my stomach wasn't all about how bad I was feeling. I was excited. And my head was feeling clearer, though my vision was a bit off. There was an odd sort of clouding at the edges of my sight, so everything was in soft focus. Maddy touched my arm. "I've got to go to the loo – come with me?"

I took a deep breath. "Nah, you're alright. I'm going to sort out my make up."

She smiled and nodded. She was worrying about me more than a mate should have to and I wanted to show her I was okay. "Go on, I'm fine."

She'd literally just left when Ollie appeared at my elbow. My face must have said it all, because his first words were, "I'm not having a go, okay? I'm saying nothing. I can't begin to put myself in your head. I'm just glad to have her back. You look shit by the way."

"Thanks." Why did boys think it was okay to point that out? I said, "Where is she?"

He pointed to the corner of the room. She was with all Ollie's mates and looked happier than I'd ever seen her. Of course she did, she had her life back, the life I took. Guilt washed through me but I pushed it away. I was putting things right. I didn't need to feel guilty any more.

I said, "She looks happy. I'm glad. Look, Ollie…"

"Yeah?"

"I'm sorry, I couldn't…god…it was complicated."

He shrugged. "I don't really understand it all, I just…" He stopped, his jaw tight as he looked over my shoulder. I turned round. It was Tommo. A lurch of something like hope rose in me and I lifted my chin.

"Tee," he said, "can we talk?"

My throat thickened but I forced myself to nod. I looked back to Ollie but he'd already gone, back to Fifteen, back to where he was comfortable.

Tommo took hold of my good hand and pulled me towards the corridor. "Come out here where it's quiet."

My heart thudded and I wished I could think straight. Maybe away from the hum of people chatter, the fuzziness filling my head would go. Erin was bustling towards us saying, "Forty minutes people, forty minutes."

Tommo found a quiet spot in the doorway to the PE cupboard. I couldn't look him in the eye. I poked at the floor with my toe and he just said, "I'm sorry. Really, really sorry."

A tear dripped from my nose to the floor. I watched it land on the grey vinyl with a soft splash. Or maybe I didn't, my eyes weren't doing so well. I said, "It's okay. It's a bit much to take in."

"It's not okay. I was rubbish. Fainting all over the place and then running out of words – not really me, is it?"

"I don't know, Tommo. I don't really know you, do I?"

"Could we fix that? Do you think?"

That made me look up.

"What?"

"Could we fix that? You not really knowing me, me not really knowing you? I'd like to get to know you better. Coffee? Sometime? Lots of times?"

I laughed. Really, genuinely laughed. My head was shaking. "You pick your moments, Tommo."

"And can you just call me Tom? I hate Tommo."

"Really?"

"Yeah. It's from *Private Peaceful*, you know? When we read it in Year Seven? I'm not a hero like Tommo and I don't plan on getting shot at dawn."

"I think that was his brother, Charlie."

"Well, there you go." He laughed.

I said, "So what is your plan?"

"I plan on getting the girl and just getting to the end."

He unbuttoned his shirt and my face flushed scarlet; he said, "I see you have a filthy mind, I'll be sure to make a note of that, Ms Webb."

I put my hands to my burning cheeks and he handed me

the pot of glitter. "Well? The show must go on."

I took the pot and burst into tears. I waited for him to say some dumb thing like, *I know, I know, this happens when you touch the body of a god*, but he just pulled me gently into his arms and, even though my skin was screaming, I didn't want him to let go.

By the time Maddy came back from the loo I was half crying, half laughing on Tommo's – Tom's – shoulder. She walked past saying loudly, "Don't mind me, just passing through."

I pulled away from him, properly embarrassed by crying all over him yet again. "Sorry, it's been a hard couple of days."

He smudged my tears away with his thumb. His touch burned a rough trail on my skin but I tilted back my head to look at him. I sniffed and said, "Your eyes are the colour of amber."

"The stuff that flies get stuck in?"

I was laugh-crying as I said, "Yeah, exactly that."

And he leaned down and kissed me so softly that, for one second, it seemed like there was nothing else in the world but the place our lips met, soft and warm and safe.

Then Erin reappeared and practically yelled in our faces, "Thirty minutes, people, costumes!"

Tom pushed a bit of hair back from my face and said, "God, you do look awful. That zombie make-up is amazing. Who painted those cuts on your face? Come on, we better get changed before Erin has a fit."

He kissed me lightly on the nose and went into the gym. I couldn't move. Icy claws gripped my shoulders. No one had painted cuts on my face. I wasn't wearing any make-up.

thirty-nine

I fumbled through my bag for a mirror. My face was a mess: tiny red cuts covered my skin. My bones went to mush. Somehow, I managed to stumble towards our clothes rack as Miss Francis flew in, squeezed my shoulders and said, "The scouts from H&S are here! Good luck!"

I went through the motions of getting into my costume. I nodded and smiled at the excited girl-chatter but I didn't register a word. I was there, and I wasn't – it was like I'd stepped outside of myself and was looking in. The boys were called to do workwear, Tom came and kissed my cheek, I saw his mouth form the words, "Good luck."

I tried to say, "You too," but I'm not sure I managed it.

I watched the chickens go out after him, and caught myself swaying. I had to lean against the clothes rail to stop myself falling. It was getting harder to hear, like listening underwater. The others in my group started to leave for the stage. I felt like I was trying to stay upright on the deck of a wobbly ship. Maddy caught my elbow as we headed into the dark backstage, and she whispered, "You alright, hon?"

I nodded but I wasn't alright. I was very much not okay. My fingers were throbbing and I knew this was it. The new Teva was trying to get out. I wondered how that would work with my clothes on and thought maybe it would help stop her. My breath came in shallow little gulps.

Alice took my hand saying, "I'm nervous too! Don't worry, we'll be great."

I could barely stand the pressure of her touch but I didn't want her to let go. I was so scared. I tried to say, *I need help, I need a doctor…* But my jaw felt numb, and for a moment, I couldn't remember how to work it. I couldn't go out there, I needed to sit down, but the chickens were coming offstage and I was being pushed on. I was flushing hot and cold. I didn't know where or what I was supposed to do, I could hardly see anything, the lights were hot and bright, dazzling through the fog of my vision. I looked around for Maddy, tried to call her.

I vaguely heard the music start, as pain ripped through me, burning every cell, tearing every inch of my skin, choking the breath from me. I screamed, "Maddy!"

My back arched and I crashed to the floor. I dimly heard some applause, the audience thought I was acting, but Erin, bless her annoying heart, must have realized something was wrong. Within seconds the curtains swooshed to a close. Through a cloud of pain, I sensed the change in atmosphere, the sudden intimacy of a hidden stage. "Maddy, help, she's killing me!"

My best friend's face swam over me, she picked up my hand as a crushing pain filled my limbs.

"My legs, my legs, take...the boots...off...please...my jeans..." I could barely get the words out but someone did what I asked and, for a second, I felt a tiny bit of relief before I was rocked again by tearing agony. White heat raged through my body.

"Teva, what can I do, tell me what to do?" Maddy was crying.

Briefly, the pain eased off. I could hear myself panting above an orchestra of shocked and panicky voices. I wanted Mum so badly but I heard someone else.

I knew his voice. After all those years, all those different versions of me, I should have forgotten it, but as soon as I heard it, I knew that croaking voice deep in my gut. I shrank into the floor. Desperate that he wouldn't see me.

"Let me through, I'm a doctor, please, that's my daughter, let me through."

Terror made me tremble. I was Six again. I didn't need to know what he'd done to feel the fear, so long locked inside, leach out.

His hands were on my face and I whimpered. Tried to turn from him. His touch set new fires alight on my skin. I tried to back away but she, the new Teva, had taken hold. She was so much stronger than me. My back arched as I tried to escape the agony of the terrible splitting. Every cell was bursting and I could feel it. *How could I be in so much pain and still be alive?* I tore at my clothes, anything that touched my skin was a burning torment. My father said, "Just try and breathe, Eva, just breathe through it."

Some inner rage gave me the strength to reach up and push my hand into his face. I took every last scrap of energy I had and shoved as hard as I could and as I did so, I realized we were doing it together, me and the new Teva, were combining our strength against him.

I heard Maddy saying my name over and over, "Tee, Tee, oh, Teva..."

I had nothing left, pushing my father away had finished me. I turned away from him, and there was Maddy, right beside me. A final shocking twist of pain ripped through me and my eyes locked with hers.

Maddy's glittering tears were the last thing I saw before I closed my eyes. The pain ebbed away and I drifted with it. Away from the heat to somewhere cooler, softer. I sank gratefully into gentle oblivion. I'd had enough of fighting to be normal. I couldn't do it any more. I wasn't Fifteen. I didn't have her strength.

It was such bliss to give in.

I let go.

Let myself float on a sea of memory: Tom's warm shoulder, Maddy's gentle laugh, Mum's open arms...

And that was how I died. Wrapped in thoughts of them.

forty
...and one

That's all I remember until I struggled to my feet, jelly legs barely able to hold me up. It took a few moments to make sense of everything. Maddy was crying over the pitiful wreck of my old body left on the stage: the skin blistered and bleeding, the limbs half ruined and bent and then she was looking up at me, like I was a devil. I was lying on the stage, bloodied and torn, barely recognizable. But I was also alive and standing, and growing stronger by the second.

I was that poor, broken creature on the floor, and I wasn't – *so who was I?* I took a step towards the body. My vision, my thoughts, were sharp and clear but there was so much information in my head – it took a while for my mind to clear. My brain was filled with Teva's memories, her thoughts and feelings and, stretching back, there were the others – not so clear maybe, but part of me. Part of me, but not me.

I had separated. I had survived.

A familiar feeling swirled through my veins. Guilt. She'd fought so hard but…

"Eva?"

That frog-like voice interrupted my thoughts. I clenched my teeth together and held my head up.

My father.

The cause of all this. I looked down at him.

He was small. That surprised me. And he didn't look like an evil scientist. That surprised me too. He was bald and middle-aged, selfish, pompous and nothing to do with me. Not really. He held out his jacket. I hesitated for a moment but then I took it, suddenly aware that I was cold and naked. I hadn't wanted to be onstage in my underwear let alone just my skin. *Teva* hadn't. *Who was I?* He opened his arms and went to hug me.

I stepped away. "Back off. You stay away from me; from my sisters…from my whole family."

"Eva, please, I've searched the country for you. We were getting on so well, you were going to meet me for coffee, you told me where to find you, Celly's blog…"

"That was you? You were Mr Fixer? Fixer! Of course. Of course you were."

I looked at the body on the floor, twisted and torn. My body. Her body. Teva, who'd fought so hard to save us all and, in the end, had lost herself. Because of me. Sorrow filled my eyes, my throat. I turned to my father, pointing at the poor girl on the floor.

"You did that. You. Are you proud, doctor? *Daddy*?" I spat the words through my tears.

I looked around. The stage was full of people. Trauma etched on their faces, eyes wide, mouths hanging open. Barnet and Lola were holding each other up, their zombie faces a picture of shock.

Frankie squeezed through the crowd with a patchwork quilt in her hands. She looked at me blankly, then turned to the broken remains of my other body and gently folded the quilt over it. She was trembling with the effort it took to hold herself together. Mr Winchester put a hand on her shoulder; she looked up at him, her face white.

"Get an ambulance, the police…call somebody."

Alice kneeled beside Maddy. She slid a thin arm around her shoulders. Maddy, dear, dear Maddy, held Teva's, *my* bloodied head and sobbed and sobbed.

Then I saw Tom. He was standing on the other side of the stage, apart from everyone else, pale as death, his eyes tracking between me and the shell I'd left on the floor. I wanted to go to him, to Maddy, but my father was still talking. "Eva, it wasn't meant to be like this. The project was about re-energizing yourself. Your whole body renewed; your cells eternally young. I gave you a gift."

I looked right into his piggy eyes and said, "You gave me a life of pain. You cursed me. Cursed us all. What kind of person experiments on their own child?"

"But can't you see how incredible this is? What an achievement? The world will know your name; you'll be famous."

"You're mad. I thought it was me, but *you're* the one who's mad."

And then I heard Mum calling me. Mum was actually there and bloody Erin wouldn't let her on the stage. I almost laughed but instead I headed towards her, strength growing in my legs, my body, my heart.

"Mum!"

"Oh, Teva, I had such a bad feeling. Are you okay?" She came towards me, ready to hug me and then she saw the other me lying on the stage and stopped. A tiny cry fluttered from her. My new heart stuttered. She always preferred the others, always the ones she'd known, like she was scared of the changes in me. It was ironic really, that broken Teva lying on the stage had been desperate for Mum to put her first. Now her chance had come and she was gone.

Of course Mum went to her. She kneeled beside her and laid her plump hand against that ragged cheek. Tears streamed down her face. I watched her squeeze Maddy's arm then lean forward to kiss that tattered forehead one last time.

Then she struggled to her feet and came to me.

She seemed smaller, diminished somehow, but when she opened her arms, I stepped into them and she held me up.

A gentle hand touched my shoulder. "Teva?"

I looked up. Tom handed me his tracksuit trousers and sweatshirt. A little sob caught in my throat. I pulled Tom's clothes on underneath my father's jacket, glad to be able to get it off me. It smelled of hospitals and cigarettes and all the things I expected my father to smell of. I didn't want it anywhere near me.

He – the cause of it all – was trying to move Maddy away from my body so he could examine the wreckage. I wanted to kick him. Instead, I held out his jacket.

"You're sixteen years too late for her."

He held his palms out. "Eva, please…"

"I'm not Eva. Eva got left behind a long time ago. My name is…" I hesitated, looking at the girl who had fought so hard, the girl who lay broken at my feet. I laid my palm on my chest. Who was I?

And then I knew. Her body had broken but she had stayed with me, would always be with me. She was locked into my DNA. We were each other. I was…

"Teva. My name is Teva and I'd like you to leave. We don't want you near us."

He paled visibly.

I carried on. "What you did to us was unforgivable but it's not going to ruin our lives. This is the last time your actions break us."

I pushed the jacket towards him and he took it, then Fifteen pushed her way through the crowd.

"Let me through, let me…"

When she could see what had happened, she stopped, a low growl rumbling from her before she spun round.

"You did this, you killed her!"

I stepped back, shaking my head. Fifteen braced herself for an attack. I flinched but she didn't go for me. She dived on our father, raining blows on his head, his arms, his legs.

"You! You did this! You!"

Seeing him seemed to trigger the memory that Six had managed to bury so well and Fifteen was wild with it. Ollie tried to pull her away but she had the strength of the devil when her temper went. The next few minutes were crazy.

An ambulance crew arrived and so did the police. My father was saved from humiliation at the hands of his fifteen-year-old daughter by the police. Not that he was going to be safe for long. I don't think mad scientists who experiment on children are very welcome in prison and I knew, even then, that's where he was heading.

They had to prise Maddy away from my broken body. She didn't want to let go. When she finally allowed herself to be moved, it was Alice she turned to for comfort, not me. From nowhere, Tom's hand found mine and I took refuge in his strength and warmth. I looked up at him. He said, "You're her, aren't you?"

I nodded, barely able to speak. It wasn't quite the truth but it nearly was.

He took my hand and held it firmly in his.

I wasn't sure what the future held for me and Tom. I wasn't sure if Maddy would ever recognize me as Teva. But I knew one thing. I had a future, and I was going to live every second of it.

epilogue

a year on

So much has happened. I don't know where to begin.

Maddy and me have kind of worked things out. It's been a long haul, and things aren't quite the same as they were, but we're friends again. I tried to explain how Eva runs like a thread through all the separations, that Teva and me are really the same person – we're tied so tightly together that I *am* her in all the ways that matter. I'm not sure she really believes it. We spend a lot of time with Alice, Lola and Barnet – more of a group than just the two of us. It's fine, I guess. I just miss the way we were – it hurts that there will always be this thing between us, unspoken, but there nonetheless. Still, she's already planning the trains for when we go away to college, so I think we'll be fine.

She got an offer from Cambridge. She's doing biology, wants to specialize in genetics apparently. I'm not sure how

I feel about that but I kind of understand. All she's got to do is get her grades and, given she never has her head out of her books, I'm pretty sure she will.

Tom was offered the summer apprenticeship by H&S but he turned it down because of his cadetship and they offered it to me instead. I leaped at the chance. I think it helped my college application. I've got a conditional place at De Montfort. I only need two Cs and my coursework has pretty much guaranteed that. I can't quite believe it.

Fifteen has taken back her name but everyone calls her T-T, Teva Too. It's quite cute, isn't it? I still have some stuff to work out with her but right now she's not talking to me, so that's proving a little difficult. She spends most of her time with Ollie anyway, so at least I don't have to put up with her dagger looks all the time. Would you believe he passed his English – only just, but a pass is a pass. He'll be joining the army soon, growing up, getting older – we don't really know what'll happen with him and Fifteen – T-T – but they're doing okay. She's back at school, doing her first year of A levels. She's chosen the exact same subjects as me. I'd lend her my work if she'd just stop being mad at me for five seconds. Sometimes I think hating me is a bit of a habit.

Mum is working up the courage to let the others go back to school too. There's still a lot to sort out. Six needs the most support; in fact, Elliepants is seeing our whole family. She's beside herself with pouty elephant-mouthed wonder. She seems to be doing Six some good though; she's spending a lot less time on the stairs. Her paper-peeling habit came from her time in hospital – peeling paint off the bed she was kept in while they tested her system with all kinds of vile treatments. She really can't remember Four and Five; it's like she's totally blocked it from her memory and I think it's probably best it stays that way. I think it'll be a while before she's able to start school, though.

The others are definitely going back. Twelve and Thirteen are already there part-time. The school really wants them but I'm not so sure that they really want school. They've all chosen new names too. Six wants to be called Peepee – Mum's working on that one. Twelve and Thirteen both wanted to be called Beyoncé so they've split the difference, one's Bee and one's Yoncee – yeah, I know, but it's not like it's written in stone. No one has a clue what our legal status should be – we don't have any birth records – so they can always change their minds later.

My father, god, my father! That's a hard one to talk about. Not just because he's clearly insane. It turns out we weren't the only family he did this to. When we left him and he couldn't track us down, he moved to India. We think we have brothers somewhere near Delhi. Half-brothers. He set up a clinic there and did the same to them as he'd done to us. We think three of them have survived. We're trying to find out more but it isn't easy because there are two governments and two police forces involved. My father could clear it all up in an instant, of course, but he won't.

He's in prison and he can stay there for all I care. I went to see him, to ask him why he did what he did. He tried to explain – his mother, my grandmother, I suppose, died giving birth to him. He wanted to find a better way for people to reproduce. To be honest, I really do think he's a bit mad and you know what? That's his story, not mine. He could never be a proper father. He doesn't care about us at all. He won't even tell us what he's done with all the records he kept. All we have is the file Mum stole and his laptop. Clever bods are trying to extract data from it – the same bods who found out about my brothers in India.

Dr Williams is helping us. He's not a geneticist but I prefer it that way. He's just a doctor, doing his best for his patients. I feel safe with him. He's working with a team to try and figure out a way to stabilize things. I've learned quite a bit of science – I know, get me! I've learned that greenfly are born with perfect copies of themselves inside their bodies. They don't need to mate, they're like little Russian dolls: one inside the other, inside the other.

Eurgh and eurgh again.

We've been in a lot of magazines. Jan from *Chatter* tried to get an interview but Mum was having none of it. She got my phone number changed because Jan wouldn't leave me alone. Mum said yes to *National Geographic*, though; we were on the front cover! It was all very exciting for a bit but now, I think, we all just want to get on with living. I don't want to start college as "Greenfly Girl". Jan from *Chatter* managed to write her story without any help from me, and what a delightful headline she came up with.

We still don't know why the body I was in before didn't

survive. It's too weird to think how we might be if that body had come through; too hard to think of it as Teva. *I* am Teva. Her thoughts and feelings and dreams, they are all in me. It's like, when I separated, she came with me. Dr Williams thinks something went wrong that night – maybe her immune system was weakened from too many separations, or maybe she just fought too hard to stop it happening. But I think…I think maybe something went *right*. I left behind my younger body but I carried forward everything that mattered.

Is it over now I've pretty much finished growing? Who knows? Whatever, I'll deal with it. I'm taking one day at a time. Elliepants is quite proud of me; *I'm* quite proud of me.

What else?

Oh yeah.

Tom.

Me and Tom. Tom and me.

We went for coffee.

We're still going for coffee. Lots and lots of lovely coffee.

And guess what? It turns out his college isn't going to be that far away from mine. Maddy's already working out the train times.

acknowledgements

If mushy sentiment brings you out in a rash, please read no further, but if I don't express my gratitude to these lovely people, I will actually burst. Thank you...

Shona Moth, through you, I met the quietly fabulous Natascha Biebow who suggested I join SCBWI and really learn how to write. I'm so glad I did.

My SCBWI YA Critique group: Nicky Schmidt, Jackie Marchant, Jeannie Waudby, Carmel Warden, Pat Walsh, Ellen Renner, Vanessa Harbour and others who dropped in and out – particularly Candy Gourlay and Teri Terry. Your insightful comments and encouragement have been my blanket on a cold night. I cannot thank you enough. Ever.

Chi-SCBWI: Elizabeth Dale, Philippa Francis, Vivienne de Costa, Liss Norton, Lizzy Strong, Jackie Wilson, Chrissie Gibson, Val Uden, Jill Atkins. Liz and Viv (you superstar), please continue to boss me into writing.

The Usborne team – I'm so glad the Sorting Hat put me

in your house, you are fabulous. Sarah Stewart, this book has so much of your deft hand in it, working with you has been a joy.

For timely encouragement: Mariam Vossough, Philip Ardagh, Fiona Dunbar, Mary Hoffman, Jackie Morris, Beverley Birch and so many other writer friends – I wish I could name you all but I'd fill a book.

Mary Collins, Leah Bradley, Denise Pickering, I'll never forget the gift of time you gave me. Leah, I hope Paula enjoyed finding herself in these pages. Ludo, Peepee and Angie Cottle; Emily Omiros, Julie Wilkie, Angus Davidson, Jane and Rebecca Hodgkiss, Mum and Dad – you said all the right things at all the right times.

The Hun Club. It's been a pleasure to sit at the edge of your lives; you are woven into this book in so many ways. Hannah Jones, rising star in contour fashion, thank you for your stunning A-level corset design that became Teva's.

Bishop Luffa School, Home of the Original Sixth Form Fashion Show – you totally rock.

Nick, my perfect fit in every way; Emily and Archie, the meaning of everything – you three are my stabilizers.

Finally, Emma Slack, for introducing me to the Agent of Never Giving Up – Sophie Hicks, you were right, it happened.

Thank you all.

about the author

In addition to writing, running a fruit farm and raising two children, Kathryn Evans loves to belly dance, fences competitively and is Finance Co-ordinator for The Society of Children's Book Writers and Illustrators. She lives on her farm near Chichester. *More of Me* is her first novel.

For more on Kathryn, check out her blog:
www.kathrynevans.ink

 @mrsbung

 kathrynevansink.tumblr.com

 And for more fabulous Usborne YA reads, news and competitions, head to usborneyashelfies.tumblr.com